D0550585

YOU
THINK
YOU
KNOW
ME

He points to me with a single finger. "You," he spits, "watch yourself. You and the other pieces of scum no one wants here."

I want to say something back. I can feel the words itching in my throat, but nothing comes out. I remember my mum's warning, almost as if she's right there next to me, saying it again for the hundredth time.

AF DABOOLAN DAHAB WAAYE.
A CLOSED MOUTH IS GOLD.

*To my Lord, for blessing me in ways I could never imagine
To Hooyo and Aabo, who have always made life a little brighter
And, to the other loves of my life: thank you for shaping me and
for your endless support*

First published in the UK in 2023 by Usborne Publishing Ltd., Usborne House,
83-85 Saffron Hill, London EC1N 8RT, England. usborne.com

Usborne Verlag, Usborne Publishing Ltd., Prüfeninger Str. 20, 93049 Regensburg,
Deutschland, VK Nr. 17560

Text copyright © Ayaan Mohamud, 2023

Author photo © Oluwayemisi Oshodi

Cover illustration by Wasima Farah © Usborne Publishing, 2023

The right of Ayaan Mohamud to be identified as the author of this work has been asserted by her in
accordance with the Copyright, Designs and Patents Act, 1988.

The name Usborne and the Balloon logo are Trade Marks of Usborne Publishing Ltd.

All rights reserved. No part of this publication may be reproduced, stored in a retrieval system or
transmitted in any form or by any means without the prior permission of the publisher.

This is a work of fiction. The characters, incidents, and dialogues are products of the author's
imagination and are not to be construed as real. Any resemblance to actual events or persons,
living or dead, is entirely coincidental.

A CIP catalogue record for this book is available from the British Library.

ISBN 9781803704500 7940/1 JFMAMJJASON /22

Printed and bound using 100% renewable energy at CPI Group (UK) Ltd, Croydon, CR0 4YY.

MIX
Paper | Supporting
responsible forestry
FSC
www.fsc.org FSC® C171272

YOU THINK YOU KNOW ME

AYAAN MOHAMUD

WITHDRAWN

ST PAULS SCHOOL
Est. 1509

Kayton Library

USBORNE

YOU THINK YOU KNOW ME

includes scenes of violence and racism
which some readers may find distressing

PART ONE:

AN APPROACHING STORM

CHAPTER ONE

The library at lunchtime.

Without realizing, and without much resistance, that's the kind of person I've become. The lunch bell rang ten minutes ago, and I was supposed to go meet my friends, but for some reason I'm still here at this empty desk in this near-empty library, trying to make a dent in this never-ending study list.

The date in my planner glares at me. I'm four weeks away from my med school admissions test and I can feel its nearness starting to bite at my heels. But I know if I don't turn up like I promised, my friends will have words for me, so I shove the planner in my bag and head out.

I see some of the others from my double maths lesson hanging around under the canopies and by the field outside. I don't see Jessica though, which is good. I try to avoid Jessica as much as realistically possible in this school, even though we share a few classes.

I already saw too much of her this morning. She'd capitalized on my best friend's absence, leaning over Andrea's empty chair when she'd noticed me flicking through the mock paper Ms Williams had handed back to us. Her hair was braided intricately, as it always was, and if you didn't know Jessica you'd probably think, *Hey, there's a friendly looking girl. She seems pretty harmless.*

"You really shouldn't worry," she'd whispered, leaning in close and keeping an eye out for Ms Williams. She indicated the mock paper in front of me with a nod of her head. "It's not the end of the world. There are plenty options."

I ignored her, but Jessica carried on.

"Look, I just mean that even if your grades don't work out and you need to fall back on something, I'm sure ISIS could use a marketing strategist. They could use your skill set."

I pursed my lips but didn't say anything. I knew if Andrea had been there, she definitely would've gone off on her. She's never been the type to let anything go, especially when it comes to Jessica and her snarkiness. But me? No, no, no. I stayed silent. I always stayed silent. It was easier that way. Easier to let these little jabs slide off you, like water over glass, than let any of it get to you.

So, I didn't tell her that I got ninety-five per cent – the highest in the class – along with three of Ms Williams's coveted smiley faces.

And my mum's words, her simple life-motto, rang in the back of my head as I watched Jessica's retreating back at the end of class.

Don't make more trouble opening your mouth, Hanan. Af daboolan dahab waaye.

I've heard it so many times growing up that it's become the theme song to my life. *A closed mouth is gold.* It sounds a lot better in Somali though.

I snake through the lunchtime crowd to find my friends, keeping an eye out for Jessica and her co-Braids. They're the other two girls in that toxic trio; three cut-throat girls with the hair of angels. All living, breathing, walking contradictions.

"Hanan, get over here!" Nasra calls out from the pigpen when she sees me walking across the courtyard. She's there with the rest of our friends, still waving frantically even though she knows she's already gotten my attention, so I head towards them.

The pigpen's a seating area with a few picnic tables for people who aren't in the mood for the chaos of the lunch hall. Its pointed blue wooden fences and latched gate always gives us the feeling of being kept animals, which is why we call it the "pigpen". It never stops us from hanging around here most days though.

Nasra's perched on the fence. I'm a little surprised that its pointed edges aren't causing her any pain. But then again, Nasra once broke her foot in a vicious game of bench-ball and spent the entire day attempting to walk on it just to prove to everyone else that it wasn't that serious.

"I'm so glad you're here," Nasra says when I reach them, extending her arms.

I lean in without question. Nasra's a chronic hugger and any hesitation in indulging her demands usually leads to questions about the integrity of our friendship.

"These two are such antisocial trash," she says, releasing me and indicating Lily and Isha, who are both absorbed with their phones. "I've had no one to talk to for the last five minutes," she complains. She slides off her gold-rimmed glasses, cleaning the lenses with the edge of her headscarf, and makes a face.

I laugh. "How is it that you make five minutes sound like five hours, Nasra?"

"Excuse you, I'm asking for support here, not judgement, Hanan," she replies drily, squinting at me. "Those two are the ones you should be looking at."

At that, Isha finally looks up, pocketing her phone.

She smiles sheepishly. "Sorry, sorry," she says. "Do you guys know the kind of dedication and commitment it takes to run an established Jimin fan account? It's basically a full-time job."

"Don't you have like fifty followers on that BTS account?" I ask.

Nasra bursts out laughing.

Isha gives her a side-eye as she draws out her favourite cherry blossom lip-gloss from her blazer, applying a generous amount. If she could have it her way, she'd be wearing full-face make-up every day for school, but she makes do with what she can get away with.

"I *did* have fifty, but I'll have you know I've got that number up to eighty-one now."

"Impressive," Nasra says, smirking. "We're going to have to throw you a party when you finally hit a hundred."

They fall into their typical light-hearted bickering, and I lean back against the fence to watch. Normally, Andrea and Lily are watching with me, but Andrea's out sick today and Lily's still glued to her phone.

It's moments like this when I'm surprised at just how well

Nasra's adjusted to our group. She only started at Grafton Grammar last year for sixth form, but it feels like she's been with us for ever.

I think back to how it all started: Andrea and me. Then the addition of Isha four years ago, in Year Nine, after her dad moved their family back from India. Then Lily, not long after that. She and Jessica had had a falling-out, after years of being friends, and one day she somehow ended up at a table with us. She's refused to ever tell us what made her walk away from that friendship, even though we've asked more times than I can count.

Andrea had had her reservations when Lily first transitioned to our group. I remember just how much time and energy it took to convince her to give Lily the benefit of the doubt.

"She was with them but never *with* them," I'd argued. "You know she's never been as bad as Jessica, Sarah or Divya. And I feel a little bad. She doesn't have anyone to hang out with."

"The fact that she used to be a Braid, and not whether she was as *bad* as them, should be argument enough, but whatever, Hanan." Andrea had thrown up her hands in defeat. "You win. Lily can join."

I look over at her now, still typing away frantically on her phone.

"What's she so obsessed with?" I ask Isha, interrupting her conversation with Nasra.

"She's texting her mum," Isha replies. "They're planning a trip to some town in Switzerland they're yet to visit."

The three of us smile at each other knowingly; Lily's

extravagant weekend trips happen at least once a month with her millionaire candle-creator mum, so we're all used to them by now. Most people wonder what Lily's doing at a place like this when they find out who her mum is, but it makes more sense when you know her mum went to Grafton thirty years ago too.

My phone vibrates in my pocket. I slide it out.

Hooyo: GET GIRLS SCHOOL
HUSSEIN SAY NO

I sigh. I'd been planning an afternoon in the library to study up on the physics that'll be in my exam, but I guess that won't be happening now.

"What are you moping about?" Isha asks.

"Just a text from my mum." I shrug my shoulders, quickly putting my phone away. "Apparently I'm on pick-up duty today."

"Isn't it your brother's turn this week?" Lily asks, finally acknowledging my presence. She clicks on a few more things before locking her phone and putting it away.

Nasra barks out a laugh. "Funny you should break focus when her brother comes up."

Lily swats her arm. "It's just an innocent question. Can't a girl ask about her friend's life without being harassed?"

I raise an eyebrow when I notice the red creeping into her cheeks. "Yeah, it was supposed to be his turn. Not sure what he's playing at, but I guess I'll find out when I get home."

"I could come over to yours and help you figure it out,

if you'd like," Lily replies, trying to appear nonchalant. She plays with a lock of her new pixie cut, twisting it around her finger.

I stifle a laugh. It's always the same with her whenever Hussein comes up. I can never quite understand what it is about him that seems so compelling. To me, he'll always just be the laziest clean-freak I know.

"Lily, you and my brother are never happening. The sooner you accept that, the quicker we can all move on with our lives."

"Never." She pouts. "I refuse to give up. Haven't you heard? Love conquers all."

Nasra looks at her with disdain and snorts. "Haven't *you* heard? Love actually *kills* all. Look at what happened to Romeo and Juliet. Both too dumb in love to stay alive for it. And anyway, Lily, stop creeping on your best friend's twin brother. You might as well claim you're in love with this one, too, because they're basically identical," she says, indicating me.

"Oh my God, Nasra! We're not identical." I let my head drop into my hands. "This is why you shouldn't have dropped biology."

"Please, I'm not that clueless." She smiles widely at me. "It's just hilarious seeing you get so worked up."

I'm about to reply when we hear the whine of sirens. We all look up at the same time, like startled meerkats. The ear-splitting noise gets closer and closer, until we see the flashing lights of an ambulance whizz past the school gates. When the sound begins to melt away, I turn back to Nasra and say, "I'm not as easy to wind up—"

I'm cut off again by more sirens. Not an ambulance this time but one, two…no, *four* police cars. I see bursts of red, white and blue through the bushes. They disappear in seconds, and we're left with the quiet rumble of regular traffic once more.

"That doesn't sound good," Isha says, craning her neck like she can see where the police cars were heading from where we're standing.

One or two police cars? Normal. But four police cars and an ambulance? That means something bad, even for London.

CHAPTER TWO

Isha and I leave school together at the end of the day and walk towards my sisters' primary school, which Isha lives right next to. I'm grateful for the company but my mind's wandering.

I see Isha's fingers floating in my periphery, trying to catch my attention.

"Hellooo? Earth to Hanan?"

I blink, trying to re-orientate myself. "Sorry," I reply quickly. "Just daydreaming."

For some reason, I hadn't been able to stop thinking about the police sirens the entire hour of last period chemistry. Even now, I can't seem to shake it off. Where I live, I'm used to hearing the police all the time, so I don't know what it is that's got me so on edge.

"About what?" she asks, mildly offended. "I don't know what's more important than the fact that I've just somehow lost a follower. I'm down to eighty now!"

"Oh, nothing's more important than that," I reply with my most serious expression. "A zombie apocalypse couldn't even match the distress you must be feeling right now."

Isha nods, appeased. "I'm glad you understand the severity of the situation." She scoffs. "I know Nasra definitely wouldn't."

We walk in comfortable silence for a few moments until we hit the busy middle of the high street. She juts her chin out at some boys ahead of us. "Ugh, look at those idiots. I literally always see them messing about like this. Wonder what year they're in."

There's no way I can miss who she's talking about because they're so loud. I can tell they're Grafton Grammar kids like us because I catch a glimpse of the school crest on their blazers and because there's a few of them I recognize. They walk like they own the road and with the kind of swagger that seems forced, unnatural. One of them jumps quickly onto the road before the incoming bus reaches the bus stop. It seems like it's some kind of dare, because when the bus honks and he jumps back onto the pavement, he's cheered on loudly by his friends.

"Two years down. Year Eleven. The idiot that's trying to get himself killed is Daniel. The one right next to him is Jacob, his biggest fanboy."

"You know them?"

"Only because they're both in the Fundraising club with me and Andrea. Heard Daniel was forced to join since teachers were fed up with giving him detentions and wanted him to do some kind of community service thing instead. Then he just turned up with Jacob one day."

Isha gasps. "Wait, is that *the* Daniel, as in Jessica's brother?"

"Yeah," I sigh. "That's him."

I will never forget the day Daniel walked into the club.

My stomach had dropped. It felt like I had lost one of the last places at Grafton that wasn't toxic for me.

But I refused to let go. It's been my favourite place since I started at Grafton and I won't let anyone take that from me, especially not Daniel and Jacob. The club gives me a chance to do something I love for the things I care about – to bake and raise money for people that really need it. Also, it doesn't hurt that it gives me an excuse not to study whenever I get sick of it.

The boys continue carelessly walking along the high street ahead of us, forcing other people to swerve around them at the last second. We follow behind, keeping a distance.

When we near the junction, Isha and I start to slow. There are huge groups of people standing at the corner.

It's crowded. *Very* crowded. Even Daniel and his cronies have stopped goofing around.

"Why is no one moving?" Isha grunts in frustration. "Faren High Street can be such a bitch sometimes."

Someone next to us overhears her complaint.

"Nah, this isn't regular. You see there?" the man says, pointing across the road. "Think something went down an hour or two ago. The police were down here so quick, never seen anything like it. Heard a guy was injured but no one's really sure."

Isha and I look at each other and I know we're both thinking the same thing.

"The police cars," we whisper at the same time. She nods, grimacing.

I try to squint past the crowd, to see if I can make out anything, but all I see is endless police tape.

I remember myself then, and what I'm meant to be doing.

"Oh my God, Isha, I need to run." I glance at my watch. "My sisters are going to be let out soon."

"Go, go," she says, gently pushing me on my way. "I'm going to hang back for a little while. See what's up."

I nod, half-turning to see if the road to the primary school is cordoned off too, but luckily it's not.

"I hope it's not serious," I say to Isha, "whatever's going on. Let me know if you find out anything?"

She nods, waving goodbye. I jog the rest of the way to my sisters' school.

The short journey gives my mind time to wander again, and I find myself doing the thing that I do at least ten times a day – planning the rest of my day. Fundamentally, I've always believed there are two types of people in this world: those who plan and those who don't. I've always considered myself to be the former and just thinking about being the opposite makes me queasy.

But while I'd love nothing more than getting through my daily to-do list, I often get distracted. Usually, that means sitting at my grandmother's feet in the evenings, listening to all her nostalgic stories. Stories where she becomes alive with the memories of Somalia and her hometown of Baydhabo: the days her family spent in search of good grazing land for their livestock; the nights she spent breathing the dry desert air as she lay staring at the brightest stars until her eyes hurt. And,

18

even though there's always so much to do, I never feel as happy as when I'm hearing the greatest love story ever told: the story of my grandmother and the grandfather I never met. Of a woman locking eyes with the handsomest shoe-shiner in all of Mogadishu on her very first trip to the city. A city of a thousand wonders. A city of endless possibilities.

She's told this story a million times, but Abooto always narrates it with the same beauty, building the story like a wave where the crescendo is always spectacular: the birth of my dad. And that's why, despite everything else, I will always sit at my grandmother's feet to hear these tales about him. To hear about the man I want to keep alive in my memories.

I reach the school and walk to the furthest corner of the playground, waiting for Sumaya. It doesn't take long for me to spot her since she's the only one wearing a yellow and orange parka. We'd tried very hard to dissuade her from that colour combination last year when we'd gone school shopping, but my eight-year-old sister wasn't having any of it. She would wear that jacket or wear nothing, she'd said, standing in the middle of the shop aisle. Hooyo had been too tired to talk her out of it.

Sumaya comes bounding from her place in the class line and her teacher, Ms Campbell, gives me a wave and a smile. Sumaya throws herself onto me, giving me a breath-obstructing hug and forcing me back a couple of steps. Where this has come from, I'm not sure. Generally, Sumaya's quite lethargic by the end of the day, probably expending all her energy on the playground drama she always seems to be in the centre of.

"Woah, sis," I laugh. "You need to be careful before we both end up on the floor."

Sumaya takes this as an invitation to hug me even tighter. It's a hug that feels desperate and raw, and I want to ask what's wrong, but for now I hug her back harder. Whatever it is, something's clearly upset her today.

I gently break our embrace after a few moments. "Here, take my hand. We'll go pick up Hafsa. I have a feeling seeing her will make you feel better."

Hafsa, my other sister, has an uncanny way of fixing everyone's problems. Although she's only eleven years old, she seems to dispense sage advice like she's handing out sweets. Usually, whenever Sumaya gets upset like this, Hafsa understands instantly, her large, bronze-coloured eyes reading the emotion expelled from Sumaya in a single breath. Our mum always says that although our dad no longer exists in this world, his character still lives on, burrowed into Hafsa, like a wayward ember from a flame.

We reach the other side of the playground just as Hafsa's class descend the yellow staircase. Hafsa looks pristine as usual, her headscarf firmly in place with the butterfly pin she'd painstakingly saved to buy, her coat zipped all the way up and her dolly shoes polished so well you can see your own reflection in them. She smiles when she spots us, but a quizzical expression soon replaces it when she sees Sumaya's face.

Sumaya releases a torrent of words as soon as Hafsa reaches us.

"No, but, Hafsa, I did what you said...they, I didn't mean,

but, but...it didn't—" Sumaya's head hangs low, the frilly tassels on her grey headscarf falling to whisper gently against her cheeks. "I'm sorry, Hafsa. I didn't get the crayons."

Hafsa and I share an amused glance before she looks back to Sumaya. She puts a hand under her chin, tipping her sister's head up.

"Hey. It's okay, Sumaya. They're just crayons. Maybe you can get them back next time."

Sumaya nods fiercely, blinking away the tears in her eyes.

"I only wanted you to start standing up for yourself." Hafsa lets her hand drop, looking at her baby sister a little sternly now. "Primary school's a jungle. You can't let people be mean to you all the time."

Sumaya wipes her nose with the sleeve of her red cardigan. "I know. Next time, I'll get my crayons back. All of them, Hafsa. I promise."

Hafsa smiles. "I'm sure you will."

A part of me wants to laugh, to tell them that crayons are the least of their worries, that the reality of secondary school will blindside them soon enough – when their lives will intersect with those who say cruel and awful things for fun. But I know they're still children and, for them, playground drama feels like the worst it'll ever get.

Still, the two of them are lucky in so many ways already. They've never had to experience what Hussein and I did when we first started at this primary school. It was ten years ago now, when both of us were only seven years old, but I don't think I'll ever forget just how painful it was. The finger-pointing, the whispering, the never-ending laughter when English words came out of my Somali mouth all wrong. In those first few months, all I wished and prayed for was to go back home to Somalia…to be in the place where I could exist without trouble – even if that existence was against a backdrop of bombs and gunshots.

I don't know how I could've gotten through all of that without Hussein. Every break and every lunch, like clockwork, Hussein would take my hand, and the two of us would find somewhere quiet, somewhere away from the intense looks and smirks of the other kids. And, like clockwork, I would cry. I would cry and cry and Hussein would cry silently too – both of us wondering why Hooyo and Aabo had promised things would get better in the place across the ocean, because things did not feel better. In fact, they felt decidedly *worse*. There was no Aabo; there was no sun, and there was no joy in this place.

And things got worse still when the class clown, Luke, decided he wanted to make me joke-of-the-week. He and his friends had followed Hussein and me at break one day and we hadn't noticed until they were only a metre or two away.

"It's true!" Luke shouted, pointing at me. "I'm telling you, she's bald under there! I'll show you guys!"

He'd lunged forward aggressively, hand extended. I remember the whole moment felt like I was trapped in jelly: Luke reaching for my hijab, his friends howling in laughter and me, in disbelief, unable to do anything about it.

But Hussein, he wasn't trapped. He'd simply stepped into

Luke's path, forcefully moved his arm away from my head and said, using the little English he knew, "No touch."

That was the moment I realized that even though Aabo was no longer with us, my family and I still had each other to protect. I would never be vulnerable. Not with them around.

Somehow, Hussein and I managed to get through the next three years together in one piece. It never stopped being hard, but it did get a little easier. We made a few new friends, began making some good memories, and we stayed well away from Luke and his mates.

The two of us went our separate ways after that. Me, to Grafton Grammar, and Hussein, to Northwell High. We became different people with different dreams, but we were always still two halves of the same whole – Hanan and Hussein. Thankfully, that's never changed; we're both still there for each other when it matters.

Sumaya's finally composed herself, holding Hafsa's hand and letting it swing between them. I hold their bookbags, trailing slightly behind, wanting to let them comfort each other for a little while longer.

Wanting them to be there for each other the way siblings should be.

When we arrive home, time becomes elusive. I swiftly enter what I call my Hooyo-sphere – doing what my mother would be doing if she didn't have to work endless shifts at the care agency to make ends meet. I cook a quick dinner in our tiny kitchen, after relieving my grandmother's carer, and then sit by Abooto to massage her hands. It's the only time of the day when she isn't holding her tusbax tightly in her arthritis afflicted hands, caressing each smooth bead and making her silent prayers to God.

I send the girls to bed while I'm sat with her, and stealthily poke my head in their bedroom a little later to make sure they're not still awake. I'd made a deal with them after homework-time that I'd read them a book and let them watch extra TV if they promised to get into bed without a fuss tonight. I had too much work to catch up on to stress about them too. I'd held up my end of the bargain, but I was slightly worried they wouldn't. The light snoring that carries through the door sounds like music to my ears.

I lose track of time until I hear a loud slam downstairs, making me jump and my pencil create a jagged line across the page. I look up at the clock.

It's late.

The creaking of the stairs gets louder as Hussein makes his way up. He's trying to tiptoe, but I don't know why he bothers. It only ever makes the noise worse. The creaking reaches a fever pitch and I stand up to tell him to stop, worried that he might wake our sisters, but then I hear him yelp, and he hurtles through my bedroom door, sprawling to the floor on his hands and knees.

"That's the fifth time my sock's caught on that stupid nail," he cries, gingerly checking for any toe damage. "It ain't right!"

I stand over him and extend a hand when he's done with his

foot inspection. He considers it for a moment before taking up my offer. He's right to second guess me. When we were younger, I'd almost always offer help before humiliating him.

"Hussein, you know you scream like a girl, right?" I ask, pulling him up.

"Well, what do you expect? I've got one for a twin," he replies, immediately throwing himself onto my tattered chair. "Probably infected me with your voice box in the womb."

"Haha," I say, rubbing at my eyes. "So funny." I stand up straighter and cross my arms. "Seriously, man, where've you been? You were meant to be home hours ago, Hussein. You know, I've got stuff going on too. Hooyo's working a late shift tonight and you just disappear?"

My stomach growls and I realize that I haven't even stopped to eat any dinner tonight. In between cooking and reading with the girls and working on university applications, I'd forgotten to eat. No wonder I'm feeling so annoyed.

Hussein has the sense to look apologetic. "Listen, I'm sorry, sis. I swear I was gonna come home earlier but football was long and then Ahmed wanted to grab food after."

I avoid rolling my eyes. There isn't any use in arguing because this isn't the first time Hussein's done this. I love my brother, but his priorities are usually all over the place.

"It's fine. Whatever. Just deal with everything else until Hooyo gets home. The girls are already in bed, but Abooto needs her night meds and someone needs to take the washing out. I've still got stuff to do," I say, indicating the pile of papers on my desk.

While I'd like nothing more than to sleep, I have to get through my list because otherwise all my plans will start to fall apart. And the truth is, I'd rather go a thousand sleepless nights than have that happen.

It's not something that's spelled out in black and white, but I know that my future and my family's future are one and the same. I know that I have to be perfect because there's no room not to be. Not when Aabo is no longer with us, and Hussein doesn't even know what his tomorrow will look like, let alone his future. I've already lost track of how many university and apprenticeship brochures he's chucked in the bin when Hooyo isn't looking.

"Don't worry, sis, I've got this," Hussein says, propping his legs on the edge of my bed, locking his arms behind his head. "I'm not entirely useless."

I give him a fake smile. "Get that stuff done and then we'll talk about how useless you are."

He sniggers. "Chill out, Hanan. You know you're gonna go bald if you keep worrying so much and then Luke would've been right about you."

I gasp, annoyed he's got the audacity to bring up that story *now*, when he's the one on thin ice. I kick him out the room, launching a string of curse words in Somali, and he runs, dodging the pillows that I throw at his back without mercy.

When Hussein's gone, and I hear the door of his room shut, it takes me a few moments to remember what I was doing before he collapsed on my floor. I'm about to get started again when I find myself staring at the wall opposite my bed.

The peeling wall is bare, apart from a few frames and my calendar, and in the centre hangs my dad's degree, bordered by an oak frame. The paper is weathered, for ever changed by the oceans we'd been forced to cross. The space to its right is empty, waiting for me to fill it with my mark, with my footsteps following in my dad's. To the left hangs a family picture from our home in Mogadishu. It's a home I barely remember now, but I can never forget the expansive courtyard with its towering acacia tree; a tree Hussein and I would play on every day. The two of us reckless, unrestrained, desperate to reach the top before the other, but always stopping to catch each other whenever we'd fall.

We're standing in front of that magnificent tree in the photo – the sun beginning to emerge from its nest as the afternoon gradually takes hold. Aabo is stood joyfully holding Hafsa in his arms with Hooyo next to him in her orange baati and garbasaar, both her arms around me and Hussein, gently squeezing us, imploring us to be still for just a moment. Unbeknown to anyone, Sumaya had also been in that picture, though she'd only come to exist in the world nine months later.

I look at these two things on the wall every day to remind myself of what's at stake – our future.

I buckle down and get back to work.

When I'm finally done with my chemistry homework, I close my books and stretch out my cramping legs.

I have no idea where the last two hours have gone but,

somehow, it's midnight. Hooyo came back from work at some point and brought me a pot of yoghurt and a cereal bar to snack on but, apart from that, everything else has been a blur.

My phone vibrates. I pull it out of the charger and see a text from Isha.

the news!

And then a moment later –

check the news!!

I throw on a robe and head downstairs, expecting to hear the usual household background noise like Abooto shouting about the remote being too complicated or Hooyo reciting the Qur'an. But, as I head down the hallway, I hear nothing except the dull drone of the TV. I can't hear Hussein either, who's normally watching random YouTube videos on his phone.

Instead, when I walk into the living room, I find Hooyo, Abooto and Hussein all fixated on the TV, a collective picture of dismay. I'm shocked that they're all watching the same programme more than anything, before I notice that they're watching the news. But it isn't a regular newscast about government policies or weather reports.

It's something much, much worse.

CHAPTER THREE

I find it difficult to sleep that night. The fuzzy images of a bloodstained pavement and weeping bystanders from the news stay with me on a never-ending loop behind my eyelids; defiant, persistent.

I hear the screams too, the soundtrack to those fuzzy images. Faintly, like when you sometimes hear the whisper of wind against a window, but there. Definitely there. The screams of people in distress, the kind of human cry that makes you instinctively recoil at first. Not because you feel nothing, but because feeling the pain of others is a different sacrifice. A harder sacrifice. As I toss and turn, fighting with my duvet because I'm both too hot and too cold, I wonder if that's what I sounded like when I saw my dad die. If those screams are the same as the ones that came from me.

Finally, I fall asleep, but it's not peaceful. The images and the shrieks from the news footage on the high street follow me into my dreams, and I wake up shaking, gasping, drenched in sweat. Somehow, I'm on the floor, though I don't remember falling off the bed. I push myself up to sit and lean against the frame behind me, drawing in huge breaths.

A moment later, Hussein bursts into my room. He kneels down on the floor next to me and grips my hand but doesn't say anything. He only waits for me to calm down, waiting for my breathing to steady again.

I lean my head against his shoulder when the worst is finally over.

"Was I screaming again?" I ask wearily.

Hussein nods.

"Was it bad?" I ask, holding my breath.

I sense him weighing up his answer. Hussein nods again but doesn't add anything else.

"I'm sorry," I whisper, willing my tears not to fall. "I thought they were finally getting better. I thought they'd stopped."

Hussein's shoulders tense up under my head. I start to think that he might be angry, but then he grips my hand tighter.

"Don't ever apologize to me, Hanan. Ever," he says fiercely. "No one lives in the present without remembering the past. No one. And anyone who pretends they can is really just fooling themselves."

I nod, wiping my nose and unshed tears on the edge of the duvet.

Hussein speaks more softly this time. "And I know you're only screaming because of what was on the news last night but the guy's still alive. He's in bad shape but in shaa Allah he'll make it."

That was true. We still didn't know much about what we'd seen on the news, what I'd seen on Faren High Street, but the reports coming through had all agreed on one thing at least:

that the man who'd been stabbed was still alive. I try not to imagine who else it could have been on the floor. If it could have been Hooyo, jumping between discount grocery shops, or Hussein, waiting for a bus that would have brought him home. I try not to think about how close this was to us and whether it could be even closer still, one day. I try not to think at all.

We sit there together, side by side, until dawn begins to peek through the curtains. I try to push away the demons of our past, the ones I've been trying to forget for most of my life, and Hussein simply holds my hand, like he's always done.

We break apart when my alarm goes off.

"Friday, sis," Hussein grins, standing up. "One more day pretending to learn."

I smile gratefully at him as he leaves to get ready and head off to his sixth-form college. He has to take two buses every morning to get there on time, so he's always the first person to leave the house. But it also means he's the first one in the bathroom and, by the time it's my turn, it's always a complete and utter mess. Hussein's the only neat-freak I know who keeps distinct parts of his life in order. His bedroom, yes; the bathroom, no.

I hop in the shower when it's finally my go and stand still under the hot water, letting my skin go numb. After a moment, I move to grab the soap, but something makes me hesitate. A weird niggling feeling ticking away at the back of my head.

I stand there for a few moments more, letting the hot water strip away all feeling from my back, trying to work it out.

31

What is it?

The question circles, but there's no answer.

I groan in frustration, give up and grab the soap.

It's ten minutes later, when I'm downstairs and halfway through my bowl of cereal, that I finally realize what's been nagging me.

Hussein said he'd been at football last night, but his weekly practices are always on a Monday and Wednesday. Yesterday was Thursday…

I chew on my Coco Pops, trying to make sense of it. Wait. Had Hussein lied to me? But why? We've never kept secrets from one another. Never. I can't believe that my powers of twin intuition failed and Hussein might have pulled one over on me.

He'd probably been too lazy to come home and do his fair share of chores but why bother to lie? And to me, of all people? Hussein knows I'm a sniffer dog when it comes to detail and if there's a bone buried somewhere, I'll sure as hell dig up the whole pitch to find it.

"He must think I'm some kind of idiot," I grumble out loud, but there's no one around to complain to. Hussein's probably reached college by now, Hooyo's already left to drop off the girls at their school breakfast club on her way to work, and Abooto's sleeping soundly in her room.

The doorbell rings as I finish washing the dishes, trying to figure out what to do about Hussein. We never lie to each other. Ever. It's an unspoken code that we've had since we were little. And he's just broken it.

As I go to unlock the door, I try to ignore the seed of a

thought that's trying to bury itself in my head – that if Hussein lied about last night, he must have been doing something I wouldn't like.

Right as I'm opening the front door, the bus app on my phone dings.

Abooto's carer, Rosa, stands in our narrow doorway, her navy uniform ironed and pressed to perfection, a snapshot of her infectious smile captured on the ID card hanging from the pocket of her shirt.

"Hiya, sweetie, how we doing today?" Rosa asks, squeezing past me in the hallway.

"I'm alright. So sorry, Rosa, I have to go. My bus is running early. You'll help yourself to tea?"

"Of course. I know my way around this kitchen like my own."

I smile gratefully. "Thanks. Have a good morning, then. I'll see you later."

Rosa chuckles. "I'll try my best sweetie, but we'll see if your grandma is feeling up to niceties this morning. You know as well as I do that winter always puts her in a foul mood."

I laugh. That was true enough. Abooto was as tough as nails but come winter, she became undone. Her usual brightness disappeared during the shorter days and colder nights and she typically became less than willing to engage in any sort of discussion where English was the primary mode of communication.

I squeeze Rosa's hand, wishing her a silent good luck, and head out for school.

Outside, I'm greeted by light rain. Maryam, the sister of Hussein's friend Ahmed, waves at me as she's coming out of her house. I quickly wave back but I don't stop to catch up. If I miss this bus, then I'll miss Andrea on it too.

I hurry along, walking under Old Booker's Arch, making sure to hug the wall of the arch as much as possible so I'm not splashed by puddles as traffic goes by. When I'm through, I cross to the other side of the road, acutely aware that I'm now entering the Crescent Boys' turf. There are no signs or flags that tell you this, but those who know, know. Across the dividing line of the Arch, there's a clear distinction. Crescent Boys on one side and the Parsons Gang on the other.

If you're harmless enough, you could probably live your entire life in Northwell without any problems. But I've heard of one too many people who *did* encounter problems, who fell into the destruction of these gangs. Their names are inscribed on the one wall deemed to be *no man's land*. Flowers, now brown and lifeless, adorn the wall, existing alongside gum-wrappers, empty vodka bottles and crisp packets.

Still, even surrounded by all of this, I'm never afraid of walking home across this invisible line of territories because I've grown up with it.

When we were younger, Hooyo would sometimes cover our eyes with her long, black, billowy jilbab whenever we heard hushed voices or saw lingering handshakes. Or, if we smelled something strange, Hooyo would tell us it was an experiment gone wrong or coloured paper being burned.

As I got older, I started to realize the truth. That those

34

strange smells were drugs, not burned paper. But I was glad that she sheltered us from what was really going on, that she still tried to protect us even after everything we'd already seen.

The funny thing is, even with gangs and no man's land nearby, my nightmares haven't bothered me for a long while. They'd only come back last night, after hearing about the Faren stabbing and seeing the footage on the news. The Crescent Boys and Parsons Gang might stir up trouble from time to time, but that trouble has never once been as close to my front door as yesterday's was. I shudder, remembering the fuzzy images and screams again.

And, despite all of this, I have never once felt out of place in Northwell, whereas I have felt out of place every single day at Grafton.

When I'd first heard of the school, it sounded like a dream to me. I'd been so excited to get to the local library that day, rushing Hooyo to get ready so I could learn as much as I could off the internet.

When I'd seen pictures of the manicured green fields, the magnificent library with its towering shelves and the well-equipped science classrooms, I knew I had to go there. I knew that that was the kind of place where I could grow up to be a doctor, like Aabo, honouring his legacy.

I'd tried my very best to pique Hussein's interest, too, but there was always a dull, faraway look in his eyes whenever I spoke about Grafton Grammar. "I don't want to go," he'd say sharply each time, and Hooyo would tell me not to push it.

Weeks later, Hooyo and I had patrolled the local charity

shops looking for textbooks to help me with the entrance exam and we'd finally found one on our third try. I wished we could've bought new ones, but I knew it wasn't possible from the landscape of bills that painted our fridge a very dull colour.

I'd felt like I was walking on sunshine when I'd passed and was offered a place. It was enough to help me forget that, for the first time in my life, my brother and I wouldn't be together at school any more.

I had walked in through the heavy wooden doors on the first day, marvelling at the history so visibly embedded in the architecture, with Hooyo right next to me. She'd been gripping my hand tightly as she took in the other students and their families milling about in the foyer. I could tell that she'd rather be anywhere but here, in this place, with these people glancing at us too many times for it to be casual. I squeezed her hand and she'd looked down at me and smiled. But it was a small smile, not her usual one. It was one that said *let's hold it together, we'll make it through*.

I'd wanted to tell Hooyo that it was just nerves, that there was nothing to worry about. That it would be better than my old school because this time, I wasn't the girl who couldn't speak or understand the words being thrown at her. This time would be different. It would be a level playing field.

But then, the whispers reached us. Quiet, at first, until they grew in confidence.

One of them
Muslim
Too many foreigners here

I'd looked up at Hooyo. The small smile was gone, and mine was, too. Then the receptionist called out *Hamam* and I knew there was no turning back. The sunshine I had walked on for all those months quickly dissipated, leaving everything grey.

Over time, I came to learn that there was no level playing field at Grafton Grammar for me. I might not have been the girl fresh off the boat, but I was the girl who looked like no one else there.

I board the bus, which arrives a few minutes late and not the three minutes early like the app had promised, and I see Andrea sat towards the back, her long black hair tied up into a high bun and her ears bejewelled with her standard eight earrings. I squeeze past a man standing in the aisle with three suitcases precariously balanced on top of each other and climb up the two steps to reach the seat she's saved for me. I want to say hello right away, but I'm still a little stung by her absence from yesterday's maths lesson. When I see her beaming at me, though, I give in.

"Hi, deserter," I say gruffly.

"Come on, now," she says. "I'm sure we can do a little better than that with our good mornings, can't we? Can't we?" Her voice acquires the tone of baby talk as she reaches over to try and squeeze my cheeks.

"Fine," I laugh, batting away her arms. "Good morning then. Hope you enjoyed truanting."

"Excuse me," she replies, clutching her chest. "You *know* my period cramps get bad sometimes. Plus, you know how irritable I get so, really, it was in your best interests. You're welcome."

I have to concede this point.

"I have to say, I'm a little surprised you haven't asked for yesterday's rundown yet. That's usually the first thing you're jumping down my throat about."

"That's because you should know the drill by now, Hanan." She shakes her head disapprovingly. "I'm trying to be less demanding with this stuff, you know."

I roll my eyes at her.

"Well, even though you *didn't* ask, I'll just tell you anyway." I tick things off on my fingers as I list them. "Isha's lost a follower on that fan account of hers. She's down to eighty now but, also, you're not allowed to mention it to Nasra. Lily's going to Switzerland this weekend with her mum. They've been intensely planning that since yesterday..." I trail off, trying to remember what else happened, but it doesn't take me long. "Oh my God. The police thing on Faren. The mugging with the elderly man. Did you see the news?"

Andrea nods sombrely. "My dad told me and then I looked it up online." She sighs. "I can't believe it literally happened down the road from Grafton."

"The school probably can't believe it either," I say, recalling the message Hooyo forwarded me last night.

Dear Parents, the police are currently investigating
an incident that occurred on Faren High Street this afternoon.
They have assured us that there are no concerns regarding
students' safety. Attendance is expected tomorrow as usual.
Best wishes, Grafton Grammar School

"Anyway," Andrea says, attempting to divert us to something a little less gloomy. "Anything else on the rundown?"

I rack my brains to see if there's anything else Andrea-worthy to share. "Uh, no."

"What about Jessica?"

"What about Jessica?" I counter.

"You know what I mean," Andrea replies, pursing her lips. "Did she say anything? You know how she loves to come at you when I'm not there in maths."

"I don't know. Maybe."

Andrea waits.

"She might have told me to tell you to get a life."

"Ha!" Andrea laughs loudly, causing the elderly man in front of us to jump in his seat. "I wish she would say that to me."

This time, I'm the one who tries to divert the conversation. Andrea knows what Jessica is like, but talking about it doesn't change anything so why bother?

"How about you just tell me what you did yesterday."

"Well, apart from almost climbing the walls, not much. Had another *Twilight* marathon actually."

I pause. "Wait, didn't you do that last month?"

"Yes. I do it every month."

Then her face changes. She swats my thigh so fast I don't even see it coming. The impact of it makes the elderly man in front of us jump again.

"Oi!" I say, rubbing my leg. "What's wrong with you?"

"You promised you'd watch those movies last weekend!

I completely forgot about that. How many times are you going to keep dodging it?"

"Andrea." I twist in my seat so I'm facing her properly. "My bad, honestly. I've just had a ton of work to get through." Even saying this, I can hear how dead it sounds. It makes me want to cringe, too, but it's true. "I didn't think some vampire films would be a big deal."

Andrea sighs, putting her arm round my shoulders. "No, babe, it's just that I worry about you sometimes. You don't know when to cool off. School, exams, all of it…it literally consumes you and I'm just worried what happened last time might happen again. So, I thought," she says, with air quotes and an exaggerated eye roll, "a little 'vampire film' might do you some good."

We both refer to my panic attack five years ago as "what happened last time". For some reason, we never really talk about it beyond those four words. And I've never talked about it with anyone else, either. Even Hussein doesn't know, and we tell each other pretty much everything.

I wonder if I should feel guilty about having never told my twin. I've always been an open book with Hussein but I never want him to worry about me more than he already does. Then I remember his football lie last night, and I decide against feeling guilty at all.

"Fine," I reluctantly agree. "I'll watch your stupid movie, even if it burns and kills me inside."

Andrea rolls her eyes as she reaches over to ring the bell, signalling the bus driver to stop. Then, she begins the arduous task of removing all but two of her earrings. Grafton has a strict policy when it comes to jewellery, and the only thing you can wear past the school gates are two stud earrings or nothing at all. I don't know how she has the dedication to do this every day, but the one time I asked she'd simply said: "Beauty is pain and effort, Hanan. Remember that."

It's in these moments, when I'm not overshadowed by Northwell and Grafton Grammar, where I feel lighter. Untangled. I love the ease with which I can talk to Andrea, the comfort I find in her, the familiarity of our friendship. It's uncomplicated. Simple. Although uncomplicated and simple isn't what I imagined when Andrea tapped me on the shoulder all those years ago to ask if my name really was *Hamam*. I'd snorted because it sounded so ridiculous, though Andrea hadn't understood why it was so funny and stood there looking stung.

"No," I'd finally managed. "My name is *Hanan*. *Hamam* is a bath. A Turkish one. And I don't think I look like a bath."

A smile slowly grew on her face and then she also descended into laughter, side by side with me, the girl who stuck out like a sore thumb in that elegant school.

"My name's Andrea," she'd said, sticking her skinny arm out to shake my hand.

I learned later that her thick accent was Romanian and I don't know if she gravitated towards me because she could sense that I was also different, because I had an accent and came from somewhere completely unlike this place, or if she was just being nice and searching for a new friend. Either way,

41

there had been something about this girl with inky black hair, pulled into a high bun, that I felt I could trust.

"Okay, Andrea," I had said. "Let's be friends."

And, today, I'm really glad we are. Although, sometimes, I do wish that our friendship was a little more friend-friend than friend-bodyguard.

CHAPTER FOUR

When we get to school, we head to the back of form to sit with Nasra, Lily and Isha. Mr Foster, our form tutor, is sat at his desk, typing furiously on his laptop. About half of the class are already here. The rest trickle in slowly after us.

Immediately, I can tell something is wrong. Nasra is sat with her arms crossed, staring daggers across the room. I follow her line of sight to…I sigh. Jessica, Divya and Sarah.

I put my bag down on the table and pull out a chair.

Lily and Isha look like they're having an intense discussion, but they look up quickly to say hi to Andrea and me.

"So," I say to Nasra, knowing I'll probably regret opening this Pandora's box, "what is it this time?"

Jessica and Nasra have the *ultimate* hate-hate relationship. When the two of them lock eyes, the world could be burning down and neither of them would flinch out of fear of being accused of backing down.

"It's Jessica! Girl tried to cuss me out again behind my back but in *front* of my face this morning."

Andrea and I look at each other, confused.

"I don't think we're following," Andrea says.

"I mean," Nasra says, placing both hands flat on the table and leaning forward, "she was whispering about me to her little friends *knowing* I was walking right behind her. Something dumb about me ruining this school when I started last year or whatever. I called her out on it, obviously, but then Lily and Isha kept pulling on my arm and telling me to stop like I was the problem."

Nasra crosses her arms, again, this time shifting her dagger-eyes to Lily and Isha, who either haven't heard themselves being name-dropped into this conversation or are choosing to ignore it.

I don't know why Nasra is upset, though. I've warned her enough times that Grafton Grammar would be nothing like her old school.

When she first started at Grafton last year and it became obvious that she was slowly being absorbed into our friendship group, I'd tried to give her a comprehensive summary about the way things worked at this school.

I'd warned her that Jessica would run her mouth every chance she got, that she would try and get under her skin by whatever means possible, and that, whenever those things happened, there would be very few people to turn to beyond me and Andrea.

It wasn't that I was trying to turn her against anyone prematurely. I just really wanted to save her all the hurt that I've been through these last six years at school. I still remember how my own hate-hate relationship with Jessica started.

Jessica had locked on to me immediately, a bullseye for her

44

vicious arrows. I heard that she'd told everyone that someone like me must be there by mistake. That she had spent weeks telling everyone in our class that I had something much worse than the lurgies and, if they valued their lives, they'd stay far, *far* away from me. I'd done my best to ignore all of it, focusing instead on why I was at Grafton; what I was there to do and the people I was there to do it for.

Bar Andrea, and now Nasra, there's no one else here who has seen things as they are. Some of the teachers – Mr Foster included – have turned a blind eye over the years, pretending not to hear some of the terrible things Jessica says, which is why I learned, very early on, not to trust a lot of people here. Even Lily and Isha seem to be living their own version of Grafton Grammar – a very different version to the one I've known.

And, as much as Andrea defends me, I know that the people who will always be the biggest target for Jessica's jokes are Nasra and me.

It doesn't matter that Andrea moved here when she was seven, like me, or that she still has a hint of a Romanian accent, when I lost my Somali accent years ago. It doesn't matter that Isha is half-Indian and moved back after living in India for five years. It doesn't matter that Lily had a falling-out with the Evil Queen herself in Year Nine, over God knows what, and vowed to never speak to her again. None of those things matter because, at the end of the day, none of them are what Nasra and I are: Muslim. And, apparently, that's the only thing you need to be to get on and *stay on* Jessica's radar.

"Just let it go," I reply, attempting to mitigate the situation. "She isn't worth it and you're wasting your breath. I've told you this a million times."

I wish Nasra would just do what I do and ignore her. It doesn't mean that any of it will stop, but, at least, she'd avoid fighting and getting into trouble.

Nasra purses her lips in displeasure but, thankfully, doesn't say anything else.

"Did you see my text, Hanan?" Isha asks, finally wading into our conversation and giving Nasra a new focus.

"What text?" Nasra swivels to face her. Her eyes look small and angry behind her glasses. "This wasn't in the group chat, Isha. And, for the millionth time, why are you lot chatting outside the group chat? This is what the group chat's bloody for!"

"Calm down," I laugh. "The group chat's still alive and kicking. She only texted me about what happened on the high street yesterday." I stop laughing when I remember what *did* happen on the high street yesterday. What I saw on the news. What followed me into my dreams.

"Oh right," Nasra replies, more quietly now. "I heard about that too. Crazy, right? Can't believe someone would do something like that on Faren, of all places."

Andrea shakes her head sadly. "Way too close. It's scary."

"Have they said anything else about the man in hospital?" Lily asks, leaning forward to be heard over the other conversations around us.

Isha shakes her head. "No, not yet. They haven't named him or the guy that put him there either."

"I just can't believe it all happened at a random ATM," Andrea says, sighing. "How a mugging can become a stabbing –" she snaps her fingers – "just like that."

"They said that the police killed the mugger though, right?" Lily asks. "I think I heard that on the news."

"Yeah," Isha confirms. "The police shot him straight away. Apparently, he was trying to go after them, too."

"After the police?" I ask, incredulously. "Who'd be dumb enough to do that?"

Isha shrugs her shoulder. "Don't shoot the messenger, Hanan. I'm just giving you the facts."

"Wow," Nasra says, slowly giving her a once-over. "That's distasteful, Isha. Very. Distasteful."

She looks at Nasra, confused, until it dawns on her. "Oh no, I didn't mean—"

Andrea and Lily stifle a laugh as Isha stutters a reply. Nasra hides her grin.

As if aware of Isha's distress, the bell rings. Everyone rises from their seats, packing their planners and books away, saying their goodbyes and hurrying off to their first period lessons.

Nasra catches sight of Jessica again. She's on the other side of the classroom, laughing at something Sarah's said. She blows Nasra a kiss when she notices her gaze. Nasra shoulders her bag and takes a step forward, lips pursed, chest heaving.

"Let it go," I say, pulling on her arm.

She hesitates for a second but lets me pull her away – from their laughter, from their nastiness – though she still has a thunderous look on her face.

* * *

The house is already busy by the time I reach home. Hooyo's back early from her care shift, which is surprising given her hectic work schedule, and both Hafsa and Sumaya run wild and carefree, playing a game of tag. They'd usually be playing outside, but the large birch tree that fell in our garden six months ago takes that option off the table. If the council weren't in an absolute shambles, I'm sure it would have been fixed by now.

Abooto is sat on the rocking chair in the living room, eyes closed, holding her black and silver tusbax. I watch the movements of her hands carefully as I take my shoes and coat off in the hallway, relieved when I see the ease with which her joints flex. I walk over to her, inhaling her sweet, old-person smell and the potent smell of jasmine-scented attar which she always demands Rosa douse her in after her morning bath.

"Hey, Abooto," I say, crouching next to her.

Abooto looks at me abruptly, startled by my arrival. She instinctively curses in Somali.

I laugh when I catch what she's saying. "Hey, I'm not a donkey!"

"You're a thousand donkeys if you're trying to send me to my grave early," she grumbles, leaning into her pillow.

I sense an audience behind me. I turn around and find Hafsa and Sumaya paused mid-action in their game of tag, trying to follow our Somali words.

Abooto laughs violently, landing a solid *thwack* on her armrest. "Ha! Your fish-and-chips crew!"

"Don't lump me with them," I splutter in indignation. "My Somali isn't as bad as theirs."

"Oh, you're all the same to me," Abooto says, waving her hand to indicate all three of us. "Fish-and-chips to the bone."

Hafsa and Sumaya still look on in confusion. They can follow simple things in Somali but following an entire conversation is sometimes too much for them. Hafsa was only a year old when we moved here and Sumaya hadn't even been born yet. They've been speaking English their whole lives, whereas Hussein and I have only spent the last ten years doing that. Usually, all my conversations with Abooto or Hooyo happen in Somali but, if I know my two little sisters are listening in or part of the chat, I'll either jump between both languages so they sort of know what's up or give them a quick English rundown.

I'm about to quickly translate for them when I remember something Abooto just said.

"I'm sorry, did you just say I'd send you to your grave early?" I shake my head with a small smile. "No one can send you anywhere you don't want to go, Abooto. Don't pretend like you're a pushover."

"True," she nods. "But I can promise I'll send *you* sprawling across this room if you try sneaking up on me again."

I don't reply to this threat. There's no point in replying to any of Abooto's threats because the woman has a way with words that no one else can ever hope to match. Instead, I angle my body to give her a hug – the one weapon I have in my small arsenal. For some reason, my grandmother has a very deep,

49

and very well-known, hatred of hugs. She's never been one of those children-doting grandmothers. This time, though, instead of pushing me away with words, Abooto brings out a weapon I hadn't even seen coming. She licks my cheek.

I jump back, disgusted. "Ugh, Abooto, why? Why can't you just be normal?"

Abooto cackles and promptly goes back to counting the beads of her tusbax, satisfied with the knowledge that I, for the foreseeable future, will be avoiding all forms of affection. Even my sisters have betrayed me, both of them in tears of laughter on the floor. An attack on my dignity is something they understand in any language.

I ignore all three of them and stalk into the kitchen, rubbing my cheek. Hooyo isn't alone in the kitchen. Hussein stands in front of the hob, wearing the pink, rose-embroidered apron we bought Hooyo three years ago for Mother's Day. We'd saved up to give our mum something nice and she'd vowed to always treasure it. Though not enough, I think, if she's letting Hussein wear it again. At this point, it might as well be Hussein's apron anyway. Hooyo doesn't get to wear it nearly as much as she used to, with all the shifts she's had to do lately.

I quickly suppress the whisper of guilt that I feel when I think about just how much Hooyo has to do on her own. It's a thought that crosses my mind a lot, but, whenever it does, I try to remind myself that going to Grafton, trying to get into uni – doing the things I'm supposed to do – are the things that will help our family in the long run. I know it's what Aabo would've wanted for me, and I know it's what Hooyo wants for me, too.

I just wish sometimes that she could have more time to do the things she loves, like cooking.

Growing up, Hooyo used to always love cooking traditional dishes for us, like suqaar, muufo and kili, even more than she loved eating them. She would tell us that she'd had dreams of becoming a chef and opening her own restaurant, before our lives turned upside down.

"Leyla's Maqaayad," she told us one night, as she kissed Hussein and I goodnight. "Your father and I were simply going to call it Leyla's Restaurant. It was going to be the greatest restaurant in Mogadishu with the greatest food and the greatest views of the Liido coastline." The beginnings of a sadness had caught in her throat then and she'd coughed to clear it. "It was going to be wonderful."

Hooyo and Aabo had started saving money together so that one day, when the time was right, Hooyo's dream could be realized. But, when the war came knocking on our door, and we had no choice but to escape, the money that would've created Leyla's Maqaayad created a door for us to come to England instead.

They haven't noticed me standing in the doorway yet. Hussein is poised over the hob, tasting the suugo and making noises which suggest he's satisfied with the sauce. It's about the only thing he can cook successfully. Whenever he makes it, his ego inflates just a bit too much for my liking.

Getting carried away, he continues to dip into it, eating a few mouthfuls until Hooyo turns around.

I beat my mum to it. "You're going to keep eating like that?

51

So uncivilized, right, Hooyo?"

Hooyo turns to look at me in the doorway and smiles. "Hanan, I'm so glad you're home. I thought you might be late, but now we can eat together."

"Not sure I want to eat that suugo, considering Hussein's DNA must be all over it."

"My DNA is your DNA," Hussein retorts, smiling sweetly.

I pointedly ignore him. The boy lied to my face less than twenty-four hours ago and I'm still pissed about it. I'd call him out on it right now if not for the fact that doing it in front of Hooyo might make him less likely to cough up the truth.

I attempt to gracefully swerve the conversation away from my brother.

"So, Hooyo, you're free this evening? Did they cancel your shift?"

Hooyo nods. "They called to tell me that one of the old ladies I usually visit went into hospital." She sighs. "Miskeen, I'm not sure she'll make it. She's got so many problems and no love at home. And, when you have no love, you have little reason to want to keep living."

Hooyo looks a little lost in thought when she says that, gazing up at a space above her head. I wonder if she's thinking about Aabo then, about losing the love of her life, or whether she's imagining Leyla's Restaurant and losing the promise of that dream.

"I'm just glad you're home now," I say after a moment, leaning against the door frame and trying to pull her back into the present.

Hooyo smiles and takes over the cooking before Hussein eats the lot.

My cursor's hovering over the *Play* button to finally start watching *Twilight* when Andrea calls me on my phone. I quickly answer, thinking she's probably calling to brainstorm for the bake sale we're doing with the Fundraising team in a couple of weeks. And if there's one thing I'm always up to do, it's planning.

"Hey. Hi. Hello." I pull out my notepad and start scribbling but no ink comes out. "Great timing actually. I was just about to—"

"Hanan, wait," Andrea says. Her voice sounds faint. Not far-away faint but hesitant. "There's something I need to tell you. Something…"

I'm cradling the phone between my shoulder and ear as I reach to grab a pen from the other side of my desk.

"Hold up. I didn't quite hear that, sorry," I reply. "But I'm glad you called because we forgot to talk about the bake sale stuff. What we need to buy, when we're practising, blah, blah, blah." I finally grab the edge of the pen holder. It topples over and I grab one.

Andrea speaks again. This time, I detect a break in her voice, a trembling.

"Hanan, I need to tell you something. It's important." She clears her throat.

"Okay," I say, leaning back against the chair and holding the phone properly again. "But I'm not sure what's more important than us dominating the bake sale this year."

"Hanan!" Andrea's voice travels more strongly now. Firmer. "Please. I need you to listen to me." She pauses. "Do you remember what happened on Faren? What we were talking about today?"

"Yeah, I remember," I reply, tensing up a little. How could I forget the police cars and tape from yesterday, the horrible news story, the sirens and screams in my nightmares?

"Right," Andrea says. There's definitely a note of hesitation in her voice now. Andrea never hesitates.

"They've released the name of the guy now. The one who was in hospital."

Was? Does that mean he's not in hospital any more?

"It's all over the news," she says. "Have you...have you heard anything?"

I'd jumped straight into revising after dinner and shut my phone off so I wouldn't be tempted. If there were any more updates, I wouldn't have caught it.

I shake my head, waiting for her to say more, but dread floods through me.

"Andrea," I say slowly. "Is it someone we know?"

The static judders as she takes in a deep breath.

"I'm really sorry, Hanan. It's Mr Fleming. He's dead."

CHAPTER FIVE

There was a time, long before I knew Lily, Isha and Nasra, when I'd had only two friends at Grafton Grammar. Just two. Though, if you'd asked anyone else at school about me back then, they'd probably have told you that I had only one. Andrea Popa – a tall, shapely girl with long, black hair and striking, blue eyes.

Andrea herself probably would've told you that she was my only friend, but I'd had another. One who I kept to myself for a long time. I'm not sure if I was embarrassed or not, but I shouldn't have been. He was a good friend to me.

Life at Grafton Grammar, especially in those first few years, hadn't been easy. My black skin and modest dress drew eyes whenever I entered a room. There was no escaping it and, at the beginning, all I dreamed about was going back to my old school. To the place where not speaking the language was my only crime because, here, my biggest crime was simply existing and it got worse the first time someone saw me pray.

I used to pretend that I was a spy, which, admittedly, is a very uncool thing to pretend to be when you're twelve years old. But it helped. It made me feel like I wasn't patrolling empty hallways at lunch because there were no teachers willing to supervise me praying, but like I was doing it because I had a mission.

But it was in one of those supposedly empty hallways, one day, that I heard scuffling and voices behind me. I froze, right in the middle of my prayer, with my forehead on the prayer mat, my heartbeat and my coursing blood loud in my ears. For a moment, it felt like I was a gazelle in one of those nature documentaries – exposed and terrified and just waiting to see if someone would pounce.

No one confronted me then, but, afterwards, the gossip spread like wildfire. I didn't doubt for a second who those voices had belonged to, so I wasn't shocked by what Andrea said when I joined her in our next lesson.

"So, the Braids," she'd started by way of explanation. "They've piped up again."

"Shocker," I replied.

"It's not great."

"It never is," I said with a sigh.

"They're telling everyone you're a devil-worshipper."

"Very creative."

Andrea pulled on my arm, turning me around to face her, but I couldn't look at her. Not properly.

"Hanan. Stop, be serious," she said, annoyed. Her voice fell as she asked me this next question. "Why didn't you tell me that's what you were doing when you went off at lunch? I would've come and stayed with you."

I looked at her then and saw the kind of dismay that couldn't be faked – the kind that made my stomach hurt. I hated keeping things from Andrea, but this was the one thing I'd been scared would make her jump ship. That she would finally abandon me and join everyone else who supported the anti-Hanan Club. For some reason, I was scared, terrified, that her knowing I prayed to God every day would mean the end of our friendship. I was scared it would make me the kind of different I could never come back from.

"It's not a big deal," I said, shrugging my shoulders. "They say crap like that all the time. This isn't any different."

"Oh...it's different," she replied slowly. "It's very, very different."

After that, Andrea refused to let me go alone to lunch. She followed me across the courtyard, past the foyer, and through the zigzag corridors of the languages department. I could never lose her. Even when I ran, she was always right behind me. We ate lunch together and then we'd *both* find an empty corridor for me to pray in while she stood guard behind me.

Andrea made me feel invincible because people thought twice before they said anything to me in front of her. When I was with Andrea, I wasn't a gazelle just waiting to be eaten – it was like being protected by a lioness.

No one bothered me again after that until, one day, Andrea wasn't in school.

I found myself in a panic that whole morning, and the Braids knew it too. Jessica's gaze kept flicking to mine and she smiled knowingly, putting an upward curved finger on either side of her head.

When the bell finally rang for lunch, I legged it from the classroom. I went around my usual spots countless times, trying to find one that might be empty for a few minutes but each time I thought I found somewhere to pray, I caught Jessica and her co-Braids either lying in wait or trailing slowly behind me.

I let my head hang against a door, willing myself not to cry.

"You alright there?" said a gruff voice behind me. I quickly wiped my eyes with the edge of my hijab. I'd rather be caught dead than let anyone see me cry at this school.

"Sorry," I said, picking up my bag which I'd dropped on the floor. "I was just leaving."

"No, no, that's alright," he said, shuffling forward a few steps. "Just wanted to offer you a room is all, for...um, your, your ritual."

Confused, I looked up from the floor I'd been staring hard at, not wanting to let this teacher, this stranger, see anything in my eyes. But that's when I noticed he wasn't a teacher.

He was an older man, dressed casually in a fleece jacket, cargo trousers and walking boots, not like the usual suit-wearing staff members who walked around here.

"Sorry, what?" I replied. "What did you say?"

He cleared his throat and put his hands in his pockets. "I, uh, I've noticed you and your friend hanging about in some of these hallways. Always during lunch, when everyone *should* be outside," he said with a small smile. "Now, I'm no Einstein, but I can put two and two together and I know, whatever it is you're doing –" he indicated the hallway – "needs a little peace and quiet. I've got the caretaker office you can use if you want."

He turned around and began to walk back the way he came. "You coming then?" he said, without turning to look back.

I hesitated, grateful for the offer but wondering if I'd be better off finding somewhere myself. After everything that had happened so far at Grafton Grammar, with Jessica, her co-Braids, with most of the teachers who refused to ever do anything about them, I was wary of everyone until I had a reason not to be.

"Wait, what's your name?" I called out.

He stopped, turning around to face me this time.

"Mr Fleming, Michael Fleming. But you're alright to call me Michael."

And though I hadn't set out to make any more friends, that was the day I met my second friend at Grafton Grammar. Michael Fleming, the caretaker.

CHAPTER SIX

Since Andrea's running late, I ride the bus to school alone. The seat next to me remains empty the whole time, as if I'm sending out a silent signal to ward everyone off. The bus is packed to the brim and the eagle-eyed passengers, whose radars are forever on the hunt for any free seat, glance at the coveted space, but it remains empty for the rest of the ride. Not only that, a few people actually look *nervous* when they board the bus and lock eyes with me. I quickly look over my shoulder to see if there's anyone scary-looking behind me, but there's only a group of nursery kids being hushed by a dishevelled woman.

I walk into form alone, winding through the tables, chairs and clustered bodies to get to Nasra, Lily and Isha, who are chatting about Lily's weekend trip to Switzerland. I muted the group chat this weekend after the phone call with Andrea, not really in the mood to hear about Swiss Alps and skiing, so I'm a little out of the loop.

"Hey, guys," I mumble, leaning in reluctantly to Nasra's open arms before sitting down.

"What's up with you?" Isha asks, raising her eyebrows.

"It's a Monday morning," Lily replies, sighing dramatically.

"That's what's wrong with all of us." She digs for something in the inside pocket of her blazer and hands it to me. "But I'm sure this gorgeous keyring will make you feel better, Hanan."

If I was going to be real with Lily, I'd tell her there's not a single keyring in the world that could magically make everything better, but I know that this is tradition and that she's just being nice, so I dutifully take out my keys and swap out the last keyring she gave me – one from a weekend trip to Paris – for this one, a slice of dangling Swiss cheese.

Lily beams at me and jumps straight into another story about her adventures with her mum but my mind just isn't there.

Nasra must notice because she pulls on my sleeve to get my attention. "You sick or something?" she asks, concern colouring her face.

"No, it's not that," I say uncertainly. I look down and fiddle with my planner, wanting to avoid her gaze. A small part of me is worried that if I give words to my feelings, it might make them more real.

The weekend had been hard enough already. I'd barely gotten any sleep because my nightmares had come back in full force. Except this time, the nightmares had been much, much worse. They weren't just fuzzy images and unrecognizable screams. They were the face and screams of Mr Fleming. And my dad. Always, my dad. And, because of that, Hussein had barely gotten any sleep either. Though, luckily for him, that meant I'd decided to let him off the hook for lying to me – for now, anyway. I'll just have to find the perfect time for an interrogation later.

"These last few days have been weird," I start to say, still fiddling with the loops of my planner's spine. "I can't even tell you why exactly. Just a feeling that something's off, you know. The vibe on the bus was really weird this morning too." I pause, fingers still on the planner.

"You know what? Never mind. I'm being dumb."

In my sleep-deprived state, of course everything is going to be *off*. How can I expect to feel normal and fine when Mr Fleming is dead?

"You aren't being dumb, Hanan. I get what you mean." Nasra drops her voice lower, speaking in a half-whisper even though there's no way anyone's going to hear over Lily squealing about the quality of Swiss hot chocolate.

If I'm being honest, I'm starting to feel like this conversation might not be for them anyway.

"Things have been starting up since what came out on Saturday," Nasra adds soberly.

"What do you mean?" I turn my body so I'm completely facing her. Our closeness makes it feel like it's just us in the classroom, like there's no one else around. "What came out on Saturday?"

Nasra looks at me incredulously. "Girl, do you have amnesia or something? I'm talking about the Muslim guy who stabbed that ex-school caretaker, Mr Fleming, on Faren? It's been all over the news."

Shit. I'd avoided the TV, my phone, everything over the weekend, because I know how these things usually go. Photos of Mr Fleming, words from family members, shots of the crime scene. Rinse, repeat. I hadn't wanted to see any of that because it would have made things a thousand times more difficult to bear.

"What do you mean he was Muslim? One of those 'death to the disbelievers' crazies?"

"Nope," she replies, shaking her head. "I mean, they're really trying to make him look like that, but he was just a regular guy. A regular criminal, I mean." She laughs, once, but it's not her usual laugh. There's something darker in it, something that sounds a little hopeless. "You know it's funny –" she continues – "they'll really claim us when Mo Farah is out here winning gold, but they won't even let us have normal criminals. Everyone's got to be an extremist." She sighs dramatically and looks away. "I'm just tired."

"But maybe it's not about that." I pull her back to look at me. "Just forget what I said. It's probably a coincidence. Me over-thinking or—"

"Let me just stop you there," Nasra says. She quickly looks over to Mr Foster and pulls out her phone. "I'm sending you a video. Watch it later. You'll see what I'm talking about."

I pull a face at her and imitate her seriousness. She scowls back at me.

Andrea hurries in seconds before Mr Foster calls her name on the register. He gives her a disapproving look but gestures for her to sit down.

"Alarm emergency," she whispers to us after she's caught her breath. "My mum changed the code again and forgot it so the bloody thing wouldn't shut up."

When the register's done, Mr Foster stands at the front of the class and calls for our attention. He clasps his hands loosely in front of him, and looks down sombrely, leaning back against his desk. I feel a twinge of pity for the five people sitting at the table nearest to him. They'll be getting a front row seat to another one of Mr Foster's regular spit-storms.

"It's very saddening, this morning, to have to stand here and discuss something with you all that's truly come as a shock to the school and our local community over the last few days," Mr Foster begins, "but I also believe it is necessary." He clears his throat. "What happened last week was a hugely tragic and unexpected event and it's one that has certainly left a mark on this school. For those of who you aren't already aware, Mr Fleming, the victim of last week's attack on Faren High Street, was an integral part of the Grafton Grammar community serving as our caretaker for over twenty years." Mr Foster paces a few steps around his desk before leaning on it again. "I know most of you will have seen Mr Fleming around the school before his retirement last year. Perhaps some of you even got to know him well in the years you've been here."

I close my eyes, wanting him to stop talking, wanting the bell to ring right this very second, so I can leave and pretend like nothing's changed. So, I can pretend that Mr Fleming's still at home, enjoying his retirement.

Andrea lightly pats my leg. She texted me a few times over the weekend to check up on me. I don't think she believed me each time I told her I was fine, even though I'd tried to be as convincing as possible.

"There's support at the school for anyone who feels like they need to talk to someone. Please don't be ashamed to seek it if you need to," Mr Foster continues. "There should be more information soon about a memorial service we'll be holding for Mr Fleming so please keep an eye out for that, as well, if you'd like to come." He gazes around at us. "Does anyone have any questions about what I've said or would like to share anything?"

The class is silent for a couple of beats. I look down at my planner, waiting for us to move onto something else. We're almost there, almost over the awkward hump of silence, when Jessica breaks it.

"I have something I'd like to say, sir. If that's okay."

"Of course," Mr Foster says, sitting back down. "Go ahead, Jessica."

I look up, sure this can't be anything good.

Jessica sits up straighter. I'm not quite sure how to describe her expression. It's like a cross between real sadness and her usual savagery. "This situation with Mr Fleming… It's really shaken me, sir. I'm sure it's shaken a lot of people."

She looks around the room, taking in the nodding heads and murmurs of quiet agreement.

"He was obviously a big part of the school before he retired," she continues, "and I just think it was such a shame that he, you know, was killed the way he was. That someone could just kill him in broad daylight. What kind of person would do something like that?"

Somehow, all in the space of a minute, the atmosphere in the class has changed. Not in any obvious way, but in a way

I can feel, and in a way I know Nasra can feel too because, when I glance at her, she's already looking my way.

Mr Foster nods solemnly, eyes cast down as he listens to Jessica. He looks up when she's done talking.

"I can appreciate that, Jessica, thank you for sharing that with us. It is, of course, a more difficult loss, given the…" Mr Foster clears his throat again. "Given the circumstances of his passing and…and it is something that may take some time for people to come to terms with. Again, if there's anyone who feels they'd like to speak to me in private, or would like any kind of support, please do let me know." He nods at Jessica and then looks to the rest of the class. His gaze circles to our table in the back. I wait for him to drag his gaze around the rest of the class, like he always does, but he doesn't. Seconds elapse and I begin to wonder if this now constitutes outright staring, when Mr Foster speaks again.

"Is there anything else that anyone wants to share?"

I look back down again, praying we can finally move onto something else, but then I see Nasra's back straighten in the corner of my vision.

"No, sir, Hanan and I don't have anything to say if that's what you mean."

My head shoots up.

Mr Foster stammers a reply. "No, I wasn't, I'm not—"

"Don't worry about it, sir. We all get a bit tongue tied sometimes, just shake it off."

I reach over to pull on Nasra's arm. *What are you doing?* I say with my eyes. There's a fine line between acceptable sass and unacceptable sass. For some reason, Nasra always likes to walk the dangerous line between the two.

"It's not my fault," she whispers angrily across the space between us. "He was the one staring at us!"

Mr Foster quickly regains his composure, expression set in displeasure. "You'd better be careful what you say next, Nasra, or you'll find yourself in Mr Davies's office."

Nasra rolls her eyes but doesn't push her luck. I put a hand on her shoulder and hope that she doesn't say anything else.

Lily squirms uncomfortably, not looking at either of us. Isha stares hard at the lines of her palms, like there's something important in them she can't decipher. Next to me, I can feel Andrea quietly seething. She leans back in her chair, crossing her arms with a snort.

I catch sight of Jessica and her co-Braids smirking across the room. The rest of the class just looks at us with disdain.

I feel my skin prickle with awkwardness. I've made it through most of my years at Grafton without having to make proper eye contact or even interact with most of these people, but now it's all eyes on us.

And they're not kind eyes either.

"Mr Foster," Jessica says curtly. "I think it's only fair that one of them *does* say something though. I'm sure it's not just me who wants to hear it. That murderer was one of theirs after all—"

My hold on Nasra breaks. Before Mr Foster can respond to Jessica, Nasra jumps up, slamming both hands on the table.

"Bitch, I will beat your ass—"

"Nasra!" Mr Foster shouts. I've never heard his voice this loud before. It shakes the room for a moment. "That's enough. To the Head's office. Now!"

Nasra's body trembles with everything she's keeping a lid on, but she does it. She doesn't speak back to Mr Foster or Jessica. She packs her things away as quickly as she can, and I help her. There is only silence around us.

Her hand grabs mine after she zips up her bag. She bends down to whisper in my ear. "The cycle begins again, sis. Don't say I didn't warn you."

Nasra looks at me intently for a second before she leaves, letting the door slam shut behind her. The sound of it echoes in my ears long after she's gone.

CHAPTER SEVEN

I can't stop thinking about Nasra's words. The certainty in her voice, the quiet anger in her eyes. I know everyone else is thinking about what just happened, too, because the silence continues after she leaves, as though the balance of the room has shifted, and people are too busy trying to find themselves again to speak. Still, neither Lily or Isha meet my gaze. Andrea just squeezes my hand.

In those few minutes before the bell rings again, I wait for Mr Foster to do *something*. Anything. To tell Jessica off, to send her to Mr Davies's office, too. To acknowledge that what she said was wrong. That there is no *us* and *them*. That the man who killed Mr Fleming, whoever he was, wasn't *ours*. At least, not in the way she meant.

But…nothing happens. Mr Foster returns to the front and sits down at his desk, turning his attention to his laptop. The bell rings and the class promptly splits off into different groups. As I'm packing my things away, I hear Mr Foster quietly call Jessica to the side.

I take the long walk to the door, winding through the tables closest to them. I'm hoping I might be able to catch a scrap of their conversation. Andrea follows me.

Jessica's voice reaches us in fragments: "…took it the wrong way…didn't mean…"

She plays with the end of her fishtail braid, but with her back to me I can't see her expression or try to lipread. Still, I don't need to hear the entire thing to catch her drift: that Jessica saying exactly what she said didn't mean exactly what it meant.

"Yes, sir…I would never…" Her voice carries a smugness that makes me want to drag her right to the Head myself.

I can see Mr Foster's expression though, since he's facing in our direction. He looks…normal. Not angry or bothered or disappointed. In fact, there is a ghost of a smile that plays on his lips as he says: "I know this was just a misunderstanding, Jessica. It seems it's one of those Mondays, that's all."

He looks out of the window as sheets of rain begin to thump against it in earnest.

"Mr Fleming's death has got us all a bit shaken up, your family more than most, I imagine," he says sombrely.

Andrea starts to pull me away before they notice us lurking around.

"That prick!" she whispers angrily as she leads us both out of class. The hallway is densely packed so we link arms to avoid being separated. "Where the hell does he get off saying 'it's a misunderstanding'? He should be chucking her out of school!"

"Wouldn't that be lovely?" I reply sarcastically.

But we do live in reality after all, and, in this reality, Jessica can say whatever she likes in front of Mr Foster and get away with it. Like she's always done.

"What do you think he meant?" I ask, processing the last bit of what Mr Foster said. "About her family being shaken up?"

She sighs. "I don't know, but I refuse to spend another second thinking about what goes on in that man's brain. He's disgusting."

Suddenly, there's a commotion that draws everyone's attention in the hallway.

"Fight! Fight! Fight!" The chant starts eagerly, gaining volume as more people join in, even the people who can't see what's going on. From where Andrea and I are though, we have the perfect view.

Daniel – Jessica's brother, and Fundraising's biggest curse – is locked in a fight with another boy. It escalates quickly and, in just a few seconds, they're both on the floor, rolling around like wild dogs.

Mr Foster runs out of the classroom, with Jessica right behind him. He breaks up the fight with the help of Mr Anand, the form teacher from next door. Jessica snakes her way through the crowd to her brother and whispers something in his ear. He tears himself away from her, clearly unhappy with whatever she said.

I look at the two of them, standing in the middle of this chaos, and wonder what my life would've looked like if I hadn't met either of them. The two most toxic people I know. And then I wonder if they've got some kind of coordinated hate against me. Maybe they burn effigies of me at home for fun.

As if he's read my thoughts, Daniel looks up. He sneers at me, narrowing his eyes. Before I can even react, Andrea gives him the finger.

71

The crowd disperses swiftly when the threat of after-school detentions is thrown around by the teachers. I say goodbye to Andrea as she hurries off to her drama lesson and I head to chemistry.

The situation with Nasra plays on a loop in my head, blocking everything else out, so I'm a little surprised when I reach the chemistry classroom. I realize I must have followed Lily and Isha instinctively. I miss the mad rush to the goggles, losing out on my favourite ones with the blue band and few smudges to Sophie Lillington. She smiles awkwardly as if to say, *Sorry, bad luck.*

Our lesson on organic chemistry seems to bend the very fabric of time because whenever I look up at the clock, the hands have barely moved. And there's a weird radio silence from Lily and Isha. For some reason, they're avoiding even *looking* at me. Part of me isn't surprised that they had nothing to say about the situation this morning, but the other part is hurt they can't seem to manage to talk to me at all.

It's strange. If someone new were to walk into this class right now, we'd look like three girls who've never even met each other before, never mind three girls who've spent hours at each other's houses and hours more on the phone every weekend talking about nothing and everything.

I'm reminded of the advice I gave to Nasra when she started last year: we might all be Grafton Grammar girls, but we're all living very different versions of it.

I think back to one time Jessica purposely tripped me up when Andrea, Isha, and I were on our way to PE. I hadn't been able to do PE for two weeks after that, which was obviously great news, but the whole thing had still been a major inconvenience. Jessica feigned innocence immediately, and Isha had ended up trying to reassure Jessica that it wasn't her fault even as my foot had swiftly swelled.

Of course it was just an accident, Jessica. These things happen all the time. Look, Hanan's fine. She's not hurt that badly.

Even knowing everything Jessica had done to try and terrorize me at Grafton, Isha hadn't hesitated to believe her. Even when it was between me – her friend – and Jessica, the choice wasn't me. And I learned then that it never would be. The same way Mr Foster would never pick Nasra over Jessica in an argument.

I head straight for the library without saying goodbye to Lily or Isha, wanting to get as far away from prying eyes as possible. I sit in an empty spot in an alcove on the first floor and pull out my phone. The video that Nasra sent me before she got sent to the Head is the most recent notification on my phone.

it's a little hard to watch but just watch

I take a deep breath, not knowing what to expect, and press play.

In the corner of the video is a TfL sign with Baker Street in large letters. There's a timestamp: Saturday. The day after the news report on Mr Fleming and his killer came out. I watch attentively, not wanting to miss whatever was important enough for Nasra to send it to me.

After thirty seconds, I wonder whether I've missed it already, but have no idea what I'm looking for. On the platform are masses of casually dressed people, a far cry from the suit-wearing flood the platform usually sees. I spot a girl, short enough that she only appears in the footage when the woman next to her moves to peer at the train status board. She's of a small build, wearing a loosely wrapped headscarf and a pair of Doc Martens that look so big she could lose herself in them. She looks left and then right, unsure where the approaching train might be coming from, gripping her satchel tightly. I catch a glimpse of her T-shirt. It has *The 1975* written across the front, bordered by a white box.

Must be one of those indie hijabis, I think wryly.

The train comes along the platform, and the girl moves back a few steps behind the yellow line. The doors open, and a huge throng of people flood out, making it hard to see her clearly any more. But, for some reason, I know now what I'm meant to be looking out for. I know why Nasra sent me this video, and I know I need to watch this girl.

I spot her standing to the side of the doors, waiting for the remaining passengers to trickle out onto the platform. Then, suddenly, she crumples to the floor. A small, folded thing. People continue to board the train, either completely unbothered or unaware she's fallen. The girl doesn't move at all. The train doors are starting to close when a man with dreadlocks sees the girl and pulls her body away from the danger of the tracks. When more people notice, a crowd gathers and then I can't see the girl any more since she's

74

swallowed up by helpers and on-lookers.

The video ends abruptly but I know there's something I've missed. I rewind the video to just before she fell, not looking at the girl this time, but looking around her. That's when I see it and that's when I understand what Nasra meant when she said, "the cycle begins again".

A man with a chubby face and too-small hat slams his fist into the side of the girl's head, knocking her against the carriage. The girl doesn't stand a chance: he comes up behind her, doing it so quickly and so viciously that there's no time for even a look of surprise on her face. She falls and then the man boards the train without a single glance back.

After lunch, I make my way to the maths department and knock on one of the classroom doors.

Ms Al-Khansaa opens it. She stands beaming in the doorway, the light reflecting off her gold nose piercing. She's the only Muslim teacher at Grafton Grammar and since she started last year, I've always been mesmerized by her ability to walk through these halls, existing and thriving, not afraid to stand out.

Not long after she'd started, Ms Al-Khansaa had pleaded with the powers-that-be at the school to make an exception to the lunchtime rules for students wishing to pray. Usually, we weren't allowed in any room during break or lunchtime without supervision, but thanks to Ms Al-Khansaa's persistence, the school had reluctantly agreed to have an informal multi-faith prayer room for anyone who wanted to use it. The timing had been perfect. Mr Fleming had been due to retire in a few months and I didn't want to assume that the new caretaker would be as accommodating.

"Hanan!" Ms Al-Khansaa says, turning around to grab her laptop and keys from the desk. "You're right on time. I've got a department meeting starting in a few minutes so I need to get going."

Ms Al-Khansaa hands me the keys before grabbing her yellow tote bag. When she reaches the door, she hesitates.

"Hanan..." She sighs sadly, looking back. "I don't want to pretend to be this cool teacher who can always relate to her students, but sometimes I can. I don't know how hard Mr Fleming's death hit you or how you're coping with everything else going on, but I want you to know I'm here for you if you need a friendly ear or space to breathe." She smiles but it doesn't reach her eyes. "I think we all need that from time to time."

I'm not sure if Ms Al-Khansaa's saying this because she knows that Mr Fleming was my friend or whether Nasra's outburst has already trickled through school. Either way, after everything that's happened this morning – with Jessica and Mr Foster; with Lily and Isha...the video – hearing this tethers me.

"Thanks, Miss. I really appreciate that."

Ms Al-Khansaa squeezes my shoulder and then leaves.

I push the first two desks and chairs out of the way before taking the carefully folded prayer mat out of my bag. It's a beautiful piece of work, the midnight blue of the mat starkly contrasted against the gold thread that runs throughout it, creating two images: the Ka'bah, and a mosque under an intricate arch that descends into two thick, ivory-white pillars.

I'm reminded of Mr Fleming then. When he'd first seen my prayer mat, he'd picked it up, turning it over in his hands and bringing it close enough to his face that it looked as though he was sniffing it. I'd stifled a laugh, not wanting to interrupt whatever he was doing, but curious to know why he was so fascinated.

After a minute or so, he handed it back to me.

"So?" I asked, walking over to the corner of the caretaker office I always prayed in. "I hope you weren't licking it or anything, Mr Fleming. You know I actually put my face on this thing."

He looked at me indignantly, crossing his arms against his chest. "Can't a man appreciate fine workmanship when he sees it?"

"Sure," I smiled. "As long as that's all it was."

I hold onto that memory tightly as I stand on the prayer mat now. The memory of his gruff voice and warm smile. The memory of the room he let me pray in, every day, without fail, for as long as I needed to. A simple space that looked almost uninhabited apart from two framed photographs and a single jacket hung behind the door, and the only space I ever felt truly safe in at Grafton Grammar.

I try not to think about it, but Nasra's right. Everything is changing, like it always does whenever a Muslim does something like this. Whenever unforgivable violence is committed, it's on all our heads. We'll all be forced to weather the storm, even if none of us had any hand in creating it.

That's why I'm not surprised when Hooyo sends me a text after I've finished praying.

Dhaqso guriga u imaaw markuu iskuulka kuu dhamado

Come home straight after school.

I shoot her a quick reply, not bothering to question her instructions, because, if the video is anything to go by, I already know why. And the fact that Hooyo's sent this in Somali and not English means she's serious.

Later on, I find Andrea and Nasra at the pigpen, deep in conversation. Lily and Isha are nowhere to be seen.

I wonder if this is the worst of the fallout we're going to see. If the two of them acting weird and distant is just a today thing or if this is going to snowball into something bigger, something uglier.

But I know that no amount of wondering is going to help. We're in uncharted territory here. I have always seen the cracks in our friendship with Lily and Isha – the differences that divide us, that we don't speak about and pretend not to see – but now, they don't just look like cracks. They're craters.

Before I sit down at the table, I lean in to give Nasra a hug. She squeezes my waist tightly before letting me go.

"So, I see you're still in one piece," I smile, trying to keep it light-hearted. "That's a good sign."

"There's nothing good about this," Nasra says, deadpan. "Only bad."

"What did Mr Davies say to you?"

"He just gave me a lecture about respect and speaking to others kindly and this and that... It was a complete waste of time. He didn't even care that Jessica said all that rubbish to me in the first place."

"Surprise, surprise," Andrea mutters.

"It's just the way it is, Nasra," I say, looking out at the manicured green fields and the library that drew me to Grafton all those years ago. "It's the way this place has always been."

"But it shouldn't be!" she shouts, throwing her hands in the air. "It's just...it's not right. None of it is right."

I think about the video Nasra sent me. About the cycle starting again.

Sometimes it feels like we're all acting in the same stage play. We all know the story and how it unfolds. We all know our roles. Bad Muslim guy. Bad Muslim people. Good guys with pitchforks and torches trying to drive out the evil. Eventually, the play comes to an end, but we're all just patiently waiting for the next showing to start.

I sigh. I wish so much that this was just a play and not my life.

CHAPTER EIGHT

Hooyo is waiting for me when I get home.

"Hanan, macaanto," Hooyo calls out from the living room. "Kaalay."

I kick off my shoes before walking in. I'm surprised to see Hussein there as well. No one looks particularly happy.

"We need to have a chat about what's going to happen," Hooyo says with a sigh.

I go over to greet her and then sit by Hussein on the sofa opposite. "A discussion about what?" I ask, still a little breathless from my walk home.

"About protecting ourselves," Hooyo says, rubbing her eyes. "The world is angry at us again."

Just then, I hear loud thumps from upstairs. The three of us look up. By the sounds of it, Sumaya and Hafsa must be practising some kind of acrobatic performance, blissfully unaware of the vibe down here.

"Me and Hooyo were talking and we thought it made sense for me to pick up the girls after school from now on…just until things blow over." Hussein sits with both hands clasped together, making circles with his thumb. "You know, for safety's sake."

His leg bounces up and down. I kick him lightly, wanting him to stop. It always makes *me* nervous when he does that.

"For how long?" I ask.

"I don't know." Hooyo shakes her head. "We'll have to see when things begin to die down in shaa Allah."

She pulls out her battered Samsung phone. "Habaryar Hodan sent me this. I want to show you, give me a second."

Hooyo puts on her reading glasses to get a better look, holding the phone at arm's length and using a single index finger to navigate the screen. She passes the phone to me when she finds it.

On the screen is a group chat with hundreds of people posting various stories: a woman wearing a hijab and abaya spat on as she takes her kids on the school run; a video of an altercation between a man wearing a qamiis and taqiyah and another man wearing an English Defence League shirt; and a kid at school having their lunch tray thrown to the ground. It doesn't stop there. There are forwarded videos and stories about countless incidents and, as I continue to scroll, I see the same video Nasra sent me earlier. I stare at the thumbnail of the fallen girl and swallow, quickly scrolling past it.

"It's not just these, other people have sent me so much more. They'll have you, uh, what's the English?" Hooyo clicks her fingers. "Spinning head."

Hussein sniggers under his breath.

"Why are you laughing?" Hooyo asks. "This is serious, Hussein."

"I think you mean it would have our heads spinning,

Hooyo," I reply, rolling my eyes at my brother. "Don't worry about him, he's just being an idiot."

Hooyo eyes me, not pleased with my choice of language. "Anyway," she continues, "we need to be more careful. Especially you and me, Hanan, because the hijab is not invisible. So, Hussein will collect the girls from school, and you need to come straight home. No excuses and no library."

"Yeah," I sigh. "I got it. No library." I look up at the calendar near the fireplace. With just under a month left until the admissions test, I'd been planning some intense cram-sessions there, but that won't be happening now.

This isn't the first library ban I've received, but this one feels…different, somehow. In a way I can't quite explain. Maybe it's because I'm studying for something I've been working towards for ever. Or because the reason this time is a mugging-gone-wrong, not someone who even claimed to terrorize in the name of their faith. Or because the library is the one place outside of this house where I can forget about the Braids and everything else and just…be.

"In shaa Allah, we'll get through this," Hooyo says, extending her hands so she can reach both of us. "We always do. We just need to have faith and hope."

Hooyo looks at us intensely and I know what else she's thinking. She doesn't need to say it. Faith and hope can get you far but so can keeping your mouth shut.

Keeping your mouth shut helps you stay under the radar and get back home in one piece.

* * *

After dinner, I stand in the hallway with my jacket on and both hands in my pockets. I eye my right pocket in the full-length mirror. After our discussion this afternoon, Hooyo insisted that I have my hand gripped around my keys whenever I'm out; sharp-end ready and poised to jab at someone if they came at me. Though "insisted" is a pretty tame word to describe what she said.

Hanan, I swear on God's name that if you ignore me, I'll be standing front and centre against you on the Day of Judgement, she'd said, as she sat braiding Sumaya's hair.

I didn't say anything else then. I knew when my mum made statements like that, she wasn't playing around. Even Sumaya had sat deathly still, not making the complaints of pain she usually did whenever Hooyo braided her hair.

I hear Hussein come in, locking the front door behind him. I peer down at him from my place on the landing. Seems like now might be a great time for a good old-fashioned interrogation.

"Look at what the cat's dragged in," I drawl. "Where've you been all evening?"

Hussein had left straight after our chat with Hooyo. According to Hafsa, he'd told our mum he was going to play football for a couple of hours. That was *five* hours ago.

Still, today's Monday so, for the moment, Hussein's football story tracks. Maybe him lying to me last week really wasn't anything more than a simple get-out-of-chores card.

Hussein looks up, shrugging off his jacket and squinting.

"Looks like you've just walked in as well." He indicates

my jacket. "Thought Hooyo was keeping you on a tight leash."

"Please," I scoff, "if anyone's the dog here, it's you."

I turn back to the mirror and grip the key in my pocket. "Hooyo's just told me to start doing that key thing again, so I can just pull it out and go *pow pow pow* if anyone comes at me." I punch the air with my key for good measure with each *pow*.

He gives me a feeble round of applause. "Doubt anyone would try coming at you with that mad weapon."

"Watch yourself, bro. Sarcasm looks bad on you," I say. "And I don't have a choice anyway."

"Ahhh," he says in understanding, leaning against the banister. "Hooyo hit you with that akhirah threat? Savage."

"It is, isn't it? I hate when she does that. She gets this scary look in her eyes—" I pause, hearing my own words. "But don't tell her I said that," I add quickly.

Hussein laughs as he comes up the stairs, lightly shoving past me. I block his way.

"And where do you think you're going?"

"To my room?" he replies, confused.

"Without telling me where you were?" I ask innocently. He's walked in without football boots again, which means that his story is no longer tracking. "I know it's not football."

He tries to shove past me again. Hussein is a lot taller than me, but I hold firm.

"And I know it wasn't football last week either," I say, jabbing a finger to his chest. "So, for future reference, if you're going to lie to me, get better at it."

If Hussein's shocked at me calling him out, he hides it well. His face remains impassive, curtains closed tightly, refusing to let anything show.

"Hanan, do you really want me to throw you down the stairs?" he asks wearily. "Because you're asking for it at this point."

"I dare you. You know Hooyo would throw you out the front door before you could blink." I pause, deciding to change tack. Clearly this course of action isn't working. "Listen, I'm just worried about you, that's all. I don't like this weird secrecy and things are scary enough as it is without you disappearing."

"I was playing FIFA with the boys. That's all. So you can stop being so dramatic," he says. "I'm sure you have better things to be wasting your energy on, like your little books and flashcards."

Hussein doesn't wait for my reply. Instead, he picks me up quickly – too quickly for me to react – and moves me to the side. Then, he stalks past me and into his room at the end of the hall, shutting the door firmly behind him.

Andrea and I go over to her house after school the next day. It's just the two of us since Lily, Nasra and Isha are out on a school history trip.

Thankfully, my mum's blanket statements about coming straight home never apply to Andrea. She's gotten to know Andrea's parents over the years and thinks they're the kind of people who are both worthy of her trust and responsible enough to keep me in one piece, which is high praise from Hooyo. For some reason, me being only a few months away from adulthood is never part of the conversation. I am a child, Hooyo says, and I will *always* be a child, regardless of any law that says otherwise. Andrea's mum always drops me back home, which has undoubtedly pushed them further into my mum's good books, though I'm sure it doesn't help my "I'm an adult" argument.

We reach her house just as her mum's stepping out. She has her back to us, standing in the open doorway with her hands on the home alarm keypad. She steps back after a moment, running her hands through her hair.

"Buna, Mama," Andrea calls in greeting when we're close enough to be heard. Her mum visibly jumps. "Did you forget the code again? We literally just changed it to one you said you'd remember this time."

Andrea's mum turns in the doorway to reply and notices me. "Hanan!" she says, beaming. "It's so lovely to see you. I've been asking Andrea when you'd be around again, but it's hard to get two words out of this girl sometimes."

"Traitorous, Mama," Andrea replies, before I can. "At least say those things about me when I'm not around."

I bat Andrea's arm. "It's so great to see you too, Auntie Camelia," I say, coming forward for a hug. "Helps remind me that Andrea comes from good people whenever I'm tempted to cut her off."

Her mum laughs loudly as we break our embrace. Andrea splutters in response behind me.

"I've missed that classic humour of yours," Auntie Camelia says with a smile. "Are you girls here to practise for this year's bake sale? I remember Andrea mentioning something about that."

"Yep." I nod. "Practice makes perfect and perfect helps us win."

Auntie Camelia looks at us. "I didn't realize this was a competition. What do you win?"

"We don't win anything," Andrea replies, sighing loudly. She pushes me through the doorway and pivots her mum so she's standing outside the house. "Hanan's just a weirdo who loves to make everything into a competition. And I'm the one who lets her drag me along."

"Well, a little healthy competition never hurt anybody," Auntie Camelia says, buttoning up her jacket and placing the strap of her handbag squarely on her shoulder. "I'll let you girls enjoy your afternoon then. I should be back in a few hou— Andrea!"

"Yes, Mama?" Andrea says sweetly.

"Stop shutting the door on me before I've even left." She waits until Andrea opens the door again. "You see what I have to deal with, Hanan?" she says, exasperated, then waves goodbye as she leaves.

"You're a real piece of work. You know that, right?" I say to her when she's shut the door.

Andrea grins as we walk into the kitchen. "Doesn't anything good need a bit of work?"

I roll my eyes at her and take a seat at the breakfast bar.

I've always loved coming over to Andrea's house. There's so much peace and quiet that it scared me the first few times I was here. I wasn't used to having that much space with very few people to share it with. Andrea is used to it though, being an only child. She's usually home alone after school until her parents come back in time for dinner.

She slides me a glass of water and sits on the stool opposite, bringing her chin to rest on clasped hands.

"I'm going to share a deeply unpopular opinion with you, but I want you to hear me out, okay?"

I nod slowly, sipping my water.

"I think we should skip the bake sale this year," she says, keeping her eyes fixed on mine. "There's just a lot going on right now. Like, a *lot*. And I'm not saying this for me. I'm saying it for you because I care about you. I know how close you and Mr Fleming were and, even if you're not talking about it, even if you keep saying you're fine every time I check on you, I know none of this is easy."

I look away from her then and stare at the countertop through the bottom of my glass. The granite looks blurry, distorted.

"Your exam's coming up too and that's a huge deal," Andrea continues. "You've been working at this med school stuff for ages and I just feel like the bake sale isn't that important this year. You need to just take a minute, you know, step back, give yourself some breathing room."

I don't respond straight away. Instead, I pick up the glass and play with that, swirling the water around, seeing how the distortions change.

"But why would we want to lose out on the chance to get a hat-trick?" I finally reply, looking up at her again. I lightly punch her on the shoulder. "We could be champions, Andrea. Don't rob us of that."

"Don't try to make this sound cool." She looks at me blankly. "It's literally a bake sale."

"A bake sale we've won two years in a row. I don't know about you, but I want to go down in the fundraiser hall of fame."

"There's literally no such thing."

"Not yet," I say with a grin. "And not with that attitude either. Come on, Andrea, please? It'll be a good distraction, if nothing else. I was really looking forward to it this year."

She scrutinizes me, scrunching up her eyes and looking me up and down. And, though she doesn't say it, I imagine she's remembering what happened the last time things got to be too much.

"Fine," she concedes, after a moment. "But, since you're basically forcing me to do this against my will, I'm establishing some new ground rules. Number one: *I'm* eating the practice doolsho this time. And the leftover brownie mix. My sweet tooth is basically a bottomless pit and it needs sustenance. No compromise there."

I smirk. "Should've seen that one coming."

"Number two: you have to stop holding me back every time Daniel and Jacob say or do something stupid at Fundraising club. Those meetings are hard enough already."

"Ugh," I groan. "Really? You've crossed into full blackmail territory now."

She tilts her head, looking up at the ceiling. "Number three: I want you to pinky promise that we'll do a *Twilight* marathon. Soon. Together. In one sitting."

I feel my heart drop in my chest. "Are you trying to kill me?"

"Please, Hanan," she scoffs, "you only really start living when you see a grown man sparkle in sunlight. I thought I taught you that."

I burst into laughter. "Okay, fine. There's clearly no way I can argue with that logic."

Andrea smiles in triumph. We make our pinky promise and then spend the rest of the afternoon in baking bliss.

CHAPTER NINE

I get home late that evening, having stayed for dinner at Andrea's. Even after so many hours, the smell of brownies and doolsho and cookies still lingers on my clothes. I hope that no one remembers exactly what I was doing at Andrea's house because I don't want any questions about leftover food. Thanks to Andrea, I've brought home nothing.

Peeking into the living room, I see Abooto sleeping, softly snoring in her favourite chair. Hooyo is sat on the sofa opposite. She brings a finger to her lip when she sees me. We both tip-toe to the kitchen to avoid waking her up. Hooyo puts the kettle on to make us some tea.

"I didn't want to wake your Abooto. She hasn't been sleeping very well lately," Hooyo says, dropping a teabag into each cup. "Rosa said she's been quieter, too, and with the anniversary next week..." Hooyo lets out a heavy sigh. "I'm not surprised. Your poor Abooto doesn't like to talk about these things, but I can see it eats her up inside, every year." She reaches for the sugar canister. "I hope you realize that your stubbornness comes from her."

Hooyo's right, I think to myself, horrified. Not the stubborn part, though that's mostly true, but the other part. The anniversary. I hadn't realized it was so close.

"Oh my God…I…" I let myself collapse onto a chair. "What kind of daughter forgets something like that?"

I've done the one thing that I promised myself I would never do: lose sight of my own father.

"I'm horrible."

"No! Hanan, you're not, macaanto. You put so much pressure on yourself, you can't remember everything. And Aabo would be so proud of everything you're doing now. But you know your Abooto… She gets lost in her grief around this time of year. I just want to make sure she gets all the rest she can."

I reflexively nod as Hooyo opens the fridge. I know she believes what she's saying, but it hasn't done anything to help the weight I feel in my stomach. If anything, it's made it worse.

I glance at the papers stuck to our fridge – a collection of bills that almost never changes – but today I can see thick black lines drawn through some of them, and I frown, wondering when I missed this. It's usually a big deal when we clear a debt.

"Hooyo, what's this?" I ask, pointing to the fridge. "When did this happen?"

"Wallahi, today was a blessing," Hooyo says, giving me my steaming cup of tea. I wrap my hands around it, letting the warmth of it seep in. She sits down next to me at the table. "Hussein walked in and said he could pay off the bills. Not all of them, but some of them. I almost fainted in shock," she says, more animated than she'd been a moment ago.

92

I let go of the warmth and walk over to the fridge. My hand reaches for the bills. My mind steadily adds up the running total. It's hundreds of pounds and counting.

"He told me he'd gotten a job at the cinema," Hooyo adds, the excitement still alive in her voice. "Can you believe it? He wanted to keep it a secret until he could surprise us with his first pay cheque."

"At the cinema? The one on Faren?"

Hooyo shakes her head. "No, further away. A new one in Haldow, I think. He applied and started last week. His friend Ahmed referred him so they both got a bonus." She runs her hand around the rim of the cup, waiting for the tea to cool some more.

"Hmmm." My eyes flick to the fridge again. "That's a pretty big bonus."

"It is," Hooyo replies, sipping her tea cautiously, "but Hussein says he's been doing overtime and referring other friends too." Hooyo puts her cup down again. "Still, I wasn't happy at first. I thought 'here's my son wanting to throw away all his hard work at school' but he's promised he'll stop working if it gets in the way of college."

"Really? Hussein said that?" I think back to what he said last week about going to school and pretending to learn.

Hooyo nods. "He promised he could do both and, if he can?" She looks at the fridge again, at the black lines erasing our debts. Hooyo shakes her head slowly and grips her cup tighter. "Then Alhamdulilah because we needed this, Hanan. I can't tell you how much we needed this."

I can see Hooyo's eyes glistening. I can see how much it means to her. It feels like there's less to worry about for the immediate future; space to relax, to take a foot off the pedal. Maybe Hooyo can even do fewer shifts at work because of it.

But even though this explains Hussein's absence lately, I can't shake the feeling that something isn't adding up. Huge sums of money don't just appear from brand-new jobs at the cinema, especially if you're still meant to be at college. Minimum-wage and bonuses can only get you so far. I know that, everyone knows that, but the black lines on the fridge tell a different story. And, if it was just about a job the whole time, why didn't Hussein tell me? I'd understand not telling Hooyo, if he was so intent on surprising her, but why did he feel the need to hide it from me too?

I don't want to burst Hooyo's bubble with my suspicions though. And I can't go slinging accusations without facts. Especially when I don't know what I'm accusing him of in the first place.

I sit down at the table opposite Hooyo again. Under the light, I can see her face looks tired. Her eyes are red and the lines around them appear accentuated.

I've always found it hard seeing Hooyo this way. It makes me remember the glow she used to have. This kind of shining light that brought a brilliance to her smile. It was a glow that disappeared when our dad died, and now I can only see it in the pictures of her youth.

I sip my tea. "I'm glad things are finally working out, Hooyo," I say with a smile.

* * *

There's so much to do in the month before my exam and too little time to waste. I don't want to sleep but, at the same time, I can't ignore the burning of my eyes. I decide to lie down for a minute, but I wake up, just after midnight, bleary-eyed and with notes stuck to my cheek. What should have been a small reprieve has transformed into three hours of being completely knocked out.

I lean into my pillow again and try to ignore the familiar feeling in my chest – the tightening like a belt fastened around my ribs. I breathe, upwards, towards the ceiling and try to ignore the blank sheets of paper around me that I've yet to fill with answers. But, most of all, I try to ignore Andrea's warning about giving myself breathing room, because she's right. She's always right. But, as close as we are, I know she doesn't fully get why I can't just step back from everything. She didn't really understand the first time I had a panic attack either, even though she's as loyal and unwavering as best friends come.

It was in my second year at Grafton, after my first ever failed physics test, and, in a little corner of the science department, I'd crouched and crumpled in on myself. It felt like everything had fallen apart, as if the seams of my life had come undone. My legs felt weak and my stomach in chaos, but the worst was my lungs. I remember thinking that my life would end in that corner, surrounded by a strange musty smell, and that that would be my legacy. It didn't seem like there was a way to come back from what felt like lung failure, so I surrendered. Dark figures danced on the edge of my vision and I welcomed them, wanting to be lost in their strange motions. Just then, Andrea turned the corner, holding her toilet pass and whistling "She'll Be Coming Round the Mountain".

She didn't panic when she saw me gasping for air. She just bent down to my level and told me to put my head between my knees. My breathing, which I thought was never going to recover, slowly evened out and the dancing figures swayed into emptiness.

Andrea held onto my arm as she walked me back to class, but it didn't take long for her to ask me why a failed physics test would affect me like that. Eventually, I admitted it sometimes felt like my past, present and future collided so powerfully it overwhelmed me; that I needed to be perfect to secure my family's future. Andrea had looked confused. I couldn't blame her though; her life is so different to my own. She doesn't carry anyone's future but her own.

But me? I carry my dad's legacy; my parent's sacrifices; my family's hopes for a good life against the undercurrents of racism in a place where people are surprised I have succeeded, *am* succeeding. I carry all of that every day, but it's a weight I've grown familiar with. Except for the few moments when it does bury me.

I look up at the family photo on my wall, at the smiles on all our faces outside our house in Mogadishu. I cherish the memory of that time as I settle back into sleep again. As I wiggle to get comfortable, I realize that my legs are brushing against something soft that wasn't there before I fell asleep.

I see a thick green blanket thrown over my body, and I smile, content that no matter what's going on with Hussein, he's still always here for me.

CHAPTER TEN

The whirlwind of gossip grows intense. I'm bombarded with texts from friends and cousins talking about girls who've decided to take off their hijabs, afraid of the violent repercussions that now come with being Muslim in London, but this steady stream of messages isn't unpredictable. It happens every time the cycle starts again. Personally, I've never been tempted to take my own hijab off even with it being the source of so much scrutiny. I know I could never bring myself to do it, because I wear my hijab for God. I refuse to take it off for anyone else.

The funny thing is that I never see any of these stories, this violence against people like me, make it onto the news. Stories of the murderer still dominate every newscast, always focused on his *alleged* radicalization. I'm starting to get the sense that these news reporters are clutching at straws, trying to force a reality that just doesn't exist. The simple fact is that a man killed my friend over a few notes of cash outside an ATM. A man who just happened to have a beard and a "foreign" sounding name and be Muslim.

But this man also happened to do this right on our doorstep.

Nothing like this has ever happened so close to home before and, while I know how the cycle usually goes, I wonder just how different I should expect it to be this time. Nasra and Jessica's fight might be as far as this thing goes, or it could be the tip of the iceberg. Especially since the man on the other end of this was Mr Fleming. Not someone unconnected to us, but someone we all knew. Someone who meant something to me and meant something to Grafton too.

My phone buzzes as I'm stepping out of my house. It's a message from Nasra on the group chat. I open it to find a link to a tabloid article and scan through it.

SCHOOL CARETAKER MURDERER DECLARED "FULL-BLOWN JIHADI" BY CLOSE SOURCES

Nasra: Can you believe this shit!!! Legit nothing here except the most desperate lies I've ever seen in my life. my 2 year-old cousin could report better than this

Andrea: Why u even reading that trash u know the daily sun only hire middle-class racists anyway

Nasra: like to know what's out there so I can trash-talk on twitter
go like my tweet please and thank you xx

Hanan: so these sources are apparently 1 random woman from his old school and 1 butthurt ex-neighbour?

how does this stuff even get to print?

Andrea: u know they're just trying to justify why
they killed him
makes the police look better right, easier if he's
a "jihadi" cos then no one bats an eyelid

Hanan: true

Nasra: i'm lowkey just wondering if there was any
bodycam footage and whether it's mysteriously
disappeared...
also guyssss wait I wanna tell u about my new
dream quickly

Andrea: Lol go on

Hanan: Bet it's dumb

Nasra: Ur dumb
but no
my dream is to grow up and be a journalist and infiltrate
the dirty institution that is the daily sun all the while hiding
my true Muslim identity and then become the chief editor
and then I'LL REVEAL MYSELF MWAHAHAHAHA and
take those pigs down from the INSIDE

Andrea: Woaaaaaah all hail Queen Nasra. That's genius

Hanan: I take it back, that's super smart, not dumb at all

I reach the bus stop and pocket my phone as the bus arrives. Andrea's sitting in our usual two-seater and I shuffle to the back to claim my space. Before I even sit down, she starts talking.

"Did you see?"

"See what?"

"Lily and Isha just *read* the messages in the chat but didn't reply." Andrea's eyes are wide. She plays with her dangling earrings, and, by the way she's looking at me, I assume she's waiting for my similarly shocked reaction.

"So?" I ask, confused. "Why are you so surprised? They've been acting weird for the last two days."

"Well, we don't know about yesterday," Andrea replies, raising both eyebrows. "They went on that history trip along with Nasra, remember? We didn't see them all day."

"Oh right." I'd completely forgotten about that. The last time I saw any of them was two days ago... Lily and Isha during our silent double chemistry lesson and Nasra during lunch. "So...we have no idea what we're walking into now?"

Andrea shrugs her shoulders. "It's either going to be the most awkward vibes I've ever experienced in my life, or they'll be overcompensating with normal-ness, and it'll still be the most awkward vibes of my life."

I make a face. "Awkward vibes either way then. Guess we'll see."

In form, Nasra's sat in her usual seat, facing the front, and clearly ignoring Lily and Isha next to her. All three of them sit at the table in silence.

Andrea pulls on my arm as we walk towards them.

"Is it too late to switch over to Mr Anand's form?" she whispers in my ear.

"I don't think there's anywhere to hide from this kind of tension," I whisper back. "It's too deadly."

We sit down at the table. I take in the three of them one by one – their stony expressions, the sourness coming off them in waves – and I wonder how it's come to this. Jessica's always been a thorn in our sides, but she's never infiltrated our group this badly before. It makes me angry that someone like her has the power to do something like this. That what she says or does and the reactions she causes somehow have the ability to bring everything crashing down.

But then my anger quickly turns to disappointment when I think about Lily and Isha. The three of us have been friends long enough now that there should be some kind of understanding at this point, some kind of loyalty or compassion or just… *something*. Because what does it mean when the friends you've known for years suddenly turn their back on you? When they decide to ignore you, for absolutely no reason other than the fact that their friend's defended herself against racist bullshit?

I think back to when Lily first joined our group after she fell out with the Braids. Maybe she never really stopped being a Jessica-sympathizer and I'm now just seeing it. Maybe Andrea was right to resist us becoming friends with her in the first place. I look over to Andrea. She meets my gaze and grimaces.

The uncharted territory we've walked into feels like it's riddled with booby traps. One wrong word or move and the whole thing could just blow up in our faces.

Nasra greets us before Andrea or I can say anything.

"Hello, my *friends*," she says with dangerous emphasis. "How are we on this fine day, my *friends*?"

I bite my lip. Something's definitely happened on this history trip. All three of them and the Braids take history and that would have been more than enough fuel to make fire.

I look over to Jessica, who's sat by Sarah and Divya near the window. Though there's always five seats to a table, they're the only three who ever sit there. Other people who tried to sit there at the start of the year came to regret it and quickly vacated the space. Theirs is the kind of popularity that hurts if you get too close.

"Good," Andrea replies, fidgeting in her chair. "And you... guys?" she asks uncertainly.

"Never been better," Nasra beams. "In fact, I've almost forgotten what happened the last time I was in form, that's how good I feel. And I've almost forgotten how this snake of a teacher, Mr Foster" – she pretend-coughs – "committed a heinous crime against me." Her smile stretches even more but, to me, it looks like it's only seconds away from cracking. "I feel like a new woman this morning."

Movement in my periphery catches my attention.

"Honestly..." Lily hesitates, fiddling with her Marrakech keyring. "You were the one who went off, Nasra. Jessica wasn't the one screaming or making threats."

My jaw drops.

"Yeah," Isha agrees. Her gaze hardens when she meets Nasra's. "We tried to tell you this yesterday. You didn't need to do that, create a whole scene when it wasn't even that big a deal. It's not like she said anything that was—"

"Stop. Talking. To. Me," Nasra says through gritted teeth.

She briefly closes her eyes and breathes in deeply through her nose. I know she's holding back. Even *I'm* holding back, and I'm usually the person who lets these things slide. It's often easier to do that than let it eat you up inside. And it's definitely easier than hearing people call you "sensitive" or say, *Hey, you're making a big deal out of nothing – just let it go.*

The thing with Lily and Isha is that I don't think they've ever really noticed or maybe cared about the little comments that sometimes stop me in my tracks, like needles trying to break into the armour I've learned to wrap around myself. Why would they when Lily's white and has a millionaire for a mum, and Isha, even being half-Indian, has been mistaken for white her whole life? It sounds ugly, saying it like that, but the truth is, they've never had to endure being singled out for anything. I've always known and accepted that we come from separate walks of life, but hearing this, today, I can't keep quiet. Today, I'm seething, and the words just fall out.

"So it's okay for Jessica to say the murderer was one of *ours*, like we're a completely different species?"

Lily glances at Isha.

"Well, no, of course not but—"

"It's okay for her to call us out and basically tell us to defend

104

ourselves? Like we need to prove to everyone else here that we're not terrorists?"

Isha jumps in this time, shaking her head. "No, Hanan, that's not what we're saying. Just that there doesn't need to be so much drama—"

I laugh, but there's no humour in it.

"Girl, please, if this was Jessica coming after your little fan account, you know you'd be jumping down her throat."

Isha huffs, turning away from me. Lily does too, shaking her head as she does so. I don't say anything more. I've always told Nasra that the status quo at Grafton should be keeping your head above water, keeping yourself out of drama and just walking the tightrope every day, but, with everything I've just said, I know I've gone against my own philosophy. And I know Andrea would have jumped into the conversation, guns-blazing, to give Lily and Isha a long-overdue wake-up call. But something about *this* time feels different. Something about this time makes me feel like I can't just close my eyes and pretend it isn't happening. Even if the price to pay is risking this friendship.

When I notice my hand shaking, I move it underneath the table. Andrea squeezes it and the two of us just hold hands until it begins to steady. The bell rings and we turn to face Mr Foster as he takes the register. Andrea squeezes my hand again. I turn to look at her.

Wow, she mouths, widening her eyes a fraction. I *can't believe you said that.*

Me either, I mouth back.

She smiles, letting go of my hand. *Ballsy.*

I know. A pause.

I know, I mouth again, when it starts to properly sink in, my eyes widening like hers.

When the shock begins to subside, something unfamiliar replaces it. It takes me a little while to recognize it, but once I do, I'm able to put a name to that strange, bubbling feeling: pride.

After form, on our way to chemistry, Nasra holds me back for a few moments. We're in the middle of the hallway, being pushed by moving bodies on both sides.

"Girl, please?" she says. The mischievous glint is back in her eyes.

"Well, what can I say?" I throw my hijab over my shoulder in that way that girls with long hair often do. "You can take the girl out of ends, but I guess you can never take ends out of the girl."

Nasra grins widely. We walk the rest of the way to class hand in hand.

I sit down next to Andrea when we get to last period maths, glad to have her back as a buffer between me and the Braids after her absence last week.

Ms Williams sets us our tasks and I fly through the questions, as usual, hoping to get through the lesson without incident. Thankfully, she doesn't ask me to answer anything today and the Braids don't share any of their unwanted opinions with me.

The class is packing up at the end of the lesson when Ms Williams calls out Jessica's name. "Jessica, can you come here a moment? You too, Hanan. I've just got an email from Mr Foster."

I stop abruptly, my hand still on the zipper of my bag. Andrea glances at me, both eyebrows raised, as if I have an answer to this.

I've always liked Ms Williams. She's one of the only teachers I know who calls Jessica on her crap whenever she steps out of line. That's probably why Jessica doesn't look as self-assured as she normally does, walking over to Ms Williams. I follow her lead, standing a little bit away, uncomfortable with the closeness to her.

"Right, girls," Ms Williams says. Her voice sounds strained. "We've got a bit of a situation here."

Jessica visibly gulps, looking slightly nauseated now.

"I've been told that Mr Foster thinks that you two would be great for the new buddy system we're setting up for different subjects. Jessica, you're struggling with some of the topics that Hanan's more confident in and, Hanan, we think you'd be great tutoring Jessica. Now, it'd only be for a few months, probably until the Easter break so it doesn't interfere with summer exams, but we'd like for you to set up regular study sessions. When and where this takes place is completely up to you since you're both mature enough to sort this out between yourselves. How does that sound to both of you?"

Ms Williams looks hopeful, both hands clasped under her chin. She gazes at us imploringly. "And if that doesn't sell you already, you're promised two glowing certificates for your portfolios."

Normally, I'd jump at any opportunity to get a certificate under my belt, but this idea is worse than anything I could've imagined. I wish, suddenly, that I could just spontaneously self-combust. Then Ms Williams would have no choice but to find someone else to voluntarily put themselves through this hell.

And there's no way that Jessica would ever accept someone like *me* tutoring someone like *her* anyway. Since day one, she's told me I don't belong here. I'm sure she's fuming at the suggestion that she could need my help.

Ms Williams looks at us intently. Neither of us has so far said a single word or moved a muscle. Most of the class have left now and the only lingering students are the other Braids and Andrea. All three of them watch the unfolding scene with huge curiosity.

Jessica breaks the silence first. I know she's going to say no. I breathe a sigh of relief and thank God under my breath. I couldn't be more grateful to have someone hate me right now.

"Umm...sure. I'm happy to do that," Jessica replies. "As long as Hanan's good with it, I'm fine."

I almost faint. They both look at me pointedly now. I can feel myself getting warmer and warmer. The seconds stretch, feeling like eternity, and I open my mouth, no words lined up, wondering what's going to come out.

"Yeah, fine. It's good with me too," I mumble, defeated.

The words feel like molten lead in my mouth, but I know that if I fight this, it'll only cause more problems and bring on more questions. I'd rather not be the girl who everyone thinks is problematic. I'd rather not be thought of at all in this school.

"Great, so it'll be up to the both of you to decide when and where you meet, although you ideally need to meet twice a week. Just keep a log of your sessions and send it through to Mr Foster." Ms Williams gets up to herd us out the classroom. "Now go, go. Enjoy your evenings. I'll see you next lesson."

I watch the Braids walk off, their hair swaying in unison and looking as if they've just come out of hair and make-up. I turn to Andrea. She doesn't say anything, only puts a comforting hand on my shoulder.

Mr Foster catches up with us just as we're leaving school. There's not much I feel like saying to him, since he's the whole reason I'm in this mess. He either doesn't seem to notice my sour mood or chooses to ignore it.

"Hanan!" he says, a little breathless, leaning against the school gate. He gives Andrea a friendly nod. The both of us take an imperceptible step back. Whatever he has to say, he can say from a spit-free distance.

"I'm glad I caught you. Ms Williams gave me the good news and I just wanted to say I'm so pleased to hear you've agreed to buddy up with Jessica."

I nod. "No problem, sir." I fight the urge to grit my teeth. "Glad to help out."

Andrea and I turn to leave but Mr Foster stands up a little straighter.

"I know the whole thing isn't ideal with your med school prep going on..." Mr Foster trails off. He looks between Andrea and me, as if uncertain. "But I thought it would be nice to try and get you a bit more integrated with the school and, you know, make you really part of the fabric here." He pauses and looks between us again. "You may not look like a Grafton student, but you are. You're absolutely one of us, and, of course, you have been for six years now, but I want you to really *feel* you are."

In the moments before I reply, there are a few things I realize:

That I was right when I wondered about the cycle being different, about whether Nasra and Jessica's fight was the tip of the iceberg.

That these differences in this skewed cycle are because it's about one of their own; someone they can put a face to, as well as a name.

And, this time, the status quo might not be enough to help me walk the tightrope. This time, if I'm not careful, I might just fall.

I can see Andrea looking at me with an expression of disbelief. Mr Foster holds my gaze. He looks wary, as if worried about what I'm going to say.

"Like I said, sir. Glad to help out."

CHAPTER ELEVEN

I go straight home, not wanting to disobey Hooyo's orders. I know if I do, things will start to get ugly. My mum's usual happy and cheerful demeanour will melt into something else if she doesn't get her way, particularly when it comes to our safety.

I remember noticing it when we first came to London ten years ago. I'd found myself completely bewitched by everything this alien city had to offer. The red buses that drove by like clockwork every few minutes, opening their mouths wide to collect and drop off all sorts of people. People of every shade under the sun, people who looked like me and people who looked nothing like me. It was remarkable, and it was enough to mask the sadness that I carried with me for a little while. But it had been a completely different story for Hooyo. She refused to walk into London starry-eyed, excited for the future that lay at our feet, a future of peace and possibilities. Instead, she saw in London what she'd seen at the border back home: that nothing is ever what it seems and, to protect the ones you love, you can never entirely trust anyone else.

So, I board the bus and go straight home, following Hooyo's orders, keeping my head low and eyes forward, trying to remain inconspicuous. When I reach Northwell, I feel my guard loosening up a bit.

The keys jiggle in the door as I open it. I follow the excitable babble coming from the kitchen and I'm surprised to find Hussein standing there with three measuring cups in his hands, Hafsa and Sumaya watching attentively.

Hussein and I have only seen each other in passing since I point-blank asked him about his recent shadiness and he unceremoniously picked me up and moved me out of the way, like I was a piece of furniture or something. I'd been waiting for him to mention something, *anything*, about his new job at the cinema or his apparently very hefty first pay cheque but... nothing. We've said hello, how's it going, goodbye and not much else over the last couple of days.

"Just do it!" Sumaya whines. "We've been waiting for ages."

Hafsa notices me and leans back. "Hussein still thinks he can juggle," she whispers, "but we don't want to hurt his feelings." She covers her mouth when she says this, to stop herself from laughing out loud, and quickly looks back to Hussein, giving him a thumbs up.

"Watch this space, people. Watch it, watch it...now!" Hussein says, launching the cups into the air. The first and second go up, but it quickly goes wrong when he launches the third. He's left standing there with only the first cup in in his hand, the other two by Hafsa's feet.

Hussein bites his lip, turning to reluctantly acknowledge me. "I did feel some negative energy coming from you there." He gestures towards the general area where I'm standing.

"Sabotager energy. So I'm going to blame this on you, Hanan."

For the first time in my life, I feel unsure about what to say around him. It's a strange feeling, to be second-guessing myself around the person who makes up the other half of my whole.

I still remember how the two of us would spend hours climbing the papaya trees near our house in Somalia when we were younger, how long we'd take deciding on the best one before splitting it exactly in half, both of us savouring the same sweet taste. We'd divide the papaya seeds evenly too, even though it took ages to count them out. I remember Aabo would laugh at us whenever he was home, amused at how engrossed we were with the task.

Sometimes, I miss how simple life was there. There were no ISIS jabs or you're-not-one-of-us subtexts. No library bans or dead friends. No single-parent household or horrible nightmares. There was war, but there was none of that, and there was all of my dad.

"Well, I don't know what a sabotager is, but glad you don't like them," I reply after a moment. "And I think the actual word you're looking for is saboteur."

Hussein mimics me under his breath though it's loud enough for all of us to hear.

"You shouldn't do that, Hussein." Sumaya swings her legs from the seat. "Copycats are bad cats. That's what Ms Campbell says when Nadia copies Alex in school."

The strain is visible on Hussein's face as he keeps himself from copying her now. I'm sure he's about to give in but, as luck would have it, Abooto calls the girls from the living room.

Hafsa groans into her lap. "I don't want to go. Hanan, can you please, please, please ask if me and Sumaya can skip today? Maybe she'll listen to you."

I give her a pained smile as I lean against the door frame behind me. "Sorry, girl, I might need to cash that in for something else one day. And, anyway, I'm sure it's not as bad as you make it out to be."

"Easy for you to say. You're not the one doing it." She glares at me as she and Sumaya walk away.

Though Hafsa has a high tolerance for most things, she hates the daily Somali lessons. Our grandmother started them spontaneously a few years ago when she realized the girls could only understand the most basic conversations. She made it her mission then to fix the mistake she blamed herself for.

No granddaughter of mine will exist in this world deaf to her own language, Abooto used to cry. *My own mother would be shaking in her grave if she could see them now.*

Abooto teaches them every day, after school, without fail. She believes it's better to fill their ears with the language of the motherland as quickly as possible, so that the English they hear all day doesn't take dominance. I'm not sure how much longer Abooto's going to keep trying with them, though, because, even after an hour of practising, they barely retain anything.

Hussein puts the measuring cups away and turns around to face me.

"So, spit it out, twinny." He jumps on the counter to take a seat. "Why so vexed? Your face has more creases than Abooto's does."

114

I laugh despite myself and then promptly feel a swell of irritation for letting that slip out. I'm shocked Hussein's even speaking to me, but I can't forget how annoyed I am with him.

"Say that a bit louder, why don't you?" I move to sit down in Sumaya's vacated seat. "I'm sure she's itching to use that broomstick."

Hussein grins. "Nah, you know I'm too fast for that." He leans back against a cupboard and kicks off his slippers. "Go on then. What's your problem?"

I grab the bag of Doritos next to me. I eat a couple, trying to psyche myself up, before I register the flavour. Cool Original, the worst of them. I open my mouth to ask him how he's bagged such a high-flying job in the space of a week, but something stops me. I clam up. Maybe it's because Hussein can't seem to give me a straight answer these days or the fact that he's still, for some strange reason, keeping me in the dark about his new job. Or maybe it's because I've just been coerced into taking part in the worst kind of torture imaginable with Jessica.

Whatever it is, I think I'm mostly scared that he'll just lie to me again. And, if he does, I'm worried that means we're growing apart, that things are changing between us in ways I don't understand.

"It's Jessica," I say.

Hussein sucks in his breath. "What about that witch?"

"I'm meant to be her study partner now. Ms Williams asked us today and I wasn't even going to agree to it, but imagine this girl said *yes*. She said *yes*, Hussein, to her and me working together."

115

He whistles low under his breath. "Wow, that's… That's…I don't even know what to say. Legit your worst nightmare, sis."

He stuffs a few more crisps in his mouth and proceeds to talk with his mouth so full that I can't make out the words.

"Ew. Can you finish chewing please and then speak?"

He swallows and washes it down with some water.

"I said, why didn't you just say you didn't want to do it? It's not hard to say no."

"Hussein, have you lost the plot?" I ask incredulously. "I've never said no to a single teacher at Grafton before. Mostly because I'm always trying to bag every certificate I can for applications. But, if I said no, now, for the first time ever? I'd have a bunch of people jumping around asking too many questions."

"And what's wrong with that?"

"There's nothing wrong with questions. It's the answers that are problematic. Who'd believe the golden child's a racist?" I laugh. "Can't expect a school of racists to call out a racist anyway. Mr Foster all but told me today that I don't even look like I should be going to that school and he's the one who set this entire thing up."

"Fairs." He tilts the bag to let the crumbs fall into his mouth. "But I still think you should've done it anyway. Told someone else maybe."

"Don't start selling lies to me, Hussein. You know you'd never report someone at your college, it would only make things worse."

Hussein's college, Bakerstone College, is worlds away from

Grafton Grammar, but I know the code's the same for schools everywhere: snitches get stitches. Maybe not literally, but snitches definitely get something undesirable.

"You're going to have to do something though. Grow a spine maybe? You've got words for me in this house, but let's be honest, you don't really have words for anyone else."

As much as I hate to hear him say it, I know he's right. Even though I said what I did to Lily and Isha, I nearly always lose my nerve when I need it most. Instead, I'll feel this thick bubble grow around me, closing in and closing off my reaction.

"I don't know…" I say more to myself than him. "I think I'm scared to find the words sometimes."

Hussein raises both eyebrows, scrunching up the empty crisp packet. I grab a juice box from the middle of the table and slurp it down before throwing the empty box at his head.

"Oi! What was that for?" Hussein massages his forehead. "I just gave you some top-class advice."

"Take your top-class advice somewhere else, please. I need this kitchen free." I stand up and put Hooyo's apron on. "I'm baking."

Andrea and I did a practice bake on all the sweet treats we are planning to sell, but since the savoury treats are my turf, I need to practise. It's the food that sells out first on our stall every year and the reason why Andrea and I are two-time Fundraising champions.

"Ahhh," he says in understanding, jumping off the counter. "This is about your little nerdy contest, isn't it?"

I ignore him and open the fridge to locate onions and beef mince.

Hussein grabs the discarded juice box, holding it up like a microphone and putting on a terrible show-host voice.

"It comes down to Blazer One versus Blazer Two in this tantalizing competition – whose food shall dominate in the hallowed halls of Grafton Grammar? Whose food shall knock the judges' socks off in the knockout? Whose food will reign supreme?" He makes a dramatic turn before dropping the juice box. "Stay tuned to find out."

I find my favourite saucepan. "If you don't tune out soon, I can promise you won't be eating a bite of any of this."

By the time I close the cupboard, Hussein's already gone. I listen out for his steps on the stairs, and then hear his bedroom door shut. I wonder what he's doing up there. I'm not sure if he's been spending less and less time at home these days or if I'm just obsessing and tracking his movements way more than any rational person should.

I refocus, pushing all of this Hussein weirdness aside. At least for a couple of hours, I'll have nothing to worry about except flour and kneading and hot oil.

CHAPTER TWELVE

Andrea and I walk over to the Fundraising meeting on the other side of school the next afternoon. We're rounding a corner when she says, "They're going to email us about Mr Fleming's memorial service later. The one the school's doing for him on Monday."

I miscalculate the turn. My shoulder hits the corner with such force that I'm scared for a moment I might have fractured something.

"Woah, you okay?" Andrea asks, slowing down.

I nod, rubbing my shoulder. I pick up the pace again, not wanting her to see how badly that hurt me. "It's fine," I re-assure her, holding my arm gingerly by my side. "But yeah, I heard this morning."

The small family funeral already happened a few days ago, away from the press, but the school wants to follow it up with its own memorial service in four days since Mr Fleming dedicated so many years of his life to Grafton Grammar. I feel my stomach clench, forceful and quick, when I think about him again. I've actively tried to avoid thinking about him lately to stay as far away from that feeling as possible, but I don't think I've been very successful. I doubt I'll be successful at the service either.

Andrea looks at me from the corner of her eyes as we round another bend. "Are you going to go?"

"Of course," I say, trying to sound convincing.

I have to go. I know I have to. Mr Fleming was so much more to me than a caretaker, even though most people will never know that. But I can't pretend that going to the memorial will be simple, especially when it's people like me who are still being looked at suspiciously since his death.

We reach the room Mrs Harris has booked for us and sit at a table near the middle. Everyone else starts to slowly trickle in. Mrs Harris follows shortly after and kicks off the meeting.

Daniel and Jacob saunter in a whole half-hour late. Mrs Harris looks at them disapprovingly as they take a seat. Though most of the room is empty, they decide to sit with us. They purposefully make too much noise, dragging their chairs across the floor and throwing themselves onto their seats.

Near the end of the meeting, Mrs Harris splits up the duties for the bake sale since it's only six days away. We agree to check back in with her if we have any issues but we all know that won't happen. We've been doing the bake sale for years without any hiccups. The ten of us are now like a well-oiled machine. Well, eight of us, to be more accurate – minus Daniel and Jacob.

Andrea and I are just standing up to leave when Daniel leans forward across the table.

"Don't you want to know why we sat here today?" he asks.

There's something in his tone that makes me think I absolutely don't want to know. "No," I say, putting my arms through the sleeves of my coat. Andrea and I turn to leave with everyone else. Mrs Harris has already left, and I don't want to be hanging around these two without her eyes on us.

Daniel leans further across the table, pushing his blond hair out of his face. He's at least six-feet tall so, even sitting down, he takes up a lot of space. Jacob stands behind him, arms crossed. He's not as tall as Daniel but the muscles he's built make up for what he lacks in height.

"Don't be like that, Muzzie," Daniel pouts. He leans on his arm, like he's modelling the school uniform. "Jacob and I just wanted to make sure you weren't going to go off and kill one of us, too, like your little terrorist friend."

Andrea gasps next to me but I don't react. I know Daniel well enough to understand that the only thing he wants is a reaction. I refuse to give it to him. I grab Andrea's arm and make for the door.

"No," she says, pulling out of my grip. She's a lot stronger than I give her credit for because she does it easily, quickly, then turns to whisper to me. "Remember our promise, Hanan? At my house? Don't think I've forgotten because I haven't." Then to Daniel she says, "Daniel, I will literally drag you to the Head myself if you don't stop being an arsehole."

He sneers at her. "Takes an arsehole to know an arsehole, doesn't it?"

Jacob sniggers behind him. Daniel turns to give him a high-five.

Andrea moves closer to where he leans on the table, bringing herself to his eye-level. She speaks in a measured tone.

"You know you're only here because you're a little shit and the school had to put you somewhere. But one word from me, from any of us here, and the Head will shift you out of this school so fast you'll get whiplash."

He stops sneering then. It solidifies into something else, something ugly. He stands up and takes a step towards us. Jacob extends a hand to stop him before he takes another step. He leans in and whispers something in Daniel's ear, but I can't make out the words.

Daniel straightens when Jacob's done. The sneer is gone now, replaced by a more sinister smirk.

He points to me with a single finger. "You," he spits, "watch yourself. You and the other pieces of scum no one wants here."

I tense up. The threat laced in his words is palpable across the room. Daniel's said a lot of things over the years, but this has got to be the worst, the most hostile.

I *want* to say something back. I can feel the words itching in my throat, but nothing comes out. I remember my mum's warning, almost as if she's right there next to me, saying it again for the hundredth time.

Af daboolan dahab waaye.

A closed mouth is gold.

I've held these words in my heart for ever. They stop me whenever I feel other ones clambering up my throat, calling out for my attention, begging me to form them on the tip of my tongue, to hit back at those who spit out hatred like it's nothing.

And what Hussein told me the other day – that I didn't have words for anybody else – starts to creep in and, for a second, there's a battle in my head, but then the familiar bubble appears, clamping down on my uncertainty.

Thankfully, the boys saunter out the room with their usual forced swagger, before Andrea has a chance to say anything more either.

"They have got to be two of the shittest humans on Earth," Andrea says, fuming next to me. "Are you okay?"

I nod, shouldering my bag and wanting to get away from here as quickly as possible. I hide the tremor in my hands, putting them behind my back.

I'm desperate to just go home and curl up in my bed to study. To lose myself in chromosomes and endothermic reactions and trigonometry. It isn't most people's idea of a peaceful afternoon, but it is mine.

We pass by the bulletin board as we walk towards the door. I glance at it. And then, I stop. Andrea turns around and comes back to where I'm standing.

"What are you doing?" she asks.

When I don't say anything, she follows my line of sight to the notice that's pulled my attention.

"Oh," Andrea says, reading the heading. She leans forward to read the rest of it. "Oh, *damn*."

She turns to face me, features knitted into an expression of pity. "What are you going to do?"

"I don't know," I say quietly.

I really don't.

I wish then that we'd been quicker and left when Mrs Harris did. Then I wouldn't have gotten tangled up with Daniel and Jacob, and I wouldn't have seen this notice that looks like it's come straight out of a dystopia.

CHAPTER THIRTEEN

I try to push the notice out of my mind. In fact, I go as far as trying to pretend it doesn't exist. If it can be tomorrow's problem, why make it today's? At least, that's how I try to rationalize it.

I get a head start on dinner when I reach home and give Abooto her afternoon meds. Hussein isn't home, having dropped the girls off from school and then presumably headed out to the cinema (my mini-investigation into his exact whereabouts proved unfruitful as he hadn't told Hafsa or Sumaya anything either), and Hooyo's on the rota for evening shifts at the care agency. So, today, it's full mum-mode for me and, it's only after sending Hafsa and Sumaya off for their baths and getting them through their homework, that I'm able to sit down and get through my own stuff.

When they're finally in bed and fast asleep, I spend the better part of an hour with my copy of the Qur'an. I feel calmer when I recite the Arabic. It gives me a clarity that I don't even know I'm looking for sometimes.

I hear a notification come through on my phone and pick it up to check.

When do u wanna do this?

It's from a number I don't recognize but I know it can only be from one person. I hadn't been expecting to start this study-buddy business anytime soon. In fact, I'd actually forgotten about it since everything else this afternoon.

I deliberate for what feels like for ever, wondering what to say. I land on a simple one-word sentence.

Monday?

It's only after I send this that I wish I'd remembered what I already have on my calendar that day.

Mr Fleming's memorial service.

I type out a message to suggest another day, but Jessica's already replying.

Fine. Library after school?

Can't do library, I type, remembering Hooyo's threat, but then I have no idea what to follow that up with.

The only solution hits me a second later.

"No," I whisper, horrified at the thought that's shoved its way into my head.

Why is it that the single solution that keeps everyone happy – the school and Hooyo – is the one that literally feels vomit-inducing?

I punch my phone into the mattress, once, twice, three

times and then I bury my head into my pillow and scream. Sadly, neither of those things are as cathartic as I'd hoped.

I pick up my phone again.

My house, if that's okay?

This time, Jessica's reply doesn't come straight away.

I wonder how my invitation might've come across. I didn't want to sound eager – the last thing I want is to seem like I'm inviting her to my house as a way to beg her friendship or anything. It's not like I want her in my house at all and, after seeing Daniel today, I definitely would prefer to steer clear of any and all Robertses. But there's no way to back out of this agreement now, especially since I told Ms Williams and Mr Foster I'd be doing it.

I glance at my phone. Still no reply.

Given everything that's happened between us over all these years at Grafton, I wonder if Jessica is afraid of coming to my house. Maybe she thinks my family are all Arabic-chanting weirdos who'll force her into some kind of barbaric initiation process.

Then:

Whatever.

It's an abrupt reply and I catch myself before I end up over-analysing it. What do I care anyway? I have one job to do: tutor Jessica and then get the hell away from her.

I debate whether to reply or one-up her by leaving her hanging. Eventually, good sense prevails over my desire to win this power struggle.

Anything u wanna revise in particular?

Not really.

Ok. Meet u in the library after school next week.

I leave the texting there, already exhausted by it even though we've only exchanged a few words. Thankfully, she doesn't send anything else.

My fingers drift to the photo album on my phone. Though I wanted to make it tomorrow's problem, I can't help looking at the notice now. I'd taken a picture of it, almost as if I knew I'd need the physical evidence to prove to myself later that I hadn't imagined it. I'm lucky that it was just Andrea and me left in the conference room otherwise I'd probably have got in trouble for taking a picture of something I'm sure I wasn't meant to see.

I zoom into it now. The three bullet points glow brightly on the page, bordered by a thick red box.

"Achieving Integration" Policy Proposal for
Grafton Grammar School

Urgent emphasis on:

- Monitoring by senior leadership of students deemed to be at risk of radicalization.
- Mandatory extracurricular involvement for students deemed to be at risk by senior leadership.
- School uniform regulation change to include banning headscarves and skirts greater than knee length.

Discussion evening on proposed policy with parents, teachers and governors to be organized in due course.

I read it again. The words begin to blur the more I read them, but I can't stop. I zoom in and out as I stare at the picture, doing it so many times that I lose count.

When I'd first read it, I couldn't believe the governors had actually met to discuss how they could best deal with us, the Muslim students at the school. There are so few of us anyway, and even fewer that wear modest dress. It's only me, Nasra, and another girl for whom the last rule would apply. A rule designed to take away part of our identity. An identity we've chosen for ourselves, as much as the school might like to believe otherwise.

I let out a groan and lie down on the floor. It dawns on me that maybe this integration thing has already started. Why else would Mr Foster pair me up with Jessica, the one girl in this entire school I've never been able to stand, and who has never been able to stand me either? It's either that, or Mr Foster's hoping to smooth over class dynamics since the incident with Nasra and the Head, and somehow thinks it's a good idea to put me in the firing line.

I roll over and bury my face in the carpet.

Up until now, I've managed to get through my years at Grafton without major incident. Sure, it hasn't always been pleasant (it's not like anyone enjoys regularly hearing they don't belong, that they should go back to where they came from or being called a devil worshipper) but it's been manageable. I've done it, and I'm still in one piece. I've done it and I'm almost within reach of my dreams and Aabo's legacy. But this notice stirs up a familiar fear inside of me. That, whether I like it or not, people will never completely leave me alone. I'm something to look at, something to be curious about, someone to be angry at, someone to question and fear – now more than ever.

Though there's no real mention of anything specific, it's obvious why the notice was written. *Who* it was written for. There's no doubt this has everything to do with Mr Fleming's murder, but the knee-jerk reaction of the school stuns me. All the claims that the murderer had been radicalized were just gossip. There were no cold, hard facts. No evidence which backed up any of those claims. But it hadn't stopped reporters from chasing down every possible lead that suited their narrative when news of the murder first broke out last week. It hadn't stop them from painting a picture they wanted to paint, no matter how inaccurate. And now? Those very rumours are coming for me and every other Muslim at Grafton Grammar.

For a second, I allowed myself to be comforted by the fact that, according to the notice, the school would be holding a discussion evening. When I read those last few sentences, I breathed a sigh of relief. *Everyone would need to agree to it first*, I'd thought. They'd need to *agree* to ban my headscarf and monitor me as if I'm some wannabe terrorist.

But then I slowly realized...after what Mr Foster said to me at school yesterday – about the "fabric" of Grafton – that I don't think people voting for this thing is such an impossible idea. That's when panic quickly replaced relief.

I pick up my phone again, this time to text Nasra. Bad things are clearly starting to brew, and I don't want to get caught out. And maybe, if I tell Nasra, she'll know what to do.

I start to type out a quick message, but I hesitate for a moment before deleting the entire thing. Whatever's going on with this integration notice, it's serious, which means a text isn't going to cut it. I need to speak to Nasra face to face. I quickly glance at the clock, but I already know it's too late to call her and dissect all of this. I'll have to wait until tomorrow.

I venture downstairs in the hope of a distraction, bringing my banged-up laptop with me.

Hooyo's sat in the living room, resting her legs on a footstool. She sits up for a moment to absent-mindedly massage her legs. Abooto has her eyes closed, sat in the chair closest to the doorway, but she grabs my hand when she senses me walking by and gives it a squeeze. I throw myself onto the sofa with a huff, eyes fixed on the ceiling. Hooyo can tell I'm in a mood, so she only smiles and goes back to watching her reruns of *Super Nanny*. It's her second favourite show, after every single David Attenborough documentary ever created.

"When did you get back, Hooyo?" I ask. I realize that I didn't hear her come home.

"Oh, not long ago…maybe an hour," she replies. "I thought you might be busy upstairs, so I didn't call out."

"Is Hussein home too?"

Hooyo shakes her head, clearly too engrossed in the episode to say more.

"Do you know where he is then?" I prompt.

"He's gone to finish up a few hours at his job. They gave him a late-night shift…last minute."

"Interesting," I mutter.

I sit there, pretending to watch the episode, but I can't stop thinking about Hussein's new job. I wonder whether Hooyo ever doubts it the way I do, or whether she's more doubtful that any of her children would ever lie to her. But the way he's acting… Hussein's apparently told Hooyo all about it, but he's still not mentioned a word to me. It doesn't make sense. If he's making enough to pay off our bills, I'd expect him to be crowing about it non-stop.

Part of me is starting to think all this sidestepping is because Hussein knows I will have lots of questions. No minimum wage, part-time job is going to bring in that much cash in just a week. It doesn't add up. He knows it and I know it. But beyond all of this, Hussein and I have always told each other everything and now this makes me wonder if there's anything else he's keeping from me.

I'd be lying if I said I'm not worried for him too, with everything that's been happening since Mr Fleming's death. Despite Hussein not looking like what some would consider typically Muslim – no long beard or a qamiis or taqiyah – things are brewing. What if someone makes the right assumption by taking one glance at his black skin? What if they look past the tracksuit and see what they want to see?

Even a week later, there are still stories trickling down the grapevine, of neighbours, friends and strangers getting accosted – on the streets, in the supermarkets and, once, even at a local council meeting – because of the man who killed Mr Fleming. Mostly, these stories are about Muslim women but, occasionally, there are stories about men. Attacks on men who are Muslim and men who aren't Muslim, but the one thing all these men have in common is that they aren't white.

My stomach rumbles. I go to the kitchen and pull out the Nutella jar from the cupboard, using a spoon to feed myself and savouring the hazelnut taste. Hooyo hates when I do this because I always double dip, so I make the most of the empty kitchen now, unloading the sugar into my body.

The fridge catches my eye as I'm turning back to the table. I walk slowly towards it, dragging the spoon out of my mouth. The black lines have crossed out everything on the pieces of paper. The bills *and* the climbing debts. Hussein's signature criss-cross pattern has put a line through every single "final notice" letter. Everything has been…erased.

I start to walk back to the living room to ask Hooyo about it, but I stop myself. I know what Hooyo will say. She will say that Hussein paid it off with another pay cheque or referral. She'll say what Hussein has told her. The question is whether he's been telling her the truth.

I sit at the kitchen table with my laptop and jar and do a quick search for any cinemas in Haldow. I've only ever been to the one on Faren but just because I haven't heard of it doesn't mean it doesn't exist. Due diligence is key to any kind of investigation and if there's one thing I'll never do, it's throw the rule book out the window.

The results come up with two cinemas in Haldow. A small independent one and a newer, franchised cinema that's recently opened. I open the website for the second one. It instantly comes up with a recruitment sign and a link to applications.

Okay, I think, reassured. I let out a breath I didn't realize I've been holding in.

The cinema is real.

It does exist.

I close the tabs, grateful that, at least on this front, Hussein isn't an outright liar. Though I'm still not certain he's been completely honest either.

Reluctantly, I turn my attention to my email. I scroll through, looking for the one I've been dreading all day. I find it quickly, underneath a few emails about other school events I couldn't care less about. It's from the Head, Mr Davies, sent to everyone on the school mailing list. A simple email with words of condolences and an attached flyer with details of the memorial service happening in a few days. I feel a lump rise in my throat as I read, and I blink to stop anything from my eyes spilling over onto the keyboard.

I scroll down. My hand pauses on the trackpad. Mr Fleming's there on my screen, staring at me. I shoot up the brightness on my laptop and zoom in until his face takes up the entire screen.

He looks slightly younger in this photo than he did the last time I saw him. There are fewer lines around the edges of his eyes and fewer grey hairs in his bushy eyebrows. But everything else looks the same, which seems a little strange. How can he look the same when he doesn't exist any more?

He's smiling in the photo but it's not clear what he's smiling at. Something outside of the frame? His hazel eyes are a little off-centre, staring at the thing that's brought such happiness to his face. And his signature moustache is there, as perfectly trimmed as ever.

It brings back a memory of the time I asked him about his moustache when I caught him stroking it in front of the mirror in the caretaker office.

"Are you thinking about getting rid of your moustache, Mr Fleming?" I had asked.

"Never in a million years!" he'd huffed. "I've had little Barry here since the moment I started sprouting this hair on my face." He'd turned around and smiled. "It's been with me for ever, Hanan, and I'll take it to my grave. I can promise you that."

Somehow, this email makes his death seem more real than before. It makes it more final, more lasting. I swallow, trying to

135

remove the lump in my throat, and I close the email, moving onto the next one without even reading the subject line. I'm just desperate to get away from the photo and the words in front of me, the ones that say, in black and white, that my friend is dead, and would I like to come and celebrate his life?

I rub my eyes quickly to clear my vision. I bring my attention back to the screen, moving the cursor to the top right-hand corner, already poised to delete what I assume is junk mail. I see something unusual in the subject line, but thanks to quick fingers used to deleting most things, the email's already gone, landing in the digital bin with a familiar crunching sound before I get a chance to read it properly.

When I recover it, I almost wish I hadn't.

CHAPTER FOURTEEN

From: anon_981@live.co.uk
To: h.ali@ggrammar.sch.uk
FWD: THE ULTIMATE MISSION

U HAVE BEEN WARNED MUZZIE...

They have hurt you, they have made your loved ones
suffer. They have caused you pain and heartache. They
have killed Michael Fleming. What are you going to do
about it? Are you a sheep like the vast majority of the
population? Sheep follow orders and are easily led.

Don't be a sheep! JOIN US ON 24TH NOVEMBER.

There will be rewards based on action taken. These
are as follows:

10 points: Verbally abuse a Muslim
25 points: Pull the headscarf off a Muslim "woman"
100 points: Beat up a Muslim

1000 points: Bomb a Mosque

2500 points: Nuke Mecca

My hand freezes on the trackpad. I blink a few times and read it again, wondering if I've just somehow imagined it. Has someone *actually* typed this out and sent it to me? I'm stuck like this for so long that my hand starts to cramp.

Still…there's something that feels strangely familiar about this email. Something in the back of my mind ticks as I read the words again, but I can't quite make the connection.

One thing I do slowly start to realize is that someone I know must've sent me this. Or, at the very least, someone from Grafton Grammar, because the only way to get a school email address is through the directory. And the only way to access the directory is…by having access to it yourself in the first place.

I wring my hands in my lap, trying to figure out who would be this spiteful. There's every chance it could be Jessica, hiding behind an anon address, probably trying to rattle me in some way before we're forced together. I know how ticked off she must be that I'm the one tutoring her – me, the foreign girl, the devil worshipper, the one who doesn't belong here and who definitely should never be thought of as smarter than her in any way. Or maybe one of her co-Braids. They obviously would've heard by now what Ms Williams had asked of us. Maybe they thought this would, in some messed-up way, be an act of loyalty for their friend.

My hand stills on my lap. Daniel and Jacob. It could be

either of them, or maybe even both of them together. They're practically joined at the hip anyway. Daniel's words from today still ring fresh in my ears.

Watch yourself. You and the other pieces of scum no one wants here.

I text Nasra.

wondering if you got any creepy emails in ur school account?

She replies quickly.

Nah. wish I did tho, everything in that email is DEAD

I put the phone down and drum my fingers on the faded table runner. *Okay, so not everyone got it then.*

"What's this?" Hooyo asks, bending down behind me and squinting at the screen. I jump. I hadn't even heard her walk into the kitchen. I close my laptop quickly before she has a chance to read it properly.

"Why you scaring me like that, Hooyo? Don't you know that's bad for my heart?"

"Don't you worry, your heart's too young for that." She straightens, eyeing me. "I was calling you from the living room, but you didn't answer..." Hooyo's gaze shifts to the laptop in front of me. "What were you looking at?"

I keep my face neutral. "Nothing. Just some work for school I was finishing."

"Don't lie to me, Hanan," Hooyo says, a little quietly now.

"I'm not lying," I try but, even to me, my words sound flimsy.

"What were you looking at? I'm not going to ask again."

I sigh, opening up my laptop. The screen jumps to brightness. The email I'd been trying in vain to hide pops up front and centre.

Hooyo bends over my shoulder again and squints.

"They…have hurt you. They…have…" She sighs, moving around to sit next to me at the table, pushing the Nutella jar away for space. "Hanan, read this out for me. I don't have the energy for this English right now."

I read it for her, not leaving anything out because I know Hooyo would be able to tell. She always can.

When I'm finished, there is a silence that stretches on for some time. Hooyo isn't even looking at me, her eyes are focused on the cupboard opposite her.

I decide to break the silence, not wanting to let this spiral out of proportion. If I'm going to get ahead of this, I need to do it now. I wish I'd never recovered the stupid email in the first place.

"I know it sounds bad," I start, "but it's just a stupid prank. I promise, it's not real. People send this stuff all the time, it's not serious."

Hooyo's gaze shifts to meet my eyes. She shakes her head sadly. "You don't remember?" she says. "We got the same thing three years ago, Hanan. It wasn't a prank then, and it's not a prank now. It's serious."

The ticking in my mind stops when she says this; the odd

140

feeling, that sense of familiarity, focuses. Hooyo's right, we did get the same thing three years ago. Except, that time, it'd been through the post and almost everyone else we knew had gotten it too.

"Don't you remember what happened to Fowsia?" Hooyo continues. "She was in the hospital for two weeks. Two weeks, Hanan! She was hurt so badly that the ribs they broke put a hole in her lungs."

Hooyo lets her head hang in her cupped hands. I reach out to hold them.

"I know, Hooyo," I whisper. "But it's just a joke this time. A stupid joke from a stupid person at school. It's not real."

I'm not sure how much I believe myself when I tell Hooyo this, but I know it's what I have to say if I have any chance of downplaying this. Because I've just realized that the date in the email is the same date as the bake sale next week and, if I know my mother, any whiff of apparent danger and I might as well be shackled to my house.

Hooyo looks up, drying her eyes with her garbasaar before turning to me. "Nothing's a joke, Hanan, not any more." She pauses. "I want you to stay home that day. All day. No school. And, before you say anything else, I'm not asking you, Hanan, I'm telling you."

I splutter in response, my Somali coming out more broken than usual.

"But, Hooyo, I've got the bake sale on that day! I can't skip that. People are depending on me. Andrea, Mrs Harris—"

"I don't care who's depending on you," Hooyo says, putting

a hand up to interrupt me. "*I'm* depending on you to stay safe. That should be enough."

She dries her eyes again then gets up to leave. I delete the email from my inbox, permanently, wishing I'd just done that the first time.

CHAPTER FIFTEEN

Andrea walks beside me on the way to school the next Monday, speaking about a million and one different things as usual, but I'm not in the same headspace today. I haven't mentioned anything about the email – even though I've had enough chances – because then I'd have to explain what my mum made me promise. And I'm not ready to accept that yet. Knowing Andrea, she'd probably go off on someone too, maybe Jessica or Daniel, and I don't want that either because I know it would snowball into something bigger. I'd rather not have all of that chaos be a backdrop for Mr Fleming's memorial service tonight.

I see the Braids up ahead in the hallway as we walk to form. I stare at the back of Jessica's head, trying to read her the way I used to try and read Hussein's thoughts when we were younger. I wish I knew if she's dreading this tutoring set-up as much as I am; if she sent that anon email to me that's gotten me stuck at home for the bake sale; if Mr Foster's roped her into this crazy integration scheme too; or if she was just as oblivious to it as I was.

She must sense what I'm trying to do because she glances back, catching my eye. Neither of us smile.

As time goes by, I wait for Nasra to turn up to form, and then to chemistry, and then to the pigpen at break, but she doesn't. Since school was closed for an inset day on Friday, and I didn't see her over the weekend, I planned on telling her today about the conference room notice, but give up when the lunch bell rings. No one walks into school this late. She probably just forgot to tell anyone that she wouldn't be in today. I make a mental note to tell her off the next time I see her.

I spend my last period in the library with Isha sat at one of the tables opposite me. She walked in after I did and looked the other way when she noticed me sitting there. We usually sit together when we have the same free period but, today, it seems we're both flying solo. I prefer it this way, to be honest. I don't have the energy to think about her or Lily. Neither of them has bothered to apologize after our fight and I'm starting to think they never will.

There was a time when I would've been more hurt and confused over their silence, over how distant we've all gotten so quickly, but I'm beginning to think that maybe some fallouts are unsalvageable. Maybe some things can never be fixed.

I glance at the grandfather clock periodically as I try to make a dent in my study list, counting down the minutes until Jessica walks through the doors to meet me. I've secretly been praying for her not to turn up since last night. I believe in miracles and that would be nothing short of miraculous.

But it looks like my prayers haven't been answered.

Jessica walks in, gazing around as if it's her first time here.

She looks a little lost without her co-Braids. I pack my bag to leave.

"This will be over before you know it, Hanan," I whisper to myself. "Like it never even happened."

A boy a few seats down looks up. I give him my most sane-person smile and hope it's done the trick.

Jessica and I walk to the bus stop in silence, then board the bus in silence and then get off the bus in silence. It's a silence that isn't awkward because we both know neither of us wants to speak. So, we stay as we are, Jessica observing the surroundings, staring and repeatedly raising her eyebrows as we get closer to my house and further away from the clean and polished-looking area near Grafton Grammar. At one point, when we see a man fly-tipping three mattresses, I even notice her jaw drop.

Since my conversation with Hooyo a few days ago, I haven't been able to focus on anything properly. Hooyo rarely makes rules but when she does, she's serious. But this rule has been harder to accept because staying home and missing the bake sale is not just about me. It's about Andrea too, because I've been non-stop pushing her about this for ages. How would it look now if I just suddenly dipped? Daniel and Jacob would probably have a laugh, yes, but that isn't the thing bothering me. There's been so much happening recently – from Mr Fleming passing away and the school's agenda, to Hussein mysteriously bagging so much cash and my friends' silence – that the bake sale was the one thing I was looking forward to staying the same. It's also the one thing at Grafton that has nothing to do with my exams and med school prep. In a way, it's kind of become my therapy dog over the years.

We reach my front door. Jessica grimaces when she takes in the state of my house's exterior: a tiny semi-detached house with broken guttering, a front door marred by countless scratches and a small front garden carpeted in shrivelled weeds. How could I have thought bringing her here made sense? That this would somehow work? If I'd been thinking straight when I texted her, I would have clocked that bringing Jessica here is like bringing a snake into a bird's nest. She'll probably eat me alive and then tell everyone about it at school tomorrow.

I open the door and we walk in. Then I hesitate.

"Do you mind taking your shoes off?" I ask. "We don't really wear shoes in the house."

"Uh…sure," Jessica replies. Confusion colours her features but she bends down to undo her laces anyway.

"Hanan, is that you?" Abooto shouts from the living room.

"Yeah, it's me, Abooto." To Jessica I say, "Wait here for me."

Jessica nods, looking very much out of place in the hallway while I go to the living room, hoping that my grandmother doesn't start any drama, today of all days.

"Hey, Abooto. You okay?"

"I'm fine, but your mother was here about an hour ago to check up on me. I think she thinks I'm losing it," Abooto says with a small chuckle. She shakes her head. "Anyway, have you got someone with you?" She pokes her head around the chair to see if she can get a better look.

146

"Abooto!" I move to stand in the doorway, blocking her. "You're too much of a snoop."

"Is it a boy?" she asks, a twinkle in her eye. "It's about time you started shukaansi, you know. I was much, much younger than you when I started dating."

I want so desperately to cringe right now, but I avoid giving her exactly the kind of reaction she's looking for.

"No. It's a girl, we're studying and I'm leaving right now so enjoy your afternoon," I reply firmly.

Abooto chuckles with delight, grabbing the remote to flick through random channels until she finds a programme she won't understand but likes the look of.

Jessica's still standing in the hallway where I left her. I think she looks a little…nervous? Her expression takes me by surprise. I've rarely seen her without her signature smirk.

"Well, my room's upstairs." I put a hand on the banister and step towards the staircase uncertainly. "Think it's better if we go there."

"Whatever you say." The smirk is back. "You are the teacher after all."

We head up to my room. A room that's always been a reprieve away from everything else in my life but now, I'm letting in the one person who might just ruin that for me too.

She sits cross-legged on the floor in my room, a little awkward, legs pulled in as though she wants to avoid touching anything. I sit opposite her, giving us a wide enough space so should either of us be tempted to lean over and strangle the other, we'll really need to work for it. I lean back to grab the folder from my bed and slide out the study notes I've made for us.

My plan is to jump right into it. No preamble, no opportunity for anything other than the stuff we need to get through. For me, this is the most pain-free solution: get it done as quickly as possible.

"I thought it would be a good idea to start with differentiation, since that's a pretty big topic," I say, indicating some of the questions I've written up.

Though I'm avoiding looking at her, I can't help but notice that Jessica hasn't got anything in front of her. No book, no pen, no papers. Is she expecting me to just *give* her these things?

I carry on, pushing those thoughts away. I'm here to tutor her, not nanny her. It's her business whether she wants to write anything down. I know I'm doing my job well enough.

"So, the first question is to differentiate with respect to x. The equation is y equals—"

"Stop," Jessica says abruptly. "Just stop. I'm not…I'm not doing this." She laughs under her breath as she stands up, dusting her skirt off for longer than seems necessary. "Yeah sorry, I thought I could do this but I'm not sitting here in this grotty place to listen to you, of all people, tell me I'm dumb. I'd rather fail my exams than do that."

My initial confusion turns to anger and then to disbelief.

"Are you being serious right now?"

Jessica doesn't answer me. She only picks up her bag and

takes out a notebook. For a moment, I start to think she might be reconsidering. That perhaps she's found a tiny bit of common sense, which is better than no sense at all, but then she pulls out a log sheet with the Grafton Grammar letterhead. She scribbles in today's date and signs her name, before putting the sheet and pen on the floor in front of me.

"Sign this. Ms Williams and Mr Foster don't need to know anything apart from what we put on this paper. So as long as you keep your mouth shut, we can stop playing pretend and get on with our lives."

Jessica stands above me, arms crossed, waiting. I pick up the pen. It feels a little slippery in my grip. I look at the sheet and pause. I think if push came to shove, I would sign this paper. As much as I hate to admit it, Jessica's right. This way, the two of us don't need to spend any time together and we can go our separate ways without getting into trouble at school but, still, I hesitate.

In my entire life, only a few situations have ever warranted deceit. Like when I was younger and Hooyo would ask if I wanted to go to the swimming pool in summer, and I would say I was ill because I'd rather stay home and read a good book. Or when Hussein went on the warpath, trying to find out who ate the last of his crisps and I shrugged my shoulders, wanting to avoid any retaliation in the future. But I never lied about anything big, anything that mattered.

I bring the nib to the page, but I don't write anything. I just watch the ink start to bleed through the paper.

"Just sign it already," she spits.

149

The spell breaks. I take the nib off the paper and stand up to face her directly. I don't think Jessica knows that she's played her hand. She's shown me how much she wants this. And I start to recognize there's something that I want out of this too. Something I've never been able to get all these years at Grafton. Answers.

"Why do you hate me so much?" I ask in an even voice. I grip the pen tightly. "Tell me, what's so terrible about me that you'd rather lie your way through this than do it for real?"

I've had to deal with so much of Jessica's crap over the years and I've never let anyone know how much it hurt, not even Andrea. I hated the idea of anything making me look weak. Letting anyone see just how much my blood boiled or how deep my anger ran. A closed mouth is gold, Hooyo always said, and it's what I whispered to myself anytime things got too bad.

I always thought that it would end one day. That Jessica would stop, get bored maybe, and find another target. But that never happened. Jessica was relentless, day after day, and here she is now, in front of me, after six years, still doing the same.

"I don't hate you," Jessica finally replies, looking out the window. "That would suggest I even waste energy thinking about you and trust me, I don't."

"What is it then? Because you act like you hate me, you look at me like you hate me. I don't know what you expect me to think." I laugh bitterly. "You can't waltz around, doing the things you do, then expect someone to shrug it off."

I can't believe what I'm saying. This is more than I've ever said to her in my entire life. The words tumble out of my mouth, like a tap resistant to closing, the pressure steadily rising.

"I just don't like you," Jessica says calmly, as if that explains everything. She looks away from the window and I wait, wondering whether she'll say more, but there's nothing.

"That's not good enough!" I say. The pressure builds and builds. I've never felt it this high before. There's a ringing in my ear, like the whistling of a kettle. "You've had it out for me since my first day at Grafton and I've dealt with it. I kept quiet, never said anything, tried to stay out your way and that's all you can say now? 'I just don't like you'," I repeat, mimicking her. It's a childish thing to do, but I can't help it. "You know, you're one of the worst things that's ever happened to me."

Jessica looks taken aback by my anger. Her eyebrows are arched in a perfect C-shape, surprised to see this side of me. Hussein told me I didn't have words for anyone else, but I'm going to show him that he's wrong.

I drop the pen onto the sheet on the floor. The impact of it, a quiet thud, sounds loud in this room.

"No," I say more calmly now. "I'm not signing this until you tell me what your problem is with me. Until then, you can show yourself out. I'm sure you remember your way to the front door."

I walk past her, releasing the tension I can feel coiling in my body, and leave my bedroom, and Jessica, behind.

When I shut the bathroom door, I look at myself in the mirror. My headscarf is still intact, the pin holding the layers in place. I rest a hand against my flushed cheeks and then briefly against my chest. I look at myself in the mirror, gripping the sink tightly with my hands.

I don't know what I've just done, but I hope I don't regret it.

When I return to my room, it's empty.

No Jessica, no book, no pen.

CHAPTER SIXTEEN

Greenham Church is filled to capacity, but my family and I get here early enough to fit behind the last pew.

While Andrea was the only person at Grafton who knew that Mr Fleming was my friend, everyone at home has always known about him and how he'd offered me his space to pray at school for years. My family never got to meet him but when they found out about the memorial service, they insisted on joining me. Even Hussein had got back home earlier than he normally does to go with us. I had tried my best to hide my surprise, but I couldn't hide the grateful smile that played on my lips.

In front of me, Hafsa and Sumaya hold hands. I'm sandwiched between Hooyo and Abooto, and Hussein stands in a gap not far behind us. I turn to look at him, but his eyes are elsewhere, roaming the church. It's the first time any of us have been in a church. The interior looks beautiful, holy. A large gold cross adorns the wall behind the priest standing at the pulpit. Two chandeliers hang majestically from the ceiling, illuminating the hundreds of faces and bodies packed inside for Michael Fleming's service.

Behind us, people try to get inside, but it's clear the church is full. I crane my neck to see if any of my friends are here. Andrea said she might be coming, but I wasn't sure about anyone else. I recognize a few people from my neighbourhood and my year – Sophie from chemistry is a few metres away and smiles at me when our gazes meet. I smile back. Sophie is clearly nice enough to not act as though she doesn't recognize me outside of school and that almost never happens in my experience.

Sophie's father, on the other hand, isn't smiling. I see his glance jump over me and, as he takes in my similarly dressed mother and my niqab-wearing grandmother, I recognize a look of contempt flash across his face. It's brief, but long enough for me to notice. He angles his body away from us, blocking my view of Sophie.

The priest begins the service. He reads various passages from the Bible, a few of which I recognize from my RE lessons a few years ago. When he concludes the sermon, the church is eerily quiet. The silence is pierced by the quiet sobs of a woman in the pew closest to the front as the priest invites her to speak. There's a heaviness that seems to bend and fold around her, like a shawl. She stands next to an enlarged photograph of Mr Fleming – the same picture from the email with him smiling.

It dawns on me, then, that I recognize the woman from the pictures I once saw in Mr Fleming's office.

"Who's this?" I'd said after my prayers one afternoon, fingers grazing a silver frame. "Is this your wife?"

His face shined like a light had burrowed beneath his skin and lit him from the inside.

"Oh, yes," he'd said smiling. "That's my Diane. Been married for thirty years now, but she's still every bit as beautiful as the day I first laid eyes on her."

I stroked the silver frame, lost in the memories of a different time, of a different place. *What a beautiful thing it is*, I thought, *to have love and to have it for so long.*

Mr Fleming stood up and walked over to where I stood near the cabinet. I hadn't even realized he was at my shoulder until he spoke again.

"Deep in thought, are we?" He held out a tissue.

I realized, suddenly, that my face was wet. I smiled gratefully as I took it, wiping off the tears.

"I was just thinking about my dad," I sniffed. "And what it would be like if…if he was still alive and married to my mum."

The words had slipped out from my mouth. I never talked about Aabo at school, ever. I never talked about my family, about what we'd lived through and survived, but, strangely, I found myself relieved that I'd shared my thoughts.

I've never forgotten what Mr Fleming said to me next. I think about his words often. I carry them with me still.

"Good fathers never leave us," he said, offering me another tissue. "They take root too deeply for that."

Then he picked up another frame. One of him and his three children. "Seems as though your old man did it right, if you're still thinking of him so fondly. I just hope I've done as good a job with my own when I'm gone one day."

I feel the tears readily flowing down my own face now as I listen to Diane, her voice ringing out across the church. I cry because I've felt the type of grief she is feeling before. I cry because I know how bitter grief tastes, how endless it feels. I cry because the world is unfair and the unfairness of it all *hurts*.

"Michael was a wonderful man, husband, father, brother, son and human." Diane's voice wavers as she speaks, but her face is the picture of resolve. "He was taken too early from this world…a world that can be as kind as it is cruel. And though Michael isn't here today, he would also tell us that the world can be deeply forgiving.

"In times of tragedy, it's important that we come together as a community. That we remember our humanity. Remember what brings us together, rather than what sets us apart. I'm sure he would tell you all, if he could, that there's no one to blame for his death." She looks up from the piece of paper in her hands briefly. It's as if her gaze meets every individual gaze in the room, like she's speaking to each and every one of us personally.

"Michael would tell you all that hate is the devil's biggest weapon and to not allow yourself to be used by the devil. Stand against hate," Diane says solemnly. "In all its forms."

The hush presides as Diane turns to the priest, an elderly man with deep-seated wrinkles. His white cassock trails the floor as he walks towards her. He holds her hand and whispers something in her ear, bringing a small smile to her face. A few teachers from the school also say a few words, followed by the Head. I don't pay attention to them but, when a familiar voice floats over the church, my head shoots straights up.

I know that voice…

Daniel stands at the front, all six feet of gangly limbs and combed-back blond hair, reading from a piece of paper in his hand. He doesn't speak for very long, perhaps a minute, maybe less, but I'm in too much shock to even hear, to process, what he's saying. He's done just as quickly as he started, stepping back down from the front to let the priest take his place again.

I'm so busy trying to figure out why Daniel's at the front, speaking at Mr Fleming's service, that I miss the priest concluding the service. But, somewhere in the confusion, I recall something.

Mr Foster's words to Jessica after the argument in class.

Mr Fleming's death has got us all a bit shaken up it seems. Your family more than most, I imagine.

Someone pulls on my arm. It's Hussein.

"What are you doing?" He pulls me again. "Everyone's going across to Belmount for the vigil. Let's go," he whispers, more insistently this time.

He's right. When I look around, I see the huge crowd has split off into groups, everyone turning towards the exit at the same time. The rest of my family are already near the door. Hussein grabs my hand so we don't lose each other.

We walk across the road to Belmount, a huge park which looks eerie under the light of the lamp posts. The candlelight vigil has been set up near the south side. We pass by the midnight black lake as we walk over. I shiver when I imagine how cold the water must be this time of year.

Abooto stumbles by my side as we walk. *It must be her*

arthritis acting up, I think as I hold her arm tighter. When we'd talked about the service earlier, I'd expected her to want to stay at home, anxious about keeping her joints out of the biting cold which usually seeps its way into her knees and hands every winter, but she'd scoffed at me, telling Hafsa and Sumaya to get ready.

"Hanan," Abooto had said, "I know what a violent loss feels like. I *will* be there today to let that family know that they're not alone, and my body will just have to deal with it." Trying to find some suitable English words to conclude with, she landed on a simple: "End story," ignoring her limp as she went to find her niqab.

We stand now, all six of us, on the edge of the gathering, looking up at the sky as dozens of balloons are released by the Flemings, who say a final goodbye to the man who was the centre of their world. The backdrop of the candlelight is beautiful in the November darkness.

My own family holds hands – our old wounds instinctively recognizing the kindred grief that exists in the air. I look across at Hussein and give him a small smile, remembering how much his very presence helped me after our dad died.

I wonder how Mr Fleming's children will survive this tragedy. If they'll grow to be bitter about how they lost their father, or if their hearts will soften with time, only remembering the good things about him.

I shut my eyes for a brief moment, praying for the Flemings and for my own family. When I open them again, I catch a glimpse of someone I recognize making their way to the front.

The girl looks behind her to make sure the person she's with isn't lost in the gathering as they snake their way through. It's Jessica. As if she's heard my thoughts, she looks at me suddenly, shock and then hesitation registering on her face, before she slowly continues moving to the front. I catch a glimpse of the person who she's pulling behind her. Daniel.

I close my eyes, not wanting to catch another glimpse of either of them again. Not wanting to know why such a spiteful person was standing up to speak about one of the kindest people I have ever known.

CHAPTER SEVENTEEN

The memorial service and Daniel are still weighing on me the next morning. For a long time, I wondered whether I had just imagined him. After all, I was standing at least twenty metres from the front so there was every chance I could have mistaken him for someone else who just happened to look and sound similar to him.

Now, walking to the bus stop this morning, I try again to make sense of why Daniel was there. I had zoned out of his speech yesterday so if there were any answers in whatever he had to say, I don't have them.

"Hanan!"

Someone calls me from behind just as I've walked through the Arch. I turn around to see Maryam. I walk back a few steps to meet her halfway.

I'm glad to see her this morning. Though the two of us aren't close friends, I can't lie, it's nice to see someone that has nothing to do with Grafton Grammar or the havoc that is currently my life.

"Hey, girl," Maryam says, coming in for a hug. "Long time no see. How you been?"

"I'm good," I say, giving her a squeeze before letting go. "And you? How's the fam?"

Maryam makes a face as she shoulders her school bag. "Fam's all over the place, honestly. Ahmed's been…" She shakes her head, making another face. "Well, I'm sure Hussein's told you anyway. My mum still hasn't recovered to be honest, and I don't know if she will."

I keep my expression neutral. "Oh, right, yeah, I can imagine." I hold my breath, waiting for her to say more, *hoping* for her to say more. I don't want Maryam to figure out I have no idea what she's talking about because, one, she'd know something's up between me and Hussein, and two, it might mean she holds back from telling me something I think I need to know.

"It's the way he thinks dropping out of college is the answer to all his problems. Does he think Bakerstone's going to welcome him back with open arms when he finally gets his head screwed on straight?" Maryam huffs, crossing her arms. "And these people he's hanging around with now…I don't know, Hanan. I don't know. But I'm sure my mum's going to lose it soon."

I'm pretty sure I've already lost it.

"Who's he hanging around with?" I ask, trying to appear casual.

Maryam looks past me to wave at one of her friends across the road.

"Just the kind of people around here who attract the wrong attention," she replies grimly, turning back to me. "You know what I mean, right?"

161

"Yeah," I whisper. "I do." Standing underneath the Arch – the dividing line of the gangs in Northwell – I know exactly what kind of "wrong attention" she means.

Maryam says bye and crosses the road to join her friend. Their laughter echoes in the Arch and dies away but her words follow me for far longer. I try to string together the pieces of information I've gathered about Hussein and his shadiness as I walk the rest of the way to the bus stop.

What I know is this: Hussein has been earning hundreds of pounds from a job he says he started less than a couple weeks ago; Hussein has been avoiding me; Hussein's friend Ahmed has dropped out of college and has been hanging out with some not-so-great influences.

I sigh. Time for me to finally figure out what the hell is going on.

I steel myself when I reach school, preparing to be hit with questions I don't want to answer. So, when Nasra and Andrea ask me, point blank, how it went with Jessica, I'm expecting it. There's even a noticeable pause in Isha and Lily's conversation, though they don't go as far as to look over.

"It was fine."

Andrea and Nasra look unimpressed. Nasra taps her nails against the table.

"Is that it?" she asks incredulously. "Come on! You and Jessica locked in a room for an hour...girl, I'm sure it wasn't a happy ending."

Obviously, Nasra's right and, in fact, one hour is a pretty generous estimation for how long we lasted. Things had pretty much gone south after five minutes, but I don't want to talk about it. Most of my brain is already preoccupied replaying the conversation with Maryam. Better to just brush it under the carpet. Also, given how much Nasra hates Jessica, it doesn't seem like such a good idea to fan the flames even more.

"Wait," I say. "You weren't even in yesterday, Nasra, how did you know I was meeting up with Jessica? I didn't tell you what day it was."

She points to Andrea.

"Of course," I sigh.

Luckily, Mr Foster calls my name out on the register, giving me a reason to turn away from the spotlight. Neither of them asks any more for the rest of form, but I don't miss the confusion in the looks they share.

I realize that I still haven't told Nasra about the notice I saw in the conference room. Since she wasn't in school yesterday, I didn't have the chance to give her the rundown.

I quickly take stock of how many people are around us and decide against sharing it here. Might be better to find her later, I think, when there are fewer ears around.

Later, in the corridor, my friends' voices carry over the cacophony of first-period chaos.

"I swear to God I'm going to lose it if I hear Jessica bitched out on Hanan yesterday," Nasra says to Andrea. "Wish I could be the one to teach her a lesson or two."

"I'm sure you would've been a great teacher," Andrea laughs.

"Maybe volunteer as tribute in Hanan's place?"

I ignore their comments, pushing harder against the swell of student bodies to get to class quicker. Really, it proves why I don't need to tell them the truth. It would undoubtedly become a whole thing and I'd much rather it didn't. Not when there are more important issues to worry about. Between Hussein, the Integration policy notice I'm trying very hard not to think about, and the strange connection between Daniel and Mr Fleming – not to mention my upcoming med school exam – there's not much left in me to give Jessica even a second thought.

The fact that it's also the twenty-fourth of November *tomorrow* doesn't help matters either. It's not so much that I'm worried about the "ultimate mission" email, but Andrea still doesn't know that I'm bailing on the bake sale, and I have no idea how I'm going to tell her.

When the double biology period ends, I'm called back by Ms Bloom.

"Hanan," she says, turning around to wipe the board. "I'm sure it isn't anything serious, but Mr Davies has asked for you to see him in his office."

"Mr Davies? The head teacher? Wants to see me?" I ask, perplexed.

Ms Bloom nods and goes back to attacking the whiteboard. It looks like that's all the information she's going to give me.

I know the Head by name only. He's new and started a few

months ago at the beginning of the school year. I've only seen glimpses of him so far since I'm not the type to get tangled into anything that would usually require meeting the Head. Most students interact with their year leaders first, so I know, objectively, that this isn't good.

I reach the East Wing of the school and walk into the Head's office. His assistant, Ms Dunaway, tells me to knock on the door. I knock and wait for a response.

"Come in!"

I poke my head around the door.

"Hi, Mr Davies. It's Hanan. Ms Bloom said you wanted to see me?"

"Right, right!" Mr Davies says jovially. He jumps up from the leather chair and leans on his hands against the oak desk. "Come in, please do come in. Take a seat, Hanan. Either one is fine."

He indicates the two chairs opposite him.

I sit down uncertainly, crossing then uncrossing my legs, leaning against the back of the chair then leaning forward. Finally, I decide on crossed legs and lean appropriately forward.

Mr Davies mumbles something about the state of his desk, strewn papers and folders, as he shuffles a few things about. I take the opportunity to look around the room, taking in the quiet grandeur of it, with the fireplace, the floral wall-mounted lamps and the green velvet curtains. The bay window overlooks a small garden feature outside. I wonder what part of the school courtyard it's in and why I've never noticed it.

With the desk somewhat neater, Mr Davies sits back down.

He brings his hands together, interlocking his fingers.

"Now, I'm sure you're wondering why I've called you in, Hanan," he begins, a picture of extreme sincerity. Even though he's barely spoken, I get the feeling Mr Davies is trying very hard to appear approachable. "I've had a complaint from one of our Year Eleven students. Daniel Roberts. He claims that you accosted him last week after a Fundraising meeting and that you threatened to…" He clears his throat uncomfortably. "…to bomb him."

My mouth falls open.

"Another student, Jacob, also claims to have witnessed this…this argument and that you made these comments unprovoked."

I can't believe what I'm hearing. I hadn't even reported Daniel for what he'd said to me. Now he and his little sidekick have the gall to *make up* lies about me? I remember myself then. I close my mouth and will myself not to burst out laughing. It would look bad, for obvious reasons. I bite down on my lip in an effort to hold it at bay.

Mr Davies sighs and spreads his hands on the large desk. Again.

"As you know, Hanan, I've only recently started at the school, but I've already heard quite a bit about Daniel's reputation. I'm aware that he's on the Fundraising committee because of behavioural concerns."

This isn't news to me. Everyone knows about Daniel and his school record. I remember the look on his face when Andrea reminded him of it at the bake sale meeting. I'm sure the only reason he picked it over any other club was because he'd thought it would require the least amount of work.

"Suffice it to say, I'm not quite sure I believe Daniel or his friend. I've also had a look at your portfolio and teacher references – which, by the way, are superb so keep up the good work," he says with a toothy smile. "So, in fewer words, I want you to know I won't be taking this matter any further, Hanan."

I nod slowly, surprised but glad that I don't need to make a case for myself. But, if Mr Davies believes that Daniel's lying, why has he called me into his office at all?

"I did want to discuss a different matter with you...entirely unrelated. We've recently had a school governors' meeting and some of the governors, uh...essentially are considering a new policy."

Mr Davies pauses, beginning to look slightly uncomfortable. A redness creeps up his neck and he pulls on his tie to loosen it slightly.

"It's confidential for the moment but they're considering putting a few things in place to help the, uh, you know, students such as yourself become more integrated with the school community. What I mean to say is, uh, Muslim students."

I pretend to be surprised at this information, widening my eyes just a little and leaning against the back of the chair.

"I don't understand, Mr Davies..." I reply. "Are they saying there's something wrong with the Muslim students here? There's barely any of us and, well, none of us have ever done anything seriously wrong. I don't think so anyway."

Unlike Daniel, I want to add but I don't.

"Quite right, Hanan. I don't particularly agree with the conclusions from this meeting. I value our Muslim community and I certainly don't want to alienate anyone." The redness creeps higher and higher up his face. "I think...I think it might help if we put you in front of some of the more worried parents and governors to...alleviate their concerns."

Now I'm genuinely surprised. What does he mean, *putting me in front of?* "I'm not sure I understand what you mean, Mr Davies," I reply slowly.

Mr Davies looks as though he'd rather be having any conversation apart from this one. "What I mean is that, as our most senior Muslim student, and with a stellar school record, you might be, let's say, best placed to speak to the parents and governors who'll be voting on the issue soon. It's my feeling that all of this is only coming about as a consequence of –" he pulls on his tie again as if it's choking him – "recent events."

So, there it is.

"You mean what happened to Mr Fleming, sir?" I whisper, but I already know what the answer is.

Mr Davies nods once.

I lean back against the chair, absorbing the full impact of what Mr Davies has just said. He wants me to *speak*, to the adults who run this school, who are meant to be the ones behaving logically and rationally, to make my case for the decent treatment of the tiny Muslim population at Grafton – something that should *be* the reality anyway.

I feel a familiar dread settle in my bones. I don't want any of this. I don't want to be the poster-girl for anything, let alone the poster-girl for Muslims. All I've ever done is follow the rules and yet, somehow, it still isn't enough. There'll always be new hoops to jump through, like I'm in a dog show that I didn't sign up for.

It dawns on me then that I'm not the only one Mr Davies could be asking this of.

"What about Nasra, sir? She's another senior student. I'm sure she could speak at this meeting. She'd be really happy to. I could talk to her and—"

Mr Davies gives a strained smile and interrupts me.

"Actually, Hanan, I'm happy for you to take this on. I feel you're probably, uh, better placed than Nasra to handle this. I want the message to the governors and parents to be clear, refined. I'm sure you understand."

Yes... Yes, I understand perfectly what he means. Mr Davies wants a palatable Muslim, a token Muslim. He doesn't want Nasra. The kind of girl who isn't afraid to be vocal, to say what she means and to mean what she says. The kind of girl who speaks the way she wants to speak. Clearly, he wants someone like me. Someone who does as they're told because they're too afraid to do anything but walk the tightrope.

I nod and look down at my shoes.

"Well, thank you very much, Hanan." He smiles at me in dismissal. "I'll give you the details of the meeting closer to the time."

When I open the door to leave, Mr Davies asks one last question.

"Hanan. I hope you don't take offence, but, uh...I've been

wondering whether you were born here? In this country, I mean. You speak very well. Very well indeed."

I shake my head, *no*, and leave.

I'm walking out of a cubicle in the girls' toilets when I finally put two and two together.

Of course.

Daniel must have sent me the anon email. Suddenly, it all makes sense. The heading was staring me right in the face and I'd completely missed it:

U HAVE BEEN WARNED MUZZIE

Don't be like that, Muzzie, he'd spat, on his way out of the conference room with Jacob that day.

Daniel's the only person I've heard use that word. And the fact that he's falsely snitched is the confirmation I needed that he's playing mind games with me. It means that, thanks to him, Hooyo's banned me from school tomorrow for no reason.

The 24th November, the "ultimate mission" – and the only reason why I can't go to the bake sale I've been planning for weeks with Andrea – is as fake as his bomb accusation.

My hands ball into fists without my realizing. It's only when I register the pain of my nails digging into my palms that I unclench them. Am I really supposed to sit back and let that idiot dictate my life? Let him control where I go and when?

I breathe through the swell of anger and take out my phone to text Nasra.

I need to talk to her. About the notice, about everything.

CHAPTER EIGHTEEN

I find Nasra later during my free period. She's sat alone in the pigpen, despite how cold it is today. I sit down next to her, pulling my coat tighter around me. She doesn't even let me catch my breath.

"Don't make me beg, Hanan. Please tell me it's about Jessica. I'm legit *dying* to hear how it went."

I groan, letting my head fall into my hands. "Oh my God. No, Nasra. It's not about her. Stop fishing for drama. It's something else."

I hesitate for only a moment, wondering what this conversation might unleash. What am I even hoping will happen? That the school drop their obvious vendetta? That everything goes back to the way it was before? A part of me questions whether going back to before is even the answer. Things weren't perfect then either.

So, I tell Nasra everything, not leaving anything out – about the notice that I'd seen pinned on the bulletin board, about the anon email, and about Daniel and Jacob. How he'd reported *me* to Mr Davies and what Mr Davies had asked of me. How I feel torn about it.

Nasra whistles once, low, under her breath. She takes a steadying breath before she speaks. Her brown eyes are wide, shocked.

"So?" I prompt.

"Sorry, just give me a sec. I'm still trying to get my head round this."

She brings her palms together in front of her face and stays like that for about a minute, eyes closed. Then she clears her throat and looks up.

"Okay, so. First off, this is crazy and, uh, secondly, this is *crazy*." She shakes her head in disbelief. "Sis…there's a lot I could say and, you know me, I could really chat for days but for now all I'll say is this." Her eyes bore into my own. The only sound that cuts through the silence is the wind that wraps itself around the trees. She reaches out to put a hand on my shoulder.

"You need to stop worrying about the world and start worrying about who you want to be, Hanan. Believe me when I say the world doesn't give any fucks for you. You can trust me on that." She doesn't blink as she holds my gaze. "So why do you keep bending over backwards for it?"

There's no savagery in the way she says this. Just calm straightforwardness.

"These people want you to do a little song and dance for them. But why? You've been doing that since you got here and look what they're trying to do to you now. It hasn't gotten you anywhere so…just think about that, sis. Think. About. It." She taps her temple with each word.

This whole time, I've been desperate to speak to Nasra, desperate to hear what she has to say – because Nasra always has something to say – hoping that in her words there might be a clear solution to what Mr Davies had asked of me. A solution that I don't need to be a part of. A solution where I can stay where I've always been and where I've always felt comfortable… out of everyone's way. But now I'm left with more questions than answers.

Later that evening, after everyone's gone to bed, I sit at my desk, rubbing my eyes. I find that I can't get up. There's a sudden heaviness bearing down on me. I drag myself down to lie on the floor and bundle myself into a foetal position. I hold an old cassette tape to my chest, pressed against me. I trail my fingers along the edges repeatedly, finding it oddly comforting, until my fingers fall numb.

Though I'd tried not to think about it today, right now – surrounded by the absence of people and the absence of sound and the absence of anything to *do* – it hits me full force: today is the anniversary of my dad's death.

We've never done anything to mark the anniversary as a family but that doesn't mean any of us think about it any less. Every year, the day goes on as seemingly normal, but beneath the surface, beneath the shell of normality, I know we're all carrying a sharper sadness than we do on all the other days of the year. Especially Abooto. She usually goes out of her way to pretend nothing's different, but all of us hear how she weeps for hours on end through her bedroom door. None of us are ever allowed to mention it.

The only outward acknowledgement of the anniversary is the hug Hussein and I share on this day. It's fleeting, but it steadies me. We'll share no words but it's enough of a comfort that it makes the rest of the day seem just a little less impossible.

But Hussein isn't around today. In fact, he hasn't been all day. I wonder whether he's gotten so caught up with his new job that he's forgotten about Aabo's anniversary? About the hug that we've shared every year for the last ten years – the one I thought we'd be sharing today too.

It's hard to believe Mr Fleming's words right now, that good fathers take root deeply, that they never leave us. It's hard to believe because Mr Fleming's gone now too, and it seems impossible to hold onto those words, to believe in them, when the person they came from no longer exists.

Right now, I can only feel the crushing sense of my dad's absence. I've searched for him in my dreams, though those very quickly become nightmares, and I've searched in the decade-old memories which are slowly starting to fade. I've tried to look for him in the words he left to me, the words I now clutch to my chest. I hold the tape there, hoping the words will seep into my heart, so I can carry him wherever I go. I do it even though I know how senseless it sounds. Still, I can't seem to put Aabo's cassette down. I don't want to listen to it… I'm not ready for that now. I listened to it once, years ago, when my mum first gave it to me but, today, I'm content to just hold it.

* * *

I'm woken by Rosa knocking gently on my door and popping her head in. I must have fallen asleep on the floor, because I'm still there with blankets strewn over my body, my limbs radiating in all directions like a starfish.

"Hi, sweetheart," Rosa begins nervously. "Your grandmother sent me up to check on you since she didn't hear you getting ready for school this morning." She opens the door a little more. "Everything okay?"

"Yeah, I'm okay," I reply. "Just not feeling great. I'll be down in a bit." I smile and hope that'll be enough for Rosa. She nods and slowly pulls the door closed behind her.

It's easier to just say I'm sick than explain my mum's gone over-the-top and won't let me go to school because of a random anon email. I cringe when I think about Andrea. I still haven't told her about bailing on the bake sale today. I'd prefer to hide under a rock for the rest of the week than face her. I was the one who dragged her into it and now I'm the one bailing.

Oooh. I perk up. Maybe this means the pinky-promise is null and void now. I'll consider it a major win if I can avoid watching a girl throw herself onto vampires and werewolves. Talk about a lack of survival instincts.

I stay lying down on the floor for a while longer, only getting up when my back starts to ache from sleeping on the carpet all night. I throw on a robe, hoping it'll make me look a little less messy and head downstairs to put Abooto's mind at ease and grab some breakfast. But when I step out of my room, I see Hussein's door is ajar and I hesitate.

175

I listen out for Abooto and Rosa's quiet chatter to confirm there's no one with them downstairs. When I'm certain they're alone, I go to Hussein's room and push the door further open.

His room is as tidy as it's ever been. His bed is neatly made, room dust-free and the floor is clear of any junk. The only thing out of place is a single sock on the floor next to his laundry hamper. I'm sometimes weirded out by how clean he likes to keep his room – and how happy he is to trash the bathroom every morning instead – but, in this very moment, I'm grateful.

The closet is nearest to me, so I start there. I'm not sure what I'm looking for, exactly, or if there's even anything to find, but after hearing what Maryam said about her brother Ahmed, I'm more worried than ever that Hussein really has fallen into something bad. This might explain the sudden cash influx and the fact that my brother's not acting himself.

When I'm done with the closet, I move to his bedside table. The first drawer is full of random things – charger cables, batteries, chocolate. The second looks about the same. The third seems empty...until I pull it all the way out.

Neatly bunched away in the corner is a navy polo shirt. I unfold it.

The logo on it reads TRU CINEMA.

So...Hussein was telling the truth.

I close my eyes tightly and take a moment. I'm not quite sure I realized just how terrified I was that his job wasn't real. Yes, I knew the Haldow cinema existed, but this is the confirmation I needed that Hussein's *job* really does exist and that he's not been lying.

I fold the shirt as neatly as I can, ready to slide it back into place, when my hand brushes against a piece of paper in the same corner of the drawer, almost invisible against the white interior. I take it out. It's addressed to Hooyo and it's from Bakerstone College.

Dear Ms Abdullahi,

We are writing to you to highlight our concerns with regards to Hussein Ali's attendance at Bakerstone College over the last several weeks…

I read the letter slowly. Then, I go back to the start and read it again. When I'm done, I put the letter back exactly how I found it and put the folded polo shirt back on top. I slot the drawer back in and I scramble to stand up, wanting to get out as quickly as I can.

I go downstairs, my mind buzzing with thoughts moving too quickly for me to catch, and then I almost bump into…Hussein.

Hussein?

I do a double-take, wondering why he's home at this time of day, but then I remember the letter I've just read.

Hussein's not been going to college. In fact, he hasn't been going for a while.

"Did you just appear out of thin air?" I ask, keeping my voice light. "Didn't hear you come in. Could've given me a heart attack."

He rolls his eyes. "Don't blame me. I came in through the front door, not some secret portal."

I almost blurt out everything I know then. I'm not sure what my game plan was going to be but seeing him in front of me now, I feel as though I'll burst if I don't say something. All we've done is dance around each other lately but I'm sick of it. I don't want to act like things aren't falling apart or that everything isn't upside down. But when I open my mouth to let it all out, something catches my eye. I step back to look at him properly.

Hussein's get-up looks like something off a JD mannequin. The white of the Nike swoosh is brightly contrasted against the olive green of his shirt and, at the edge of his collarbone, I can make out the glimmer of a silver chain. I look down at his feet. I'm not surprised when I see two immaculate, white Nike trainers. The black of the Nike swoosh on them glints wickedly in the light of the hallway.

When I'm done assessing his outfit, I can tell Hussein's braced for impact. His arms are crossed against his chest, making his new silver watch all the more obvious.

"Well," Hussein starts, his head cocked to one side. "You got a problem?"

"Me? No, I don't have a problem. Just admiring your new outfit."

Hussein purses his lips, pushing past me to run up the stairs. When he gets to his bedroom, he slams the door.

I stand in the hallway for a few seconds, listening keenly. When I'm confident he isn't coming back out, I go over to the coat rack and delve into Hussein's jacket pockets. My hand brushes against some crumbs and I grimace, not wanting to know what I've just touched.

I feel a piece of paper and pull it out. I glance back up at the landing again to check Hussein's not there, then turn my attention to my discovery.

It's a note with two words in block capitals:

BRINLEY ROAD

Already I'm certain that this note has nothing to do with TRU Cinema. This note is about something else that I pray I'm wrong about, even though Hussein's strange behaviour and expensive clothes point to the one thing that would explain all this. The same thing that Hussein's friend Ahmed has apparently gotten himself involved in.

There's more written underneath the address on the note. A date and time. It takes me a moment to realize that the date on the note is *today's* date and, when I do, I almost drop it.

I take a quick picture of it with my phone before placing the note back in the same pocket and position as before. Then I take the stairs two at a time back to my bedroom and lie down on top of the blankets on the floor, deliberating about what to do next.

Hooyo said I couldn't leave the house today, after the anon email – and she's already called the school about my absence. And while I know she doesn't play around with her rules, it feels like those rules were for a specific set of circumstances. Ones that have now changed.

I pick up the cassette tape on the floor next to me and hold it close to my chest again. Aabo would want me to do whatever it takes to protect our family, I tell myself. Even if it means breaking a few rules.

I open up my chat with Andrea, scrolling through the countless messages she's sent and the six calls I missed with my phone silenced. I text her back, ignoring the email about my med school test that flashes up. I clear it from the screen. The admissions test is only two weeks away, but I don't have the time to worry about it right now, especially when there might be bigger things at stake for my family. I press send on the message and hope Andrea hasn't blocked me in anger.

wasn't feeling great this morn but I'll be in soon

After a few hours of swearing and sweating in the kitchen getting the bake sale food ready, I shower and then jump in my uniform. When I'm ready, I head downstairs to tell Abooto and Rosa that I'm feeling much better, and that I have an important test at school I can't miss. I hold my breath, waiting for Abooto to contradict me, wondering if Hooyo's told her about my school ban today, but breathe a sigh of relief when she only says goodbye.

I leave and head to school. With each step to the bus stop, I tell myself that today isn't the day I'm meant to stay at home. That the whole conversation with Hooyo was just a dream. When I exhaust those thoughts, I try to convince myself that everything's fine. I haven't got any more emails from Daniel which probably means it was just a silly prank. And there's no way I'm staying locked up at home over a prank. Definitely not when Hussein could be up to something bad. And especially not when me missing the bake sale would make me the worst friend ever.

Plus, if I don't go, it'll look like I'm scared of Daniel, and that's not something I'm willing to accept because I'm not scared. I'm not scared of anyone at Grafton Grammar and that isn't going to start today.

I get on the bus and plan the day: bake sale first, head to Brinley Road to follow Hussein after, get home before Hooyo realizes anything's amiss. It's a foolproof plan. What could possibly go wrong?

CHAPTER NINETEEN

I find Andrea in the Great Hall setting up our stall with the other fundraisers. She looks up from arranging cupcakes the second I walk in through the doors and she doesn't look happy.

I do a quick round saying hi to everyone else first, "admiring" their set-up. Daniella and Flo have upped their game this year. They've got their OG brownies, the undeniable crowning glory of their stall, and slices of carrot cake, cake pops and lemon squares. The lemon squares are a new addition. I stop myself from biting my lip and try my best to sound sincere when I wish them good luck.

Andrea doesn't look up when I reach our stall on the far side of the Hall close to the back entrance – a prime location for an event like this. I lean back on my heels and click my teeth. When that doesn't do anything, I whistle. Then, I sigh. Nothing. Andrea doesn't even pause as she moves onto arranging the rose gold bunting.

I sigh louder.

"What do you want, Hanan? Don't you have someone else to ghost right now instead of bothering me?"

I move to the other side of the table to stand next to her and put the bag of goods down, making sure none of the containers inside topple over. I'd hate myself if I carried it all the way here only to have it fall in front of me.

"I thought you might want to know what the competition looks like." I pout but she doesn't see. "I've scoped it out and... initial impressions? Honestly, Daniella and Flo are moving confident this year. I'm not loving how good their lemon squares look. But everyone else looks fine, thank God – no one's done anything special. And don't even get me started on Daniel and Jacob's stall. All they've got is a Walkers multipack—"

"The competition doesn't look like anything because there is no competition." Andrea looks up. "And I'm still waiting on my apology. That's three minutes you've gone now without coughing one up. I'm not getting any younger."

I hide my smile. "You're right. I'm sorry. That should've been the first thing I said to you."

She purses her lips. "Good. Did you bring everything then?"

"Yep, we got the sambuus, bajiyo, bur, doolsho..." I fish for each of the containers in the bag and bring them out one by one. They're still steaming and warm from being cooked only a couple of hours ago. Since my plans changed this morning, I'd had to cook them very quickly though I'm praying they taste as good as they usually do. *Technically*, they aren't all baked goods, but I've always felt like a bake sale is only really a bake sale in spirit, and not in the letter of the law.

"And are you going to tell me why you were ghosting me?"

My hand instinctively stills as I'm digging out the last container. I can tell she notices.

183

"No reason really. Just wasn't feeling myself."

Andrea side-eyes me but doesn't push it. "Well, anyway." She clears her throat. "Thought you might want to know you've got a new crush. Jacob's been flitting about here asking about you."

"If you're joking, let the record show that I hate you and hate you deeply."

"You know you only love me for my sardonic sense of humour," she grins. "But I'm not joking. He really was."

"What the hell did he want?"

Andrea shrugs her shoulders. "Apparently, nothing. Maybe you're not the only one who thinks this is a competition."

We finish setting up our stall and, by the end of it, even I can't help but think we've done the best job we ever have. The rose gold bunting and gold confetti littered about the plates of food look next-level and Mrs Harris even circles our table a few times taking photos for the Grafton newsletter and commenting on what she can't wait to buy. When the flood of students arrives after school, we're ready.

Andrea and I stand shoulder to shoulder, all beaming smiles and warm persuasion. As per tradition, I stand on the savoury side and Andrea handles the sweet side. The cash box is in between us.

There are students and teachers flooding in from both entrances. The ones coming in through the second gravitate towards our stall, beckoned by scents of sweet cinnamon, vanilla, caramelized onion and the earthy smell of minced meat. It's obvious our stall is getting the most attention, compared to everyone else around us, but, very quickly, it also becomes obvious that something's unbalanced. Something's thrown us off our game this year. Something isn't right.

Next to me, Andrea's hands dart in and out of the money box, in and out of the napkin pile between us. My hand stays still, barely moving. *No one's buying my stuff*, it dawns on me. The food which usually sells out first – the sambuus, the bur, the bajiyo – remains untouched on the table, the heat of them quickly seeping out and into the surrounding air. I'm staring down at my savoury side for a few moments, trying to work out if something about them looks wrong. Maybe I cooked them too quickly this morning and they've come out bad?

But then something makes me look up. That sensation that someone's watching you from afar…watching you, hoping that you'll notice. I look up, knowing it'd be way smarter to just ignore the feeling, but it's too strong.

Daniel stands at the entrance nearest to us. He's not standing with Jacob at their stall, like he should be. He smiles when he knows he's caught my attention, putting a hand up to wave at me, and when the next person walks through the doors, he turns to speak to them, nodding as he does so, then points to our stall when he's done. The girl looks up to follow his finger. She locks eyes with me and then veers in the opposite direction. Away from our side of the Great Hall.

I feel my chest start to constrict and I know what's coming then. *I can't be here any more*, I think to myself, *I can't*. I turn to Andrea, to tell her that I need the toilet, that I'll be back in a few minutes, but her mouth and hands are moving too quick for me to catch her attention. I slink away without her noticing, not looking back at Daniel and avoiding the doors that he's guarding.

I run to the toilets, ignoring people's looks as I fly by them. The only thing that matters right now is getting the hell away from people, away from their looks and their sneers and their whispering. The only thing that matters is not letting them see me like this.

I refuse to let them see me like this.

I come back once I'm sure everything's over. Thankfully, when I walk in again, there are only a few stragglers. Most people have already closed up shop and have started to clear up.

"Hanan!" Andrea exclaims when she sees me. She waves me over excitedly and it's all I can do to try and hide what's written on my face.

"Where were you?" she continues, when I come nearer the table. "You were there one second and then you were gone."

"I'm still feeling a bit sick from this morning," I lie. "Think I've caught a bug or something."

As Andrea starts counting what's in the cash box, I look away.

"Well, congrats," she says. "Because you missed the most shocking development. Someone just swooped in and—"

That's when I notice the table's empty. Not just Andrea's side, but my side too.

"Wait," I interrupt her. "Where's the food gone? My stuff was still here when I left."

Andrea looks up at me to roll her eyes. She waves a £20 note in my face. "That's what I'm trying to tell you! Someone came in and bought the whole lot. All the samosas and those little fried balls. Delicious, by the way. I snuck one in my mouth when you weren't looking."

"But who'd do that? There was enough there to feed like thirty elephants."

She shrugs her shoulders and moves on to separating the coins.

"Who was it then? You can't say that and not tell me who it was."

Andrea doesn't shrug her shoulders this time. She stays quiet.

"Andrea."

She drops the coins loudly into the cash box.

"Ugh fine, stop pestering me. It was Jessica, okay? It was Jessica. Stinky, ice-queen Jessica."

I'm too shocked to speak but, eventually, my thoughts come together and all I can think is: *I hate that bloody family and their mind games.*

The bus stop comes closer into view as I walk down the road. There's about an hour until the time on the note from Hussein's pocket, but I also need to get there with enough time to stake out the place first and figure out where I'm most likely to spot him *and* follow him to wherever the final destination is. Brinley Road is just a road after all, and I doubt that will be the end of the line. The only problem is…I have no idea where I'm going. I've run out of data on my phone, so I have no choice but to go old school on this.

At the bus stop, a drunken man sits half-on, half-off the bench, nursing a bottle of whisky. He mumbles incoherently.

Alright, I think. *There's no way I'm asking him for directions.* I consciously take a few steps further away from his bench.

I glance around, hoping someone else will come to the bus stop so I can ask them instead. I spy a head behind some bushes a few metres away. A brown mop of hair, the collar of a white shirt and the dark blue of a blazer. Definitely someone from school but, from where I stand, I can't see who it is. I don't bother asking them either. I'm sure they're too busy sticking their tongue down someone's throat.

Everything on the information display is too scratched out to read so I resign myself to wait. When the bus arrives, I step onto it first, ahead of the drunken man.

"Hi, do you know which bus will take me closest to Brinley Road?"

The bus driver nods languidly, chewing his gum with his mouth open. He knocks on the door of his cab with two fingers.

"It's this bus?"

He nods again. I resist the temptation to do a little dance as I tap my oyster card against the reader. I can't believe how easy that was.

I sit downstairs and spot the mystery person with the mop of brown hair from the hedges as they clamber up the stairs. I haven't spied whoever was with them, but I've seen *that* movie enough times to know that where there's one floating head, there's usually another. People are serious about a make-out sesh when they want to be, and the top deck is usually the place to go.

My phone vibrates in my pocket. I'm contemplating ignoring it but then another one comes through.

WHERE YU HANAN

And the second:

ABOOTO SAY YOU GONE

I turn off my phone and quickly slide it back into my pocket. Though I'm sure my logic will definitely come back to bite me in the butt, at least for now, if I can't see anything my mum sends me, then maybe, just *maybe*, I'll be a little less of an caasi. After all, I usually always do what my mum tells me to do but, if I feign ignorance, maybe I'll score slightly lower on the disrespect scale.

I lean my head against the window of the bus, listening to the rhythmic grunts and sighs of the engine. The power of it makes me judder, but I find it oddly comforting.

I hadn't planned on Hooyo finding out I'm gone, but this is necessary, I tell myself. Yes, it's very necessary. Hooyo already has enough on her plate to worry about and, though she'll probably kill me for doing this, someone needs to get to the bottom of all the secrecy surrounding Hussein's new job.

I need proof that what I'm thinking isn't true. I've never been this desperate to be wrong about anything in my life, but I've heard stories about this kind of thing. Stories of aunties with sons like Hussein, young and ambitious. Sons who'd also found well-paying jobs from thin air and became virtually well-off overnight. Sons who'd ended up on the wrong side of the law.

I don't want to believe Hussein's taken the same dubious path, but I also can't ignore the pit that's slowly been growing in my stomach since I first found out he miraculously pressed the reset button on our debts and since my conversation yesterday with Maryam about her brother. And finding that letter from Bakerstone College, hidden away in his room, has pushed all of those worries over the edge. Hussein may have stopped sharing his secrets with me, but that doesn't mean that I can just ignore my gut feelings. We're still two halves of the same whole, even if one half isn't acting like it any more.

The bus audio system announces the next stop as Brinley Road. I ring the bell and hop off when the bus stops. There's a thunderous run down the stairs from the top deck behind me as the door starts to close. A guy wearing a hoodie and cap somehow makes it out without getting clipped by the doors, which is no mean feat. He turns a corner and disappears, with the same hurried energy.

Stepping out from the bus stop, I walk towards a dingy café on the other side of the road. It's near-empty inside, decorated with a brown and white motif. The sign is tilted. *Lou's Cuppa*. Even before I reach it, a strong waft of coffee and bacon hits

190

me. It doesn't give me the greatest hygiene vibes but it's the only place with outdoor seating that I can see and the perfect place to stage my stake-out. I use a tissue to gingerly wipe down the metal armchair and table before sitting down. I prop the menu open in front of me, using it to hide the bottom half of my face. There aren't many people about so there's less chance to miss Hussein and whatever he's doing.

"Afternoon, miss. What you after?"

I jump. The menu drops to the table. I pick it back up and arrange it properly so I'm hidden again.

"Sorry," I reply, only half-scanning the menu. "Just a cup of tea please. Milk and two sugars."

"Coming up." The waiter pockets his little notebook and reaches for my menu.

"Is it okay if I keep it, actually? I like looking at menus. Bit of a weird habit."

Why did I say that? Ugh, I'm definitely not cut out for this.

"Uh, sure," the waiter replies uncertainly, turning to walk back into the café. In the reflection of the shop window, I see him glance back at me.

After I get my tea, I sit there for a while, sipping it and savouring its warmth. There's about thirty minutes left until the time on the note, but I realize there's no guarantee Hussein will even turn up. A note in a jacket doesn't mean anything for sure. And who's to say Hussein will even take the bus? Maybe he'll take a cab to Brinley Road and then I'll miss him. But I try to keep faith that he'll turn up.

I glance at my watch, every so often, willing the seconds

to move faster, wanting to just see him, follow him, *now*. My mind flies through a hundred different scenarios, each worse than the one before. I close my eyes and breathe, tell myself to calm down. To get a grip.

When I open them again, Hussein's there. I blink a few times but nothing changes. Out of nowhere, he's appeared on the road opposite, like all of my thinking and spiralling has suddenly conjured him up. He's there!

I almost drop the menu again in shock. I get a better view of him when the bus departs and, for a moment, it feels like everything's normal. Like he's here to meet me, at this random café, to catch up about nothing important, to have a laugh. How it's always been…me and him, together, the same way we were brought into this world.

Hussein stands at the bus stop, braced against the cold in a black puffer jacket and tracksuit. The white of his trainers is bright, even from where I sit across the road. He takes out the note from his pocket and glances at it briefly before shoving it back. Then he takes in a steadying breath. Whispers, as if trying to convince himself of something. I see him make a fist with his hands, then open them.

Hussein crosses the road. When he's far enough ahead, I drop some coins on the table and follow him.

CHAPTER TWENTY

Against the backdrop of a setting sun, I follow him. Though my phone is off and there are no vibrations to catch me off-guard, it feels heavy in my pocket. I wrap my hand around it in the warmth of my wool coat and head straight down Brinley Road, past a charity shop, three 99p stores, and a pawn shop. I hold the phone, tightly, and remember why I'm doing this and who I'm doing this for.

Our whole lives, Hussein and I have always looked out for each other and if he's gotten himself into trouble, if he's done something reckless and needs my help to get him out of it, I'll be there for him, even if he doesn't want me to be.

I press on. Hussein doesn't stop to look at the note again. While he walks, and I follow, a light rain begins. He brings the hood of his jacket up, obscuring my view of his head and blocking my twin-telepathic connection or, rather, my hopes of securing one. My coat doesn't have a hood so the rain falls unobstructed, into the dips my wrapped hijab has created around my covered neck and into my eyes.

Brinley Road feels like it'll never end. I stay on Hussein's tail, so focused on him that I accidentally bump into an elderly lady's shopping trolley. I pause to apologize, and then, almost immediately after, swerve to avoid someone's dog. For a second, I'm worried the yelps might carry to Hussein's ear, make him turn around to see what's going on, but the slap of his steps on the pavement continues unchanged.

I jog a few steps to make up for the distance my clumsiness has created, but Hussein makes a sudden sharp left and vanishes out of my sight. I rub my eyes to clear the rain from my vision. It's like he's disappeared in broad daylight. I slow down when I get nearer to the spot he was a minute ago. *Maybe he's onto me*, I think. *Maybe he's hiding around the corner to jump out at me*. But when I get there, it makes sense.

A familiar sign with its person-in-mid-step icon points towards a footpath, obscured by the overhanging branches of a tree.

Brinley Road ←→ Fulram Road

The distance marker reads a half-mile long.

I spy him quite far up ahead now. He's almost concealed by the darkness pressing in around him, and his black jacket doesn't help matters either. I walk on, stepping onto the footpath.

Usually, I'm not bothered by darkness. I've never been one of those kids who had to sleep with a night light growing up or who wet themselves at the prospect of a monster in the shadows of their room (I already had monsters of my own to reckon with), but there's something about this darkness in particular.

It seems to grow, uninhibited, snaking along the shadowed walls of the houses framing this footpath, and it feels terrifyingly empty.

Some of the lamp posts stand as sentinels without light, others create merely a flickering glare. It's only six o'clock but, with the sun already set, I have to look down frequently to avoid the barely illuminated puddles and discarded plastic bottles. There's still a fair bit of distance between me and Hussein but I can't risk making a noise. I can't risk anything that might make him turn around and see me, because I need to know what he's up to without giving him the chance to lie and cover up the truth again.

The white of his Nike trainers glows up ahead, like a homing beacon, and, just like me, Hussein sidesteps to avoid the stagnant water coating his new shoes.

I keep my eyes fixed on him. He doesn't turn around once to look back, which is lucky because I'm sure that he'd be able to recognize me even from this distance.

Then, I hear something. A heavy step in a puddle, the kick of a plastic bottle. The sound makes me flinch. I hadn't realized how accustomed I'd gotten to the silence.

I cast my eyes from Hussein, still up ahead but nearing the end of the footpath, and look behind me, squinting into the dimly lit night.

Someone's there, behind me, approaching fast. I can see a silhouette but only the shape of it. A set of shoulders, the swing of arms...

A cap on the head.

The same hurried energy of the guy who jumped off the bus after me.

Of the person with the mop of brown hair who'd run up to the top deck before that too…?

No, no.

I'm just imagining it.

I must be imagining it.

Hussein reaches the end of the footpath and steps onto Fulram Road. He fumbles for something in his pocket…the note, his phone?

The silhouette behind me quickens its pace. I quicken mine, not caring now about whether Hussein hears me. I *want* him to hear, I need him to hear, because this person behind is coming for me. I'm sure of it.

The hairs on my arms go up. I grip the key in my pocket tightly, letting its teeth sink into my fingers. Hussein's still there. He looks left, onto the main road, leaning forward to peer at something.

"Oi!" A voice from behind. The silhouette.

The familiarity of that voice…I can't ignore it now. I know who it is.

"Muzzie!"

I can hear Jacob getting closer. I quicken my pace to the point that I'm running, sprinting.

"Hussein!" I scream, hoping it'll carry over the traffic on the main road.

The fear tastes metallic in my mouth. It gets stronger when I bite down on my lip and taste blood. I bite harder, welcoming

196

the pain. It gives me the power to run at a speed I didn't know I could. Hussein's head turns. Alhamdulilah, I think. *Praise be to God.*

My feet take on a life of their own, slapping the concrete path with such force that I'm surprised each time I see my feet are still attached to my body. The brogues I wear hold their own, the laces miraculously staying tied when they've come undone so easily in the past.

"Hussein!" I scream again. There's a fire in my throat, a fire in my head. My vision blurs.

Hussein takes a step. Then he disappears into the swell of people on the main road.

He's gone. *Gone.*

Suddenly, a hand clamps down on my shoulder and I feel nails dig into me through my coat. Another hand grabs my head and yanks it back at such great velocity that the rest of my body falls backward, hitting the concrete path. I hear a *crack.*

I'm not sure if it's the sound of my body or the sound of something I've fallen against. I hope it's the latter but then a white-hot pain shoots up my spine.

Jacob stands over me, cap skewed, breathing heavily.

"You bitch," he sneers. He brings a hand to circle my neck, pinning me to the ground. "Thought you'd get off scot-free after what your lot did to Mr Fleming, did you?" I try to push against his hands, but his grip is too strong. "I even warned you I'd come for you...but you were dumb enough to come to school anyway."

It was him. The thought dawns on me suddenly, distracting

197

me from my struggle. It wasn't Daniel…it was Jacob. Just Jacob.

The sidekick without the kick, the fanboy on his own – Jacob was the one I should've been worrying about, not his friend.

Another thought immediately follows: *So this is why Jacob was asking Andrea about me.*

And then the most painful thought of all: *Hooyo was right, I should've stayed at home.*

Jacob grips my throat tighter, bringing his free hand to my hijab.

No fucking way is this boy going to touch my headscarf, is all I think before I bring my right arm up, my hand gripping the key with the teeth of it exposed. I scratch it along his face. Jacob cries out in surprise and pain, reeling backwards. His cap falls off completely.

The adrenaline pumps hard through my body. I leap up from the ground. I don't look back to see where my bag is. I just run forward, building momentum. I hear him get up behind me.

My leg comes out from underneath me and, suddenly, I'm falling, falling, falling. I see something dark at the edge of my vision as I struggle to find my footing again.

"Hanan!" Hussein cries.

Somehow, he's there, right next to me, pulling me up to my feet. For a moment, I wonder whether I'm imagining him.

It can't be him, my mind registers briefly.

Hussein is gone, he turned a corner and left. Maybe this vision of him is a coping mechanism. Maybe it's just my brain's way of trying to calm me because it knows there's no way out of this.

Everything seems to happen in slow motion after that. Hussein pulls hard on both my arms, hard enough that I think he's dislocated something. I can hear his voice in my ears, but I don't know what he's saying. I try to read his mouth, make out the words as best I can under the weak light of the lamp post.

Hurry up, he says. I think. *Quick. Come on. Let's get out of here.*

Jacob grunts in anger and mutters something unintelligible. I don't turn back to look at him. Hussein does though, and he must see something because he does the opposite of what he's just told me to do. He lets go of me and walks towards Jacob, towards the engulfing darkness of the footpath, instead of the main road.

Jacob steps towards Hussein and raises his arm. He's holding something. It glints under the flickering light.

"Hussein! Move!" I run forward, hand outstretched, wanting to save him, wanting to protect him as I have done, as we have done for each other, our whole lives.

Jacob's hand swoops down in an arc. Hussein clutches his stomach and crumples to the ground. He doesn't move. He doesn't make a sound. Jacob brings his foot to Hussein's head and lands a single kick to his temple.

I scream but my voice doesn't reach me. It feels like my head's underwater. When I look down, all I see is black.

Black, black, black…seeping through the grey of Hussein's tracksuit. Dark spots blooming on him, getting bigger by the second.

I throw myself down next to him, ignoring the pain singing

through my knees. I've forgotten that Jacob's still here but when he drops the knife, I look up.

Before I can say anything, he charges at me. He pushes me hard, and I lose my balance. My head hits the concrete. The force of it hums through my whole body.

Then he disappears.

I can't get up. I can't speak.

I hear his running and receding breaths.

No one else comes.

PART TWO: UNCHAINED

CHAPTER TWENTY-ONE

I am not on the footpath any more.

I'm sat in the back of a beaten-up Jeep slowly making its way through town. With every few metres we drive, our bodies shake from the impact of the car climbing over mountains of debris and humps of sand.

Sometimes, Hooyo talks of the beauty of Mogadishu before its destruction, showing me pictures as proof. Pictures of wide, well-built roads bordered by magnificent, towering palm trees. My brain can't make sense of it when I see these pictures. Why would someone want to destroy something so perfect?

I don't fully understand what's happening or where we're going, but Hooyo and Aabo say we're going somewhere better, somewhere where the sky is always clear, and the air never smells like dead flesh.

Someone is saying something. I can hear it, but I can't *hear* it. It feels like my head's still underwater.

I don't want to hear anyway. I'm happier where I am. Aabo is with me.

I'm sat quietly, biting my lip and listening to the quiet banter between Aabo and the driver he's hired to get us to the border. It helps to ground me, listening to my dad who has always been carefree, warm and inviting with everyone he meets. A man whose very nickname, qalbi furan, means "one with an open heart".

Hooyo's different though. Not closed off, but more reserved than Aabo is. Our aunties and uncles always said that the match between Ibrahim Ali and Leyla Abdullahi was a sturdy one; tough enough to weather the storms of life and of marriage because they tempered each other the same way that the sun and moon are in perfect balance.

I can feel my body being moved. It hurts.

A dull, faraway pain.

I ignore it. I drift back to where I'm happy, to where I feel no pain.

I squeeze Hussein's hand, glad that my twin is sat right next to me. I don't mind where we're going as long as Hussein's with me. We've always been together, side by side for the seven years we've lived in this life, and I know everything will be fine as long as I have his hand to squeeze. I find the familiar dip in the nail of his thumb and press on it, to get his attention. He gives me a wide-toothed smile, but his eyes are eager, roaming the landscape, hungry to see more of the world and what it has to offer. While Mogadishu is all we've ever known, Hussein has always been excited to see everything else around him and by the idea of what's beyond it.

Hooyo and Aabo have always shielded us from the death that hangs in the sea breeze here so, for the most part, it's been a distant, unfamiliar reality. But lately, violence has brewed, and death has crept closer and closer, so much so that I notice it now. It's there, even when I close my eyes. Hooyo and Aabo say that when we travel across the oceans and reach our final destination, it will be a place where fear doesn't even take its first breath.

Little Hafsa snores next to us, nestled against Hooyo and drooling on her jilbab. It's light grey and one of Hooyo's best, but because Hafsa's only a baby, no one will be angry with her for drooling so much. I've also followed suit, choosing to wear my best baati because I want to look nice for the new place we're going to. The colours are a vibrant mix of blue, yellow and white with a motif of flowers along the seams.

We're nearing the border now. I look behind to see Abooto lying in the back, snoring loudly. Our journey has been a long one and has taken us west through Afgooye, Baydhabo and Luuq but we're almost at the border. I notice Aabo is a little more on edge now. His easy-going nature has gradually been replaced by heavy apprehension. Our driver, Hassan ilko-boqol, a man with a hundred teeth, is continuing to happily chatter away, but Aabo gazes far out into the barren land which surrounds us. He glances back at us and smiles when he sees his mother still fast asleep.

There is a light. I can see it through my eyelids and then it hits my pupils directly.

Stop, I want to tell them. I can see you. I can see the light.

Soon, we approach a makeshift checkpoint, guarded by five

205

soldiers with rifles hanging loosely from their shoulders. The guards are laughing boisterously but their laughter stills as the car rolls up to them. They snap to attention as if a credible threat has just approached. I look around. I can't see anyone else but us.

One of the guards, a lanky one wearing sunglasses and with ears so big they stick out of his cap, approaches us. Aabo rolls down his window to speak to him and the guard leans against the door.

"What's your business, aboowe?" he says, chewing on something green. I can tell it's khaat. I've seen it being sold at the market. I remember once Aabo told me that it's a drug. That people don't realize it's khaat that chews them and spits them out, not the other way around.

"Aboowe, I'm just trying to get across to see some family in Kenya," Aabo says. His voice is resolutely firm as he tells this lie, not a single part of him shaking to give it away. "It's been a while since we've seen them."

The guard considers this and asks Aabo to step outside for a moment. They pat Aabo down for a long time, but he only looks ahead at the never-ending blue sky, his face expressionless.

Aabo and the guards talk for what seems like for ever. I squeeze Hussein's hand again, but my grip feels slippery.

The heat is intense. I can feel the leather seat of the car itching the back of my thighs, but I can't scratch right now. Aabo told us we needed to be completely still when we reached the checkpoint because any sudden movements might scare the guards. It hadn't made sense to me when he had said it. What guard would be silly enough to fear children? Still, I stay as motionless as I can, willing Hafsa and Abooto to stay asleep, to not make a sound.

I look out the window. I can see arms pointing towards the car. The guards are saying something about the Jeep, but I'm not sure what. Aabo invites them to take a look and they do, checking the glovebox and under the seats and the boot of the car. Another guard, short and wiry, tries to smile at me when he asks me to lift my legs up, but I refuse to smile back.

I sense my dad's shoulders loosen as he jokes with the guards, trying to charm them so we can get across without any trouble. He points towards the Jeep again but this time he walks towards the car alone, leaning through the window to rummage in a brown paper bag.

Aabo smiles as he leans the top half of his body through, reassuring us without words, though I wish I could hear the reassurance in his voice. He finds what he needs, quickly counting the wad of cash in his hand.

A pain, a fire, cuts through my body. They're trying to move me, I think.

Leave me alone, I try to say. Please, leave me. I'm happy where I am.

I am fine.

"What are you doing?" one of the guards asks nervously. It's the short, wiry one. "You've been gone there for a while." He taps his foot, apprehensive and impatient.

My mind falters here, between dream and nightmare. Between what I wish happened and what did happen.

I follow the dream, my mind creating another reality to shield me from the truth.

Aabo turns around then, having counted the money he plans to hand over and satisfied he's got it right. He walks over to them and hands the money to the short guard.

"Haye," Aabo begins cautiously. "Can we pass through?"

Aabo keeps his voice firm and emotionless, as if the answer he's waiting for is not the answer that will keep us alive. He doesn't turn to look back at his family in the car, even though Hooyo, Hussein and I all gaze intently at the scene unfolding before us.

They're calling my name.

Calling me back to reality.

The guards count the money carefully, huddling a few metres away to give the pretence of superiority but they only look like little boys playing with guns and money in the sand. The shorter one saunters to Aabo with a cocky grin.

"You're all good," he says. "Drive safely in shaa Allah. And be careful. There are those who would wish you ill in these lands."

Aabo nods sombrely. He gets into the car and pats Hassan ilko-boqol on the shoulder. We drive on.

That pain again, as they try to move me.

Where is Hussein? Where is he? I try to lift a finger and the pain courses through my body to focus there, but I ignore it. I lift another finger, trying to seek his hand.

Something sucks me back into the nightmare, away from my dream and into the truth of my past.

"What are you doing?" One of the guards asks nervously. It's the short, wiry one. "You've been gone there for a while." He taps his foot, apprehensive and impatient.

Aabo straightens up then, having counted the money and satisfied he's got it right. His head is halfway back through the window when we hear the whine of a gun and, suddenly, the car rocks with the impact of the bullet hitting his body. Aabo is thrown against the door, the money falling from his hand. His body slides down the side of the car and he disappears.

I look over at Hooyo. Her face is contorted as if she's wailing but I can't hear anything. I look down at my baati, seeing the blue, yellow and white marred by splatters of blood. Aabo's blood. I grip Hussein's hand even tighter.

I scream out for God, but I can't hear my own voice. When I look over at Hussein, he's frozen. Not moving, barely blinking.

The guards drag Aabo's body away, prising the last few remaining notes of cash out of his hand and collecting the fallen notes from the dusty ground. They don't say anything at all. The shorter guard approaches the car to speak to Hassan, the driver.

"Iga raali noqo, aboowe," he says, but his voice is entirely devoid of remorse. "You're free to continue with the rest of your journey now."

He sneers before hitting the car twice on the hood and turning back to speak to the others. I can no longer see my dad's body.

Hooyo hits Hassan from her seat in the back as he accelerates away, but Hassan ignores her, not giving the guards another chance to take a life. She punches his seat, her mouth forming fury, anguish, but Hassan just shakes his head.

Little Hafsa wakes up in the chaos, laying still in the crook of Hooyo's left arm as my mother continues to punch with her right. My baby sister stays silent, as if she knows there are matters here greater than her needs. Abooto is still fast asleep, snoring in the back of the car, oblivious to the fact that her only son has departed from this life.

I look at the sky ahead of us. A wide, cloudless sky. Rusty-coloured and desolate.

"Hi, Hanan, can you hear us?" a woman with a strong Northern accent shouts in my ear. "We're the ambulance service. My name's Ally. Give us a squeeze if you can hear us."

I realize then that there's a warmth in my hand I hadn't noticed. It must be Ally's hand. Ally grips tightly. It feels like a safe grip. But where's Hussein? Where's my brother?

"Can you give us a small squeeze if you can hear us, Hanan?" Ally asks again. There's a note of desperation in her voice. "Just like this, you see," she says, perceptibly tightening her hold.

I want to pull my hand away. *No, no, no. I need my brother's hand*, I want to tell her. Just him, only him, because it's always been the two of us, together. Hanan and Hussein.

CHAPTER TWENTY-TWO

Weights sit on my eyes, heavy as stones. I can't open them. I've tried, and it's only now that I appreciate the blessings of such simple things. The opening of eyes, the puckering of a mouth in sadness, in anger, the wriggling of fingers to say yes, I'm here, yes, I can feel your hand. Because someone is holding my hand – though I don't know who.

I try and try and try, but my eyes stay shut. I'm starting to think that maybe someone has placed stones here. To stop me from seeing.

In the Book that people fear but don't understand, God says –

When the sky breaks apart
And when the stars fall scattering
And when the seas are erupted

that

A soul will know what it has put forth and kept back

I think about my soul, what it holds for everyone to see and for no one to see, in case this is the end.

CHAPTER TWENTY-THREE

The next time I try to open my eyes, it's a fraction easier. It still feels as though I'm battling dead weights, but now the stones have shifted slightly – they are off-kilter. It takes me a few goes but I manage to open them halfway. It seems to be enough. I hear Hooyo's sharp intake of breath before she comes into view. I only see her legs, at first, and then even less as she leans over me on the bed.

I'm desperate to lift my arms so I can put them around her and hold her tight. To ask Hooyo to never let go. To feel her arms encircle me, comfort me, calm me. To feel the gift of having someone to love and to hold. And to have that person love and hold you back. But I can't. I can't move my arms. Where Hooyo lies over me and cries, a small area of dampness grows. I can feel the warmth of it through the blankets, which I hope is a good sign.

I try to speak but my throat is so parched that I only manage a grunt. Hooyo jumps up, drying her tears. She pours me some water and holds a straw to my lips. I notice then that her hands are shaking. The water shakes in concert to her trembling, creating waves in the plastic cup.

Hooyo puts the cup down when I'm done. She looks at me for a long time, not saying anything. Her hand reaches out and she holds mine, anchoring me.

"Alhamdulilah," Hooyo says, voice faint, head upturned. "Alhamdulilah, Alhamdulilah, Alhamdulilah."

I feel myself slowly falling back into the somewhere I just emerged from. I don't try to resist it. But when the last of the light disappears behind my closed eyes, when the touch of Hooyo's hand feels fainter and fainter, I remember something.

Is he alive? I want to ask. *Is he breathing?*

But I'm too far gone to come back.

Whether it's been minutes or hours since I last woke up, I don't know, but I wake to the sound of low voices speaking in the room. I can make out Hooyo's voice, but the other voice sounds unfamiliar.

"…progress is good," the unfamiliar voice murmurs. It sounds like it's coming from the far side of the room. "CT scan and X-ray…no concerns…"

Is it Hussein? Are they talking about Hussein? I open my mouth, ignoring the ache of my jaw, about to ask if—

"Hanan, she go home soon?" My mum's voice, her broken English.

Even from here I can sense the air shift as the unfamiliar voice speaks again.

"Yes, Hanan's doing well. The scans are all clear and she regained consciousness very quickly, which is good news."

I hear feet shifting.

"We'll be keeping a close observation over the next couple of days since it appears she's concussed but, if there are no issues, she'll be fine for discharge."

Discharge? They're planning to send me home?

I can't.

I won't.

Where is my brother?

When I wake up for the third time, the room is immersed in darkness. The curtains are drawn but I can tell it's night-time outside.

I'm not alone in the room. Hooyo's light snoring carries to me. I don't wake her up. I'm not ready for that yet. Instead, I spend a moment taking stock of my body.

I breathe in. I breathe out.

I feel.

I feel the constriction of my head, as though a snake is ever so slowly twisting around it, crushing me from the outside.

I feel the burning of a throat chafed by screams and thirst.

I feel a pain that migrates from place to place on my body, from my knee to my eyebrow, from my stomach to my tongue. A paradoxical pain – a pain that migrates but one that exists everywhere too.

And I feel that missing piece again. A piece in the shape of my brother, a piece from my heart.

I stop feeling. I focus on Hooyo, who lies sleeping on a small sofa bed next to me, her head at a crooked angle. I have no way of knowing how long I stare at her, wondering whether her sleeping here, next to me, means that she has no one else here to sleep next to, to care for, to watch over.

Hooyo wakes up groggy and yawns a few times before she stands up to switch on the lamp. She jumps back with a start when she sees my gaze fixed on her.

"Ya Rabbi," Hooyo says breathlessly. "I didn't know you were awake, Hanan."

I don't say anything. I'm too scared to.

She reaches over to smooth down the strands of my hair. Her hands feel like they're holding back as they move over my scalp, as if she's afraid to hurt me.

"I have good news," she whispers. "The doctor said you can go home soon."

I don't tell her that, to me, that sounds like the worst news in the world. That I'd rather stay here for ever than go back out there.

"You can rest at home then in shaa Allah," Hooyo continues, moving to smooth down my eyebrows. "With your family, where you belong."

I prepare to ask the question. I have to. The drumming in my chest quickens, beating faster and faster and faster, outpacing the speed of my racing mind. Heart, blood, thoughts – all falling over each other.

I speak, ignoring the fire that burns my throat.

"Where's Hussein?"

* * *

Hooyo busies herself with finding her overnight bag and then locating the plastic bowl and jug that she's packed. She disappears into the adjoining toilet to get water for my wudhu and then holds the jug for me as I gingerly wipe the water on my hands, face, and hair. Hooyo helps me with my feet.

I wrap a headscarf around my banged and concussed head and try to sit a little upright in the bed, pausing when the movement brings on a wave of nausea.

Then, when it steadies, I pray. I feel the tension uncoiling from my body as I whisper the Arabic, letting the words of healing linger on my tongue. I find some peace in those few minutes speaking to God.

Hooyo sits next to me when she finishes praying. She holds Abooto's tusbax in her hands. I look at her curiously and point to it, trying to find an explanation. Abooto is rarely seen anywhere without her beads, so much so that I consider them an extension of her fingers. Whenever she falls asleep at home, we always have to gently prise the beads out of her stiff hands, and they're always the first thing she picks up the next morning.

"Oh, yes," Hooyo says in understanding. "Your Abooto, she's a woman with a lot of hikmo, though wisdom is hard to come by these days. She knew I'd need something to occupy my heart, and my hands, while I was here." Hooyo continues to slowly run her fingers over the beads. Her eyes become unfocused. "It helped me to remember faith when I needed it most."

Under the pale-yellow light, Hooyo's tears look like tracks of silver. I look at her face now, and really look, for the first time since I've woken up. I look at its youthful glow that's been diminished with every mountain she needed to climb, with every bill that needed to be paid and every mouth that needed to be fed. The weight of the world squarely on her shoulders. My beautiful, strong, resilient mother, graced with an unbearable load.

When I look at her, I choose not to see the dark and heavy eyebags accentuating the tiredness etched on her face, or the wisps of grey hair protruding from the shaash she'll messily wrap around her head at home. I choose to see the lines cupping her mouth, deep and cavernous, holding years of undiluted laughter, and the small area of roughened skin on her forehead, a mark of prostration in prayer and a mark of hope.

Hooyo leaves not long after, promising to come back once she's dropped off Hafsa and Sumaya at school. She smiles and squeezes my hand before she goes and then, suddenly, it's just me, alone, in this room that feels too big for one person.

I sit myself fully upright, ignoring the clamouring of my muscles and bones that scream at me to stop. I ignore Hooyo's fresh words in the back of my mind, the words she'd shared only moments before she left. *You'll need to take it easy, macaanto. These things, this healing, takes time.* And I ignore the sweat that plasters my forehead in layers.

I remove the needle from my hand, ignoring the sharp sting, and push the blanket off my legs. Though it takes me a good few minutes, I manage to bring myself to a standing position. My legs feel shaky, like spent matchsticks that have been trusted to bear too much weight, and my head feels like it's about to explode beneath the bandage. But I don't stop. I can't stop.

I walk to the door, slowly, taking it step by step, not rushing to get out because, if I do, I know I'll topple over and then it'll be back to square one. I pause when I reach the door, trying to steady myself and my breathing.

I open the door. Not all the way – I can't be sure what creaks will echo down these halls if I push the hinges too far. The dim hallway is empty, bounded by portable monitors, a wheelchair on one side and a trolley on the other.

I hear voices from around the corner on my right and, when I hear the click-clack of shoes coming my way, I quickly shut the door – wait ten, twenty, thirty seconds – then open it again. I slide my body completely out this time, stepping into the hallway. The door whispers as it settles back into its frame.

I walk left, past two bays filled with six patients each. I don't stop at either of these bays because I know where I'm going. I know what I'm looking for isn't here. What I'm looking for is already tugging at me, as though a rope is tied around my middle, telling me where to go.

I stop at a room that's right next to the nurses' station on the other side of the ward. When I look at the name on the door, it's an act that confirms, not an act that reveals. The tugging has stopped, and the rope has loosened.

I slip into the room, closing the door gently. I don't turn on the light because my feet know where to go in this darkness. I sit on the chair next to the bed and hold his warm hand, finding the familiar dip in the nail of his thumb.

My missing piece.

CHAPTER TWENTY-FOUR

When I find the courage, I turn on the lamp near the bed to see my brother and stare at him under the yellow light.

Hussein looks the same. Exactly the same, as if nothing's changed. His smooth, peaceful face conceals the reason that he's here – hides the rip in his abdomen and the blood that he's lost.

It's clear now how similar he looks to Aabo. It isn't always easy to see at other times, when emotion colours his face differently. But with everything stripped away, with the reset button pressed, it's obvious. He's Aabo's son, through and through. From the inconsistent arch of his eyebrows to the shape of his nostrils that flare as he breathes. The contour of his nose, sharp, then quickly flattening out, and the colour that shades his skin beautifully black.

Then there are other things I notice. Things not of my father, but of him, Hussein. The things that made him and changed him after Aabo was stolen from us. Like the jagged scar that runs along his left cheek, accompanying the angle of his jaw – a scar he received once he realized that asking nicely only gets you so far. That people won't stop calling you a pirate if you only say *please*, that sometimes the only language that people hear in the playground are fists and sticks. Like the bottom corner of his lip that rarely goes up when he smiles or laughs, as if he's afraid of letting joy completely take over. And like the hair that grows unruly, wild and reckless, whenever we get close to Aabo's anniversary, as if the sorrow is seeping so quickly out of his body that it has nowhere else to go but up.

I whisper his name. He doesn't respond. He doesn't shift in the bed.

"Hussein," I say again. Over and over.

I'm not sure what I expect. Hooyo had said that things with Hussein were bad. When I'd finally managed to say his name, she hadn't lied to me like I thought she would. She'd kept her words short, but honest.

"Hussein is…" Hooyo began, sighing. "Hanan, your brother's in a bad place. He lost a lot of blood and when they took him to surgery, he was in there a long time." Her hand had rested on Abooto's prayer beads. "They say…they say that the next few days will be important to see if he'll be okay. To see if he'll wake up, after everything his body has been through." She stopped talking and I thought that was the end, but she spoke again a moment later. "Make dua for him, Hanan. Make dua for your brother. The only way he'll survive is by God's mercy."

I sit listening now to the quiet hum of the monitors telling me that his heart's still beating. The regular *beep beep beep* calms me down but, occasionally, there's a change in the rhythm and I shoot forward and grip his hand just that much tighter. It takes me a few breaths to settle back into my chair again.

For the first time since waking up, I think about that moment – when Hussein turned away from me, armed with steely determination and clenched fists, and walked towards Jacob. I wonder whether he'd seen the knife in that boy's hand and decided that his own unarmed hands would be a match. I wonder what he thought would happen. Or whether he'd seen something else in Jacob's face, and not the knife in his hands, and decided that he didn't want to walk away, that he wanted to stand up and fight, not knowing then that it might cost him his life.

I call out his name again, one last time.

"Hussein?"

No response.

The monitor continues to emit the sound of his heart's rhythm. A rhythm that sounds the same as any other person's but sounds priceless to me.

I sit with him, holding his hand, and pray.

I'm shaken awake by someone.

"You got to wake up, girl." A loud voice. "Got a whole lot of drool falling out that open mouth of yours and, let me tell you, it ain't pretty."

My eyes reluctantly open. I flinch when I see a head only centimetres from my own.

"Oh my God," I scream.

The nurse laughs, taking a few steps back. She leans against the foot of Hussein's bed, shoulders shaking.

"Must've been a good dream," she says when she catches her breath. She points to my face. I quickly wipe away the evidence of my falling asleep.

I hadn't planned on being found here. I'd planned on sneaking back into my room and pretending I'd been there all night. I was even going to attempt putting my own drip back in to keep up appearances. I don't say anything, only look sourly at this boisterous nurse with her boisterous attitude.

"Ahhh." She nods in understanding, turning to flip open Hussein's chart. "You must be the one they warned me about."

Warned her about? What's this woman on?

"Excuse me?"

The nurse puts the chart down. "Heard there'd be a wild one out here on Ward 319. And that she'd be the sister of this handsome fella right here." She looks up from the machine and puts both hands up defensively. "Not my words, sweetie. Your mother's."

Of course.

"Right." I smile begrudgingly. "That sounds like her."

The nurse continues to go about her business, noting down Hussein's vitals and then moving onto his cannula. She cleans the port and then stands there for a few minutes giving him some medication. She doesn't say anything about my hand which still holds his. She just works around us.

I ask her the question that's been on my mind since she woke me up.

"Are you going to snitch on me?"

She picks up the chart again. "Gertrude."

"Pardon?"

"Are you going to snitch on me, *Gertrude*?" she says.

For some reason, I choose now to be a smart-arse when I need this woman on my side.

"But my name's not Gertrude," I reply.

She doesn't say anything, only *humphs*, puts the chart back down, and walks towards the door, pulling the trolley alongside her.

"Okay, okay, I'm sorry." I pause. "I'm sorry. I don't know why I said that. Let me try again." I clear my throat. "Are you going to snitch on me, Gertrude?"

She turns around. "No, sweetie. I won't snitch. Not unless you start kicking up a fuss about the cannula that needs to go back in your own hand."

I breathe a sigh of relief. I don't think I could handle Hooyo on my case right now.

"I can live with that." I smile at her gratefully.

I give Hussein's hand a final squeeze.

"I'll be back before you know it, bro," I whisper to him. "And I'll be here when you wake up in shaa Allah."

When, not if. Never if.

I sit in the silence of my room after Gertrude finishes setting up my line again, and the breakfast lady drops off a bowl of sad-looking porridge.

It feels strange to be sitting here, only a few doors from Hussein. There's an uneasiness that sits in my stomach, churning and churning away, and by the time I manage a fifth bite of the porridge, I'm gagging. I push the bowl away. How can I eat, how can I drink, how can I do anything knowing that my brother is lying comatose so close to me? It feels like the worst kind of betrayal – worse than stealing his crisps or making fun of his terrible juggling – because this is a betrayal of *life*. Me, sitting here, awake, barely hurt, with only a minor concussion, while he lies dead to the world, with stitches holding his skin together.

Because of *me*.

Because I followed him when I should've been at home. Because I ignored my mum when she told me no. Because I didn't believe that anything would follow angry, hurtful words shot through a random email. Because I believed, for some *stupid fucking* reason, that following the rules, staying under the radar, somehow meant that people would eventually see me differently. That they'd see *me* instead of what they wanted to see. That people would look at me and see a girl trying to make her way in the world. Not as someone hell-bent on ripping it apart.

The unease digs deeper. It's only now that my mind moves to Jacob. I hear a grating sound coming from me and I realize that I'm grinding my teeth. The guilt in my stomach quickly morphs into anger. The churning turns to boiling.

I grip the sides of the breakfast tray to ground myself. To subdue this anger that feels all-consuming and that could destroy me if I don't pull back on its reins. I try to think about what Mr Fleming would say in this moment – what words he might share, wrapped in a wisdom that somehow always spoke to me. I think about what his wife, Diane, said at the memorial service. How the world can be deeply forgiving. How hate is the devil's biggest weapon. How right she is, but how wrong she is too, right now, in this moment.

CHAPTER TWENTY-FIVE

Hooyo returns to the hospital soon after with Abooto in tow.

"Hanan, I'm going to see Hussein," she says, holding the door open for Abooto to walk through. "I'll be back later, okay?"

I want to tell her no. She can't leave me with Abooto. Abooto will be kind and loving and compassionate but straight-talking in a way I can't deal with now. Abooto never minces her words, and I don't think I'm ready for them yet.

My grandmother shuffles inside, walking past the chair to stand next to the bed. She bends down slowly and painfully, and it takes a few seconds before I realize that she's about to break her life-long no hug policy. She embraces me tightly, holds me there for a long time, and then lets go. She shuffles back to the chair and groans when she finally sits down. Then she removes a new set of prayer beads from her handbag and begins rolling the beads through her fingers, as if a miracle hasn't just taken place.

"I know you've already had enough happen, Hanan, enough to burden you for the rest of your life, but I'll say this and then I will leave the matter alone," Abooto says gravely, stopping the rhythmic movement of her fingers.

"Everything in life – *everything*," she emphasizes, "happens for a reason, whether we like it or not, whether it's what we sought or what we avoided, but there is something to be learned from everything. Never forget that. Otherwise, our lives, our experiences, are wasted and then…" She shakes her head. "Then we are nothing more than a rubber band which goes back to what it was before. And, I may be an old woman," the corner of her lips edge into a half-smile, "but I have some value, and I know that you will be okay, in shaa Allah, whatever comes next."

I want to ask her how she can say that with such confidence. The fact is, things almost never work out the way you expect or want them to. The only certain thing is uncertainty.

And death.

My stomach churns again.

Hooyo comes back after a little while and swaps places with Abooto, who goes over to Hussein. A hospital-style family tag-team. Hooyo settles into the chair. I'm not expecting her to say what she does next – at least, not so soon.

"Hanan, macaanto," she says, not meeting my eyes. "The police are telling me things I have a hard time believing."

I stay very still when Hooyo says this, as though any sudden movements might invite a catastrophe. I stop my fidgeting, I don't blink. I even manage to quieten the churning of my stomach.

Hooyo sighs. Her warm breath reaches me. "Hanan… they're telling me things about your brother. Things that don't sound like him. Things I know my Hussein would never do…"

229

Hooyo shakes her head. "Is it true?"

When I don't say anything, Hooyo asks, "Is that why you were with him? Were you following him?"

Silence.

"The police said you were following him before…before everything happened?"

Somehow, those three words seem like the only way to describe that day now.

Before everything happened.

"Hanan?" Hooyo asks. Her voice trembles before she reaches the end of my name.

I bite on my lower lip, wondering whether I should bend the words before they leave my mouth. Make them easier for Hooyo to hear, so she doesn't fall apart.

"Yes." My voice comes out in a whisper. I let my head fall back against the pillow and stare hard at the ceiling. I say the hard words. I tell her the truth.

"Hussein was acting weird…different. I wanted to see for myself if there was something to worry about."

Hooyo perceptibly deflates when I confirm this and, though neither of us say it out loud, we both know what I mean. That I followed him because I wanted to know if Hussein had fallen into the very thing Hooyo protected us from ever since we came to London all those years ago. If he'd fallen prey to the destruction and chaos that existed on our doorstep but that we leaped over anytime we ventured outside. If he'd somehow found himself around drugs and bad money.

Hooyo doesn't ask me anything else. She remains sitting,

tapping her left foot in a slow beat. After a while, the tapping gets slower, slower, slower…until it stops.

She looks at me and holds my gaze this time. Her eyes still look tired but now, they look bloodshot too.

"I don't want you to worry any more, Hanan," Hooyo says, her voice firm even though her eyes betray her. "I know that you've had to worry about everyone else for too long." She sits forward to hold my wrist. "But I want you to know that's my job, macaanto, and it's my job alone. I need you to focus on getting better now and leave the rest to me."

Hearing Hooyo say those words does something to me. It feels sudden, like a switch has been turned on or a button's been pressed and everything that I've kept a lid on comes rushing to the surface. I breathe in huge gulps of air, waiting for it to pass, and Hooyo just holds me, soothes me, running her hands up and down my back in circles. The dam inside of me bursts and I cry and cry and cry, wailing into her jilbab for a long time.

Later, when Hooyo is getting ready to leave again, she leaves with a message.

"You'll probably have to speak to the police soon, Hanan, now that you're awake," Hooyo says. "I want you to be prepared. I want you to tell the truth, no matter how painful it might be to share it."

CHAPTER TWENTY-SIX

The next morning, after another failed breakfast, there's a whirlwind of commotion outside my room. The sound is so loud that it carries up the hallway almost a full minute before the appearance of my sisters. The door, which I'd accidentally left ajar after coming back from seeing Hussein, suddenly swings open. Hafsa and Sumaya swarm in. I can't help but wonder how two small humans can have such a large presence. They run up to me, stopping short of the bed, and look at me uncertainly.

"Hooyo says we can't touch you," Sumaya says, sniffling. Her face tremors as she avoids breaking into a sob.

Hafsa nods her head sombrely. "Hooyo said we need to be careful because you're not very strong right now."

They hold each other's hands as they look to me for confirmation and, I don't know if it's the fact that I haven't seen my sisters in so long or that I miss their strange dynamic, but I end up being the one to burst into tears.

"Oh *no*," Sumaya says anxiously. She blinks back tears. "What if we get in trouble for making her cry, Hafsa?"

"No, no, you're not going to get in trouble," I laugh,

hiccupping through my words. "I'm sorry. I'm just so happy to see you guys. You know you're my babies."

"Actually," Hafsa replies defensively, her nose in the air, "me and Sumaya have been doing a lot since you've been gone so you can't call us that any more. Hooyo even made us change our beds yesterday."

Sumaya nods her head vigorously. "Yeah, Hooyo made us change *everything* and even when I said my arms were about to fall off she didn't let me stop."

I purse my lips to avoid laughing again.

"Okay, okay, fine," I concede. "Miniature adult-babies then. Better than just babies, right?"

Hafsa sniffs, crossing her arms but doesn't disagree. Sumaya copies her.

"Anyway," Hafsa says. "We got you something to help you feel better."

She holds out her arm with a gift bag I hadn't noticed. Hafsa passes the bag to Sumaya first, who then passes it to me. I can't hold back my laugh this time. I'm sure they've rehearsed this.

There's a small bear and homemade card inside. I give the bear a peck, before setting it down on the breakfast tray. Then I read the card.

"So," Sumaya ventures nervously. "Do you like it, Hanan?"

I swallow the stone stuck tight in my throat. I don't want them to hear anything in my voice.

"Of course. Of course, I love it," I whisper. I stand the card next to the bear. I angle it so that the writing inside faces away from me. "Thank you. I'm going to leave it right here, so I can look at it all day."

Hafsa lets out the breath she'd been holding. "That's good," she says, sitting down on the bed near my legs. "We were scared it might make you sad."

Sumaya sits down on the other side, the mirror image of her.

"Yeah," she says, gazing outside at the clouds beginning to gather. "Hafsa and me spent *soooo* long drawing and colouring it in but we were scared you wouldn't like it."

I look out the window along with Sumaya, watching the steel-coloured clouds roll by. They float lazily across the small expanse of sky captured by the window, eclipsing one another before becoming solitary again. Endlessly moving and shifting and floating, but to where?

Hafsa turns to follow our gaze too.

"That's silly," I say. "How could I not like anything you give me?"

I hope to them I sound convincing because I can hear the discomfort in my own words.

Later, before the doctor comes around for an update, I sneak back into Hussein's room. I've not paid attention to any of the visiting hours since I first snuck into his room yesterday. I figured that those rules are designed for people *visiting* the hospital and not for people like me who are already inside.

I sit down and listen to the familiar beeping of his heart.

The rhythm is the same. The same, repetitive, comforting pace. A part of me feels a little lighter with this reassurance.

I open up the card from our sisters, looking at the message I've avoided reading again since they gave it to me.

"Hussein," I say, though I don't wait for a response like last time, "Hafsa and Sumaya made a card for me, you know. Proper homemade with glitter and everything. I mean, I guess they made it for us really. But kind of for me since, you know, you're not really available right now. So…so, let's just say it's for me *and* for us, if that makes sense."

Why have I somehow lost the ability to speak?

"Anyway." I thumb the corner of the card. "They drew us a nice picture. They gave you some funky-looking eyes though, so your face looks a bit dodgy. And, for some reason, they've drawn the ugliest hijab ever on my head."

I laugh when I say this, but only because it seems appropriate to laugh. Like, if this was a script, the most natural thing to follow would be: *and then she laughs*. But the sound of it is flat in my ears.

"They wrote a nice caption underneath too," I continue. "But the handwriting is awful so I'm one hundred per cent sure it was Sumaya." Again, the same flat laugh finds its way out of my mouth.

I reach over to prop the card on Hussein's bedside table. If he were to turn over, to just move his head a fraction to the left, he'd be able to see it. He'd be able to see what's made a big, fat rock lodge itself in my throat.

But he can't.

"Hanan and Hussein, best friends for ever," I whisper, staring at his expressionless face. "That's what they wrote in the card, Hussein. For ever."

Beep, beep, beep.

"And for ever means a long time." The rock in my throat gets bigger. "For ever doesn't end anytime soon."

Hooyo and I are waiting patiently for Dr Singh to come around and discuss my progress. But when the door swings open, it's one of the other nurses I've seen around here instead.

"Hiya, just wanted to let you know the police are here," Nurse Jenny says, all bright eyes and cheery smile. "There's only a couple of them. They want to have a chat with you, Hanan, and you as well, Mum. Is that alright? Shall I send them straight in?"

"Umm sorry, just give one minute please," Hooyo says in a breathless voice.

Hooyo has never been a huge fan of the police and sometimes even seeing a random patrol car is enough to get her nerves going. Those same nerves seem to be kicking in now.

Nurse Jenny agrees to send them inside in a few minutes and when the door shuts behind her, Hooyo busies herself with tidying a room that is already fairly tidy. Then, her hands reach for me. She neatens the blanket, gently easing out the creases and adjusts my hijab slightly.

That's when I notice her hands shaking. It dawns on me then that Hooyo's nerves might not be random. It might not be because of some strange, general fear of police officers. Hooyo will hear everything in detail for the first time and hear things that I haven't told anyone yet.

"Hooyo," I say gently, holding her hands to stop them from running over the blanket. "It will be fine. I promise."

"I know, macaanto," she says a little sadly. "I know."

But I'm not sure she believes me.

Jenny pops her head back in and I give her a thumbs up. She opens the door a little wider to let in the two uniformed police offers. They introduce themselves as Police Constables Patel and Lundy.

"Hi, Hanan, it's nice to meet you. How are you?" PC Patel asks. His voice is deep and vibrates across the room.

"Fine." I shrug my shoulders. "As fine as I can be after surviving an assault, I guess."

I see Hooyo side-eye me in the way that says *don't talk like that, be respectful*. I pretend not to notice.

PC Patel coughs and shuffles on his feet. "Of course," he says. "You've been through quite an ordeal. Our job now is to make the rest of this process as simple as we can for you."

PC Lundy nods the whole time his colleague's speaking but the motion of it looks loose, like his head is flopping around without direction.

"We'd like to get a statement from you first, Hanan, before we get you up to speed with where the investigation's currently at," PC Patel says, flipping open a notebook from the breast pocket of his uniform. "And I'm sure you already know this, but it's really important that you give us as much information

237

as possible. That means anything and everything. We would have preferred a video-recorded statement but, given the circumstances, we'll be taking a written statement today."

PC Lundy follows suit, taking out an identical notebook and holding a pen poised over the page. They both look at me expectantly.

"Okay," I say. "Okay."

This part is meant to be simple right? The worst has already happened; all that's left now is to sweep up the broken glass. To get rid of the remnants of that night before anyone else steps on them and gets hurt again. To share with these people, whose job it is to protect me, to protect Hussein, the truth of what happened that night.

I take a deep breath in, then out. I ignore the knots I can feel forming in the pit of my stomach. I ignore the panic I can feel rising up in my chest, like a wave gaining momentum.

And I tell them. I tell them everything.

It's quiet when I finish speaking, as if all my words have taken up the space in this room that now feels too small for these four bodies to be packed into. Hooyo's turned away from me, looking down at the polished white floor beneath her feet. I wish she would look at me.

"Thank you, Hanan," PC Patel says. His voice feels too loud. "We appreciate you speaking about this in detail despite the difficulty." He coughs again and shuffles on his feet. PC Lundy's head stays still this time. "We do have some questions to follow up your statement, if that's alright?"

"Yeah, sure," I say wearily. "That's fine."

He waves his pen around. "So, you said that you were out following your brother because you were worried about him."

I nod.

"What worried you so much that you decided to do that? Even, as you put it," PC Patel looks down, "against your mother's wishes?"

"I was just looking out for him," I reply, trying to avoid sounding defensive. "Is that a crime?"

"No, no, of course not," he says, trying to smooth over his words. "It just helps us to paint a clearer picture of what happened that night."

PC Lundy resumes his nodding. *God*, I think. *Can this man not keep his head still for two minutes?*

I know what these people are getting at. I *know*. It's not a hard conclusion to jump to. What they're saying seeps out in thick tones, not undertones. But I have a hard time believing that after hearing everything I just said, they're zeroing in on this first. What about the boy who knifed my brother? The one who smashed my head against the ground? The one who was ready to rip the dignity from my head?

What about him?

"I know what you're trying to say but I don't think that's all that matters right now." Hooyo looks up from the floor. "Yeah, I thought my brother got mixed up in some bad stuff and yeah, I wanted to check it out for myself. But I didn't ask to have a racist prick follow me and try to kill us."

239

PC Patel nods now too, alongside Lundy. His features have knitted themselves into something I'd probably describe as sympathetic but feels a little placating.

"Of course, of course, Hanan. Sorry to have upset you. These questions are difficult but necessary, so thank you for your cooperation." He looks down at his notebook again. "When you mentioned the attack, you said that your brother had come back to help you and that you were both ready to try and get away. But that he then turned around and walked towards the boy you've identified as Jacob."

"Yes."

"Instead of trying to get away?"

"Yes."

"And then you saw a knife in Jacob's hand moments before your brother was...was stabbed."

"Yeah," I sigh. "That's exactly what happened."

Hooyo side-eyes me once again but I can't help it. I'm getting tired of a conversation that seems to be going nowhere.

"And are you certain that this knife belonged to Jacob?"

Am I certain? What kind of a question is that? I pause to remind myself of the statement I've just given. The statement where I just told them that that boy hurt Hussein, brought his arm down with such force to tear my brother down.

"What do you mean?"

"I realize this is a sensitive question, Hanan, but..." PC Patel hesitates. He looks up at the ceiling for a few moments as if trying to craft the right words in the right order. "But is there a possibility that the knife belonged to your brother?"

My mum's head swivels to the officers at the exact moment my own swivels towards her.

It turns out that Jacob had concocted his own story, with the help of a fancy lawyer. According to him, he did write that anon email, out of a "temporary and misplaced anger", but that was as far as his misdeeds went. Apparently, Jacob had followed me from school only out of concern for *me*. Apparently, I'd left the bake sale so angry that he thought I'd do something stupid. That he'd heard me say some bad things. That he'd pivoted to avoid being hit by the knife in Hussein's hand on the footpath and grappled with him in self-defence, stabbing him in the process.

The questions finally ended not long after they told us this, and thankfully, it became clear that even PC Patel and Lundy were aware that Jacob's story wasn't quite adding up.

"The evidence is coming through and it's being verified. Of course," PC Patel said, putting his hands in his pockets, "what will also help is having your brother's version of events to inform the investigation. We'll be back if he wakes up to get that official statement."

When, I want to correct him.

When, not *if*. Never if.

Dr Singh stops by after the officers leave. I'm sure she reads the room perfectly because she doesn't deliver her news with a smile.

"Good news, Hanan," she says, holding a folder under her arm. She's brought along some apprentice this time. A short, mousy boy who stands a few steps behind her and avoids looking at me. "We'll be discharging you tomorrow if everything comes back fine with the last set of bloods."

"Okay, thanks," I say.

There really isn't anything left to say beyond that. I mean, there could be. I could say: *Thanks for all your help, Dr Singh, and thanks for kicking me out when my brother needs me now, more than ever*. But I don't say that because that would be rude.

Hooyo tries to cover for my glaringly poor conversational skills. "Thank you, Dr Singh," she says. "You been such good doctor to Hanan. We really lucky."

"That's not a problem, Mrs Ali," she says, turning towards the door. The mousy boy does the same. "I wish you both all the best for the future."

"It's not Mrs Ali," I say, interrupting her escape. The lid on my simmering anger moves out of place. The smoke of it edges out. It's not her fault that she's walked in after the police officers and that disastrous conversation, but she's the one in front of me right now. "My dad's dead and she didn't take his name anyway. It's Ms Abdullahi."

"Hanan!" Hooyo shouts. "Afkaaga xir!"

"No, no," Dr Singh protests. She looks at me apologetically and I can't help but feel a little bad. "You're right. I'm very sorry. I should've been careful with how I addressed you… Ms Abdullahi."

She smiles a little awkwardly.

I nod my head once but don't say anything else. Dr Singh then makes her quick escape, the mousy boy trailing closely behind her.

"Hanan," Hooyo shakes her head, getting up to leave. The evidence of her disappointment is there in the wrinkling of her forehead and in the curve of her mouth. "Anger becomes an ugly, dangerous thing when you fling it around with your eyes closed. I did not raise you to do that." She shoulders her bag. "Neither did your father."

She bends down to kiss my forehead and wrap me in an embrace. I don't feel her disappointment in the way she holds me, only in the words she says.

"Open your eyes, macaanto," Hooyo says with her arms around me, "before you hurt someone with your words."

I murmur my goodbye, not quite hugging her back, though Hooyo must sense the tension in my body because she releases me and leaves without saying more. And then it's just me, alone again, in the room that I'm sick of but also don't want to leave.

Why doesn't anyone understand that leaving isn't some amazing, joyous occasion but a betrayal? How can I explain to Hooyo, to Dr Singh, that leaving Hussein here, by himself, when I'm the one that put him here feels like I've thrust a second knife into him?

I let my head fall into the pillow on my lap, ignoring the pain that shoots through my skull, and I scream. I scream and scream until there's no sound left in my body. I scream until the emptiness inside threatens to overwhelm me and I feel like if I scream any more, I might cease to exist.

Hooyo had said that throwing anger around when you couldn't see was a dangerous thing but what she doesn't get is that all I crave is closing my eyes. I *want* to be blind to my anger. I don't want to see it and control it and hold it back the way I have been for so long. I want to be reckless and free with it, the same way everyone else is.

I don't want to care about anything because caring *hurts* and I'm so done with hurting.

Outside, the sun sets very quickly, the yellow glow of it slowly replaced by greyness, the colour of steel. And the emptiness inside of me grows, leaving me hollow.

CHAPTER TWENTY-SEVEN

The next morning, after the results of my blood test have been cleared and the nurse hands me my discharge papers, I sit on the bed and stare at the ceiling, waiting for Hooyo to come collect me. My phone sits on the table in front of me, but I don't reach for it. Hooyo gave it to me yesterday with clear instructions to contact my friends, who were, apparently, busy knocking on our front door every day for updates.

Since then, all I've managed to do is pick up the phone and hover over the power button. I haven't yet built up the courage to press it and I'm not sure when I will.

Gertrude knocks on the door and walks in. "Hey, sweetie," she says, a wide smile lighting up her face. My own face instinctively breaks into a smile too. There's just something about Gertrude that makes you break into a grin when you see her. "Wanted to see you before my shift is done."

"You're probably going to beg me to stay, right?"

She barks out a laugh. "Well, I'd be lying if I said I won't miss that cheek of yours."

My smile widens. "I can bottle it up and leave it for you if you want. Like a goodbye present?"

"Only you," Gertrude replies, wagging a finger at me. "Only you." She walks over to me and points to the phone, then looks at me expectantly.

"Go on then," she prompts. "Don't think I haven't noticed you avoiding that thing like it's on fire."

I sigh. I thought I'd managed to distract her.

"It's not that simple," I say, using a finger to spin the phone on the table and hoping my deflated mood will be enough to signal the end of this conversation. But, of course, Gertrude is unbothered by any mood, deflated or otherwise.

"Well, I ain't thick," she responds. "So, go on."

"I just don't want to speak to anyone right now, but all of my friends are asking about me, and my mum wants me to call them back."

"Simple enough."

"It's not though," I protest. "I'm still not ready to talk to them. To answer their questions and for them to look at me like" – I swallow – "like, I don't know. Like I'm a victim or something."

Gertrude nods her head, listening carefully and making sounds of agreement.

"So, you get it now, right?" I ask.

"No."

"Wow, well, your body language is very misleading then, Gertrude."

She chuckles, leaning against the side rail. "Hanan, sweetie, can I be honest with you?"

"I feel like you're going to be anyway."

"True, but I like a good warning shot first." She shifts her weight onto her other foot. "Sweetie, sometimes…and we're all guilty of this, not just you, but…we run scared from others because, well, we don't want to see the thing we're scared of, even if it ain't there. You get what I'm saying?"

"Uh, no. Not really."

"What I mean is," she says slowly, holding my gaze, "you don't want to be a victim, and you're scared that when you look into their eyes, that's what you'll see."

I nod. I get that.

"But you need to get that what you see in their eyes is a reflection of what's in yours. If you feel like a victim, they'll see a victim. If you're not a victim, they'll see…whatever else. You get it now?"

I nod, still holding her gaze.

"So, go out and be you. Don't be running scared of something you ain't or you'll spend your whole life running. Trust me on that."

Gertrude reaches out to hold my hands in hers. "And I'll look after that brother of yours while you're not here." She squeezes my hands. "I can promise you that. Wouldn't want him snitching on me when he wakes up."

I feel the tears spring up in my eyes. Even without me saying it, Gertrude knows that it's when, not if. Never if. Not with Hussein.

After we say our goodbyes, I pick up my phone, holding it firmly in my grip and make the calls I've been avoiding.

*   *   *

It's hard saying goodbye to Hussein when I leave so I don't. I pack my things neatly in a holdall, focusing instead on the Qur'an playing in the background. The voice of the reciter carries melodiously and, for the fifth time that morning, I find myself wishing that my voice could be that beautiful so I could carry it with me wherever I go.

I play Surah Ad-Dhuha in Hussein's room after I've finished packing in mine. If I'm leaving him with anything, it'll be the words of this chapter that he loves so much, instead of a goodbye that carries with it an unnecessary and burdensome pain. I'll be back for Hussein, there can never be any doubt about that. And when I am, he'll be awake. Eyes wide open and with a face full of life, instead of this expressionless mask he now wears. I try not to think about the anger that those eyes might bleed when he does wake up.

Worries for the future, I tell myself, not for today.

Hooyo takes me home and guides my aching body back into a bed that feels unfamiliar and cold. Abooto sits by my side. For the first time in a long while, she's made the slow and difficult climb to the first floor of our house. She usually only ever stays downstairs, as if the floor above her is part of a different realm entirely. But she's sat here next to me now as if she senses that I need this, that I feel lost in my own home and that the only thing to anchor me is something solid and real with a beating heart.

I must have fallen asleep at some point after Hooyo leaves to pick up the girls because I feel myself being shaken and look up to see Hafsa peering at me with wide, worried eyes.

"You were calling out," Hafsa says, taking a step back and eyeing me uncertainly. "What were you dreaming about?"

"Nothing," I say drowsily. "Where's Abooto?"

"Oh, she went down to eat. She said I was in charge of looking after you." Hafsa smiles triumphantly. She waves a book in the air in front of me. "I was just reading my spy book but then you started –" she squints at me – "saying some weird stuff."

"Probably not as weird as some of the stuff you say."

She sticks her tongue out at me. I stick mine back out at her.

The doorbell rings. Hafsa sits up a little straighter and turns her head towards the sound.

"Who's that?" she asks.

Then, the immediate, familiar everyday panic of our household sets in. "Oh, I need to get my hijab!" she shrieks, throwing her book down on the bed. "Hanan, don't worry, I'll get one for you as well—"

I'd been holding my laughter in, wanting to see her terror play out for a little longer, but it comes bursting out of my mouth.

"It's not funny!" Hafsa screams. She's somehow teleported over to my drawers while I struggle to get a hold of myself. "It could be someone random or an adeer—"

"Hafsa," I reply, finally able to breathe again. "It's not anyone random, don't worry. It's just my friends."

Her hands immediately still on the handle of the third drawer. "What?"

"It's just my friends," I say again. "You know, Andrea and Nasra. They wanted to come see me."

She walks back over to the bed and snatches up the fallen book. "I feel like you did that on purpose."

I burst into laughter again. Hafsa glares at me and leaves, letting the door slam shut behind her. The force of it makes the calendar on my wall flutter. My eyes catch on the date ten days from now that's circled.

My med school admissions test.

I blink and look away.

A few moments later, I hear a faint knock on the door. Then I hear a scuffle and Nasra's loud whisper, followed by a louder knock on the door.

"Come in," I call out.

The door opens. Nasra steps inside, ahead of Andrea.

"These bitches were out here trying to do a non-existent *rat-a-tat-tat* on the door, you know. I had to take over."

These?

"What do you mean?" I ask. "There's only two of you."

My confusion is swiftly cleared up when Nasra and Andrea sidestep out of the way to reveal the other two in their party.

Lily and Isha.

They stand awkwardly in the doorway, all bowed heads and sheepish smiles.

"Oh, right…there's four of you."

"Quick maths," Nasra replies with a smirk.

Before anyone can say anything else, Andrea lets out a strange sound, like a cross between a whine and a howl. Her crying face comes into full-force, and she falls onto the bed next to me, lying her head on my lap and wrapping both arms around me.

"I actually believed this girl when she said she wouldn't cry." Nasra shakes her head. She sits down on the chair next to my desk, leaving Lily and Isha the only ones still standing up.

"Ho-how can I-I-I not cry," Andrea hiccups, "when my-my best friend is-is hurt?" I feel her hold tighten around me and I let my head lean over hers, matching her embrace.

Though I'd been afraid to see my friends since everything went down, I can't make sense of that fear now as I sit here surrounded by them. In their eyes, I see only love and warmth.

"Look," I say, in part trying to convince myself as much as Andrea. "I'm fine, honestly. Healthy as a horse. It's only a few days of bed rest and then I'm back to normal."

"Debatable," Nasra murmurs. "If you're saying nonsense like that. What does healthy as a horse even mean?"

Lily clears her throat. We both turn our heads at the exact same moment to look at her. Even Andrea raises her head from my lap to glance over. I'd forgotten Lily and Isha were still in the doorway, they'd been that quiet.

"Now seems like a good time to…" Lily says, glancing at Isha. "To jump in."

The initial shock when I'd first seen them standing in the doorway has disappeared. That shock has quickly become confusion and that confusion has settled very obviously on my face in the form of raised eyebrows.

"Jump away."

They both come to sit at the foot of the bed. It's all I can do not to shift from their nearness. They feel like strangers, not people who I once thought were my best friends.

Lily clears her throat again. "Me and Isha just want to say... we just want to say we're sorry. For everything." She crosses her legs, looking to Isha for support.

Isha looks down at her hands, eyes following the ridges of her palms. It takes me longer than it should do to realize that she isn't wearing anything on her face. No lip-gloss, no eyeshadow, no blush. I don't remember the last time I saw her without any make-up.

"Sorry doesn't seem like enough but..." She pauses and looks up from the lines criss-crossing her hands. "We are sorry. Really sorry." She runs a hand through her hair. "That day when Jessica said those things and Nasra went off...it was like Nasra was the only one I could see. For some reason, Jessica didn't matter. The alarms went off in my head with Nasra because I'm used to always hearing her go off about something, and all I could think was 'here we go again'. It didn't register that she was actually going off about something that mattered. About something...you know, justified."

Behind her, Nasra mimes grabbing Isha's shoulders and throttling her.

Isha looks down at her hands again, oblivious. "And there's no way to explain how shit me and Lily both feel. What we did, to you and Nasra that day, was..." She shakes her head. "Like, we're meant to be best friends and we couldn't even see the kind of shit that people said to you, even when it was happening right in front of us."

"Amen to that," Nasra cuts in, unable to help herself this time.

Isha turns back to look at her and roll her eyes. "Pipe down, you already got your apology."

Nasra grins.

"The thing is," Lily continues, "we couldn't see why this whole thing became an issue in the first place. I think part of me thought, well, Jessica's been talking shit for years, why is everyone making such a fuss now? Why can't we go back to ignoring it and ignoring her like we've been doing for ever?"

Lily shuffles back to lean against the bed frame.

"And I think we were probably more confused by you, Hanan," she says. "Because you've never gotten so worked up over anything like that before and then we got angry, because we thought you were taking it out on us, when we hadn't done anything to begin with." She grimaces. "Obviously now, I get it. I know that what she said that day was *way* out of line and so much worse than what she's said before, but it took us a while to get there."

She plays with the straps of her tote bag, biting her lip. "You know, I've never told you guys about what happened in Year Nine, when I stopped being friends with Jessica."

Nasra shoots up, not even bothering to hide her intrigue.

"It seems like such a small thing to me now, but I remember how much it upset me back then. It was basically some throwaway comment about my mum's candle business. Something about how Jessica would never want to get sucked into corporate stuff when she grows up because it's such a soul-destroying gig and everyone in that world is just a monster, even if they've gotten good at pretending they aren't, like 'some people's parents'." Lily pulls a face. "It sounds silly saying it out loud and that's why I've never said anything about it before, but it really got to me because I know how much my mum already worries about the business taking her away from me. Obviously, it's nowhere near as bad as the things she's said to you, and I think the reason why I didn't understand this whole situation in the first place is because I remember, all those years ago, I walked away when she said that crap to me. I was too scared to stand up to her and say something, but I shouldn't have been. I should have stood up for myself and I should have stood up for you guys too."

We're all quiet for a few moments after that. While I've always known that Lily – and Isha – would never understand what it felt like to have consistently been on the receiving end of Jessica's hate all these years – to an *undeniably* more terrible degree – it's nice to know that a little part of her understands it now. And, weirdly, it even makes me slightly grateful for the fight that brought us here.

Nasra's the first to break the silence.

"Knock, knock," she says with a sly smile.

"Who's there?" Isha replies. She starts giggling for some reason and then promptly descends into shoulder-shaking laughter.

"We're not even at the punch line, yet!" I say, shaking my head.

"Jessica."

"Jessica who?' Andrea asks, blowing her nose on a tissue.

"Jessica 'I'm already a soulless monster so please hire me Lily's mum'."

Isha's laughter abruptly stops. "Okay, that was bad Nasra. That was bad."

"Yeah," Lily agrees. She uncrosses her legs and pushes her bag away to make space. "That was way too long to be funny."

Something slips out of Lily's bag. It looks like a newspaper. I'm wondering why she's got one when I see part of the headline.

"What's that?" I ask, sitting up. I point to the edge of the newspaper. "Is that about me?"

She looks to Isha who looks to Andrea who doesn't look at me.

"Why are you guys being weird?" I ask, leaning forward to grab it out of her bag. "I want to read it."

Andrea tries to put her hand out to stop me, but I've already got it.

"ANGEL" SCHOOLBOY LEFT REELING AFTER MENTAL BREAKDOWN
BY DOUGLAS WHITE

A schoolboy, aged 15, from a local secondary school, has left two other students injured after his "mental breakdown" near Brinley Road, with one of those injured reported to be in critical condition at Ledway Hospital.

Sources close to the schoolboy allege that he was "pressured" in the preceding weeks by another student at the school and subsequently "snapped". The school has declined to comment on the events beyond their "well-wishes and prayers that all parties involved find a speedy recovery".

The police have opened an investigation into the events although, at this time, no charges have been made.

I stop reading. "Wow," I say. I let the paper fall from my hand to land on my lap. I don't want to touch these words. I don't want to feel the lies there. I don't want these words to stain me.

"Sorry…" Lily ventures, leaning forward to pick it up. "You weren't supposed to read this. It's my fault, I shouldn't have had it in my bag."

My hand reaches out to stop her. "No, it's fine. I want to keep it please."

She nods uncertainly and withdraws her hand.

"And thank you for the apology. Both of you. It means a lot to me."

More nods, then silence. Andrea must sense the change in mood because she sits up and leans against the headboard next to me.

"So, do you want to hear all the hot-goss you missed out on at school?" she says, but it's obviously a rhetorical question. She takes a deep breath in and is about to launch into it when I shoot her down.

"No, not really." She pauses. "I'm not feeling it so much."

"That's okay." Andrea shuffles closer to me. "Do you have anything you want to get off your chest?"

My chest? It feels like it's already caved in from the weight of everything that's been thrown onto it.

"Not really."

"What about cards?" Nasra suggests. "We brought a deck. Maybe a nice, aggressive game of bullshit will make you feel better?"

I sigh. "Maybe another time, guys. I think I just want to be alone now. Sorry."

They all murmur "Of course", "Hope you feel better soon" and "We're praying for your brother". Nasra adds in, "No one bounces back quickly from this kind of thing, Hanan, but we're here for you, we're your ride-or-dies."

Lily takes something out of her bag as she says goodbye. She puts it on my bedside table.

"It's one of Mum's candles," she says, zipping up her jacket. "Vanilla and honeysuckle. I remember how much you liked it the last time you were at my house."

Andrea lingers behind after the others begin to head out. Her fingers hesitate on the zip of her bag before she opens it.

"It's not as nice as a candle but I got you this," she says, handing me a simple black leather notebook. "I thought you might want to write stuff down. Stuff you might not want to say out loud yet, and that's okay, but at least you'll have somewhere to hold it until you're ready."

I take it from her outstretched hand, turning the notebook over and running my hands over the leather.

"Thank you," I reply, surprised.

It really is a beautifully crafted notebook. I hold it delicately, afraid to touch it. I've never been much of a writer, and probably never will be, but I still appreciate Andrea for the thought.

When they're all gone, I pick up the newspaper from my lap again and tear out the article. I stare at it for a long time, long enough that I could recite the words by heart if I wanted to. Everything else around it seems to blur. My own hands gripping the paper tightly and the duvet underneath become unfocused.

It baffles me that someone could sit down and write these words, one after the other, without stopping, without hesitating. Without seeking the voices of anyone else who was there that night.

I wonder how different these words would've been if it had been Hussein there that night with a knife in his hands and hate in his heart. How different this story would've looked and whether they would've called him an angel boy or a devil. If they would've called his violence *an act of terrorism* instead of something mild, wrapped in a bow of deceit and justification, like a *breakdown*.

I stop wondering very quickly because I already know the answer to my own question. I know it from the way the news unhesitatingly painted a picture of the man who killed my friend – a man who was a terrorist, first, before he was anything else.

I know that people like me are devils before we are angels.

Somehow, I find myself outside, walking towards the tree opposite my house. I don't remember walking down the stairs and out the door but here I am. There's nothing special about this ancient willow tree but I've always loved it. Somehow, the evening light always makes it seem magical. Celestial. The shadows of the dimming light banish the spliffs and empty bottles that circle the tree. What remains for me is the magic that seems to pulsate around it as twilight becomes night. When I'm around this tree, it somehow grounds me, as if its roots extend to me too.

I lean against the trunk. I'm not wearing a coat but I feel numb anyway, so the cold doesn't bother me. I am numb to everything except the thoughts I'm desperate to escape.

Reading that article has reminded me of the disastrous meeting with the police officers. Their questions, too wide in some angles, too narrow in others…it seemed like they were chasing the wrong thing. Too many questions about Hussein. Not enough about Jacob. Their curiosity had jumped when I mentioned anything about my brother and all of his weirdness these last few weeks, but it would flatline whenever I talked about Jacob's threats or his email or the living hatred in his eyes whenever he looked at me. Their pens would move slower on the pages of their open notebooks when they stopped hearing what they were looking for.

I slide against the trunk to sit down, my legs tired. I stretch the newspaper clipping between my hands until it starts to rip. Then I rip it over and over again until I'm left with confetti of lies. I bring my hands together to blow them away.

Maybe if I sit very still under this tree, I will stop existing, just for a moment.

I like this thought. I try to hold onto it as I watch the sky being devoured by darkness. Wishing I could disappear for the night like the sun does.

CHAPTER TWENTY-EIGHT

My nightmares start again now that I'm home. The ones that pull shouts from my body and make me sweat and shiver and fall out of bed onto the floor. Except, this time, Hussein isn't here to hold my hand and so it takes me far, far longer to get out of their grip.

I wake up and hop into a cold shower. I tear down the calendar from my wall, tear down the reminder of an exam and a dream that feels like it's slipping away with every minute that my brother's in hospital, fighting for his life, because of a sadistic boy and his hateful ideas. I eat breakfast. I ignore the clamouring of my bones, my muscles. I try to convince my mum I am okay.

I go with Hooyo to drop the girls off at school and then we go to the hospital. I sit by Hussein's bed for hours. I put some fresh flowers into a newly bought vase. I play the Qur'an in the voice of his favourite reciter. I listen to the sound of monitors speaking the language of his body. I pray my afternoon prayers.

I pray.

* * *

Hooyo and I reluctantly leave Hussein's side today. We've been here every visiting hour since I was discharged three days ago but even with all the time we spend here, it still never feels like enough.

"Hanan," Hooyo murmurs. She speaks quietly as if Hussein's only sleeping and not trapped in a coma. "We need to go now. To the school."

"What time did they say again?" For some reason, I find myself murmuring too.

Hooyo checks her watch. "We have about twenty minutes."

Hooyo had told me that Mr Davies himself had called to set up a meeting at school. He'd spoken to Hooyo and asked when a good time would be and my mum, being my mum, had said as early as possible. She didn't believe that unavoidable things in life should ever be delayed but, if it was up to me – which Hooyo quickly reminded me it wasn't – I'd want to schedule this meeting for…never. The last time I'd been in Mr Davies's office, it hadn't gone great. I don't have high hopes for this meeting either. According to Hooyo, Mr Davies hadn't really explained why he wanted to meet, just that he thought it'd be better to speak face to face.

Stepping back into Grafton Grammar now feels strange. Though it's been just six days since the last time I was here – selling food at the bake sale with Andrea – the school, its high walls and vinyl floors and arched windows…it all feels unfamiliar now.

We see a few other students and teachers around as we make our way to the East Wing. I meet all the gazes that linger on me without flinching and without looking away. I know, today of all days, it's not because of the way my mum and I are dressed. It's because they know about *it*. About everything that happened.

Outside the Head's Office, Ms Dunaway smiles and tells us to take a seat. We wait a few minutes and then Mr Davies steps out to usher us in.

Unlike last time, I don't think about which seat to take or how to sit. I let Hooyo sit on the left and I sit on the right. I cross my hands on my lap and wait for him to speak.

Mr Davies is a bundle of nerves, as usual. I can't help but wonder how a man like this could command an entire school, or even get the job for that matter.

He clears his throat. "So, Hanan and Mrs Ali…would, would you—"

"Ms Abdullahi," I correct him.

"Oh gosh, my apologies. I'm really sorry about that." Right on schedule, the red begins to creep up his neck and flush his cheeks. "Would either of you like some water?"

He indicates the water bottles on the cabinet behind him. I shake my head and Hooyo politely declines too. I think this throws him off for a moment because there's an awkward silence until he speaks again.

"Right, so, uh, first of all, I'm terribly sorry to hear about… about what happened to you and to your brother, Hanan," he begins. "And, of course, Ms Abdullahi," his eyes flick to me, "this must be hugely, hugely distressing for you."

Hooyo nods. I see her hand grip the arm of the chair a little more.

"We here at Grafton, well, we want to express our deepest sympathies for your family and, of course, wishes for your son's speedy recovery."

Speedy recovery. Those same words from the article in Lily's bag.

Nice words. Polite words.

Meaningless.

"But, of course, given that it's Hanan's final year at Grafton, I think it's important that we discuss, uh, next steps moving forward." He pauses to take a sip of water and directs the rest to me. "Obviously, Hanan, you've got your admissions test to be sitting in about a week's time and it's important that you don't fall behind with your schoolwork either. We want you to be ready for when those medical offers start rolling in." A wink.

Hold up. Is this man seriously winking at me right now?

Does he not understand that the last thing I'm thinking about right now is an exam? With Hussein lying in hospital, put there by a boy who wanted nothing more than to see *me* brought down, Mr Davies is really bringing this up?

"And, uh, of course, there is the matter of the parent–governor meeting happening in two weeks I wanted to discuss with you again." The red has covered his entire face now. He looks like a smartly dressed plum tomato. "We'd still like you to come if that's—"

"Is Jacob being excluded?"

Mr Davies splutters. "That's, that's, um, a very difficult question to answer, Hanan." He looks to my mum in what I assume is a plea for support. "There is the ongoing police investigation, of course, and, and a decision like this, it's not, it's often made on the basis of several—"

"So, Jacob's not being excluded?"

Mr Davies pulls on the knot of his tie. "It's difficult, now, to let you know what will happen and these things…such decisions, they, they're often confidential until discussed with—"

"I don't think it's difficult to kick someone out if they've stabbed someone," I say simply. "That seems like a pretty easy decision to make."

"I'm sorry, Hanan." Mr Davies removes his hands from his tie and places them on the desk. "This is just not a matter I can discuss with you at this time."

Hooyo cuts in, thankfully. I'm not sure what words would've come out of my mouth next if she hadn't. The anger Hooyo told me not to throw around had been dangerously close to being smeared all over the walls of this office.

"Thank you so much," Hooyo says, standing up from the chair. "Me and Hanan, we gonna go now."

"I'm sorry if I've offended either of you." Mr Davies jumps up from his seat. "This is a painfully sensitive matter and—"

Hooyo puts up a hand. Mr Davies stops speaking.

"This not difficult," Hooyo replies. There is an icy look on her face that scares even me. "You *choose* this boy over my son and daughter. You are bad, bad teacher, Mr Davies." She points a finger at him and punctuates the air with each word she says. "You careless teacher."

I turn to look at my mum with awe.

265

Have I just witnessed my mother throw down with Mr Davies, the Head of my school, in this office, right now?

There've been very few moments in my life where Hooyo's been fired-up about something. Her life motto, for the most part, is af daboolan dahab waaye – that a closed mouth is worth gold and, in her opinion, why would a mouth want to be anything other than gold? But now, all bets are off. Hooyo's angry and no amount of mouth-gold is going to change it.

Without looking at me, Hooyo grabs my hand, and we walk out of the office together. We ignore Mr Davies's stammered goodbyes, and we don't look back. When we round the corner and we're safely out of the East Wing, headed back to Reception, I lose my cool.

"Oh my God, Hooyo!" I squeal. "That was so amazing! I can't believe you said that to *Mr Davies* of all people. I'm not even kidding you—"

"Hanan?"

I pause mid-squeal. I know that voice. I don't like that voice.

I turn around to see Jessica standing in the hallway. Hooyo looks back and forth between the two of us. She can read my face and I know she knows from my reaction who this girl must be. That this is the girl who has tried to make my life miserable from the first day we met and who has never lost steam since.

Jessica leans forward hesitantly. "Um, I know this isn't like great timing or anything but…I was hoping to speak to you?"

I don't think about the words that come out of my mouth next. Whatever filter that existed in my brain is no longer there.

"Funny. I was hoping I'd never have to speak to you again."

Hooyo shifts next to me. "Hanan, I'll wait in the car for you, okay?"

She doesn't wait for me to object, only gives me her signature look and exits through the Reception doors at the end of the hallway. I get a strong urge to run after Hooyo, pretend like Jessica isn't in front of me, trying to speak to me. Why does she want to speak to me?

"That's fair," she says.

I roll my eyes.

"Look…" Jessica sighs. She squeezes her eyes shut then opens them again. "Things were…things were bad the last time we spoke at your house. Mostly my fault."

I look at her deadpan.

"Okay, *all* my fault. But I just want you to know I'm really sorry for what happened and…and for everything else as well. I've been a complete arse to you."

I move to step away from this conversation.

Jessica puts her hands up in protest. "Wait. Wait, please, Hanan. Please." Though I want to kick myself for it, there's something in her voice that makes me hesitate. It takes me a long time to make out it sounds like…regret?

"I know that you don't want to listen to me and that's fair, but I just wanted you to hear it from me. I wanted you to know that Daniel had nothing to do with what Jacob did. That was all him, all on his own." She looks at me intently, trying to gauge my reaction.

"Daniel would've reported him if he knew what he was

267

going to do, I swear. My brother's a lot of things but he'd never do that. Not in a million years. And I know he's been a complete arse to you as well. Trying to push people away from you at the bake sale was so wrong and I don't know what he was thinking..." Jessica stops to take in a breath. Her hands drop down to their sides.

"I tried to fix what he did, but I know it's not enough. I'm sorry. This whole thing with Mr Fleming...I think it just pushed Daniel over the edge. That was his godfather, you know? Well, maybe you didn't. It wasn't something everyone knew but...Mr Fleming and my grandad were best friends." Jessica looks down at her hands. The movement brings her hair to fall in a curtain around her face and it's then that I notice her hair isn't braided the way it normally is. I'm not sure I've ever seen her like this.

Her voices comes out faint this time, paper-thin.

"I'm sorry, Hanan. I'm so, so sorry for how I've treated you all this time...for everything. I know I've said a lot to you over the years, but I want you to know that I'd never do what Jacob did. I'd never hurt anyone like that."

When it's clear that she's finished speaking, I walk towards the Reception doors at the end of the hallway, and I don't look back.

Hooyo doesn't bring up my conversation with Jessica in the car or our conversation with Mr Davies for that matter. I'm glad she doesn't because I'm still reeling from everything I've just heard.

The mystery of Jessica buying out our stall now makes sense. Still weird, because it's almost impossible to imagine Jessica doing anything nice for anyone, let alone for me, but not as strange as hearing what else she had to say.

The thing I'm most trying to wrap my head around, to accept, to process, is the fact that Mr Fleming was Daniel's *godfather*. Not just someone he knew but someone who knew him and knew his family for a long time. There's nothing in that truth that I can fight, but knowing it makes me feel things I'd rather not feel. That Mr Fleming sold me out. That my second friend at Grafton Grammar, the friend who'd helped me when I'd been driven out of hallways to pray in, the friend I'd confided in when I refused to confide in the teachers who paid me no mind, had been in alliance with the very people who'd tried to drive me out. There's no logic to my thoughts but there is a power in them that I can't quieten.

Of course it wasn't Mr Fleming's fault that he was Daniel's godfather. It wasn't something he'd orchestrated to hurt me. It was just fact, coincidence. But it hurts now to find out like this. It hurts because it feels like a betrayal, even though it's not.

Hooyo and I pick up the girls from school on the way home. I let them distract me for the evening, dragging me off to a little corner of the living room they've remade into a funny-looking fort. They've put up a makeshift flag – seven white stars against a blue backdrop because *don't be silly, Hanan, we have seven stars in our family* – and a banner with the name of their newly-formed country in bubble letters. SomALI. They're really quite proud of that one.

"Okay, okay so now," Sumaya begins excitedly, "we should do some painting. If I ask very nicely, Hooyo might let me use my own colours. I'll let you share mine, Hanan," she says begrudgingly.

"Why don't you have your set? What happened to it?"

My sisters share a look. Sumaya sighs and looks away, pulling at her thumb. "Hooyo said she'd take it away if I didn't clean up after myself and I didn't."

I stifle a laugh.

"And I have my set but it's nearly running out," Hafsa explains. She shrugs. "So, we need another one."

"Well, I'm ready to get my Picasso skills on so someone get this paint set you keep talking so much about."

Sumaya grins. She sticks her head out of the fort.

"Hooyo!" she calls out.

No response.

"She's in the kitchen," Hafsa says. "Maybe she can't hear you."

"Hooyo!" Sumaya screams again. The girl has the body of a chihuahua but the roar of a lion. It never fails to impress me.

It's this second silence that makes me start to think that something isn't right. Hooyo always answers whenever someone calls for her; even if only to ask why we aren't being respectful and standing up to find her in the first place.

The three of us look at each other under the cover of our duvet fort.

"You guys stay here," I say, injecting reassurance into my voice. "I'll find Hooyo and come back with the paints."

I wiggle out of the small space and go into the kitchen. *Maybe Hooyo isn't even in the kitchen*, I tell myself. *She probably popped down to the shops and we missed her saying so.*

My conjured reassurance disappears when I see Hooyo's trembling body sitting at the dining table. Abooto stands over her, arms around my mum's shaking form, as though to shield her.

"Hooyo, what's going on?"

The words I've been saying to myself all along – *when, not if* – words that have become my mantra, words that are never far from my mind, have been replaced by a sinking feeling in my chest, a yawning hole in my heart.

"Hooyo?"

My mum raises her head from the table. Her face looks ballooned by sadness.

"They've moved Hussein to another hospital," Hooyo says in a shaky breath. "Things are worse. They say he might not make it through the next couple of days."

If, not when. In the space of seconds, Hussein has become an if.

A possibility instead of a certainty.

~~When, not~~ if. ~~Never~~ if.

The yawning hole in my heart sucks me in.

I find myself at my willow tree in the dark again.

Hooyo called out for me when I walked out of the front door, but I couldn't turn around. It was like I was being controlled by a puppeteer. I could hear her words and I *wanted* to turn around, but my legs continued to propel me forward, towards the towering, branching form some hundred metres away.

Now, I lean against the wide, wrinkled trunk of my tree. My chest heaves in and out, my lungs inflating and collapsing dangerously fast. I feel dizzy and a little sick but I'm afraid that if I move to sit, I will collapse. No, it's better to stand and wait for this to pass.

Because it will pass. It will.

These panic attacks always do, even if it feels completely and utterly impossible in this very moment.

CHAPTER TWENTY-NINE

Life is no longer fluid. I begin to see my life in freeze-frames. Single, motionless events with no life between them.

My friends try to visit me. I tell Hooyo I don't want to see them. She tells them I'm sleeping.

Mr Davies calls the house phone again. He leaves a voicemail. He is ignored.

Jessica texts me. Then she calls. I throw my phone across the room. Later, I pick it back up. I block her number.

My phone dings. I look at the notification. An email from the exam centre. Deleted.

My friends are back again. They're persistent, but I am too. I'm still sleeping, I tell Hooyo. And I'll be sleeping every time they're here. She shakes her head. She leaves me alone.

The house phone again. But it's not Mr Davies. It's Douglas White, the reporter. He has finally crawled to the source. He leaves a voicemail. Deleted.

Hooyo asks me if I want to see Hussein. She has asked me exactly seven times already. For the seventh time, I say no.

I do not have the heart to keep seeing my brother in a coma.

I do not have the heart for anything at all.

* * *

There's one thing Hooyo will not accept from me, as much as I beg, and that's ignoring the aunts and uncles and their children – all unrelated to me – who have been coming to our house. I can't call them mourners because Hussein isn't dead yet, but I have trouble coming up with another word to describe the steady stream of people who enter and leave our home.

Most of these people I've never seen before. They're friends of my mum and, in some cases, even old friends of my dad. Others are people of our tribe, people who've heard about Hussein's situation through the grapevine, and who come to express their sympathies. Most of the time though, these people, whether known or unknown to us, turn up unannounced. It's as though they think their good intentions somehow erase the need to tell us they're coming. As if our grief anchors us to this house, like a ship that has stalled in water and one they expect to remain unmoving.

Personally, even though it's a Somali custom, I'm still highly offended anytime the doorbell rings and it's one of these people. I've decided to call them well-wishers, for now.

Hooyo never misses a beat. She's always there within seconds of the doorbell ringing – smiling, warm and inviting. She ushers these people in as if she herself has invited them. She feeds them and listens to them, even though I'm sure her heart's aching to be alone. And I can't help but appreciate that Hooyo's learned to shield herself over the years. This art, because it is an art form – hiding her heart away, swept under an emotional carpet, in between layers of hurt – is one she

274

must've spent years preparing herself for. It becomes clear to me that Hooyo must've expected that grief would hit our family a second time. That crossing oceans would not mean we had escaped tragedy.

I hear Hooyo walking up the stairs. From the way her feet hit the steps, I can already tell she's not happy.

My door swings open.

"Why have you not come downstairs yet, Hanan?" Hooyo asks.

I sigh and pull my duvet closer around me. My room is dark but Hooyo, opening the door, lets in a light I don't want to see.

"Hooyo, please," I plead. "I just can't talk to anyone right now."

"Well, that's good." Hooyo walks over to the window and throws back the curtains.

Too much light. I cringe.

"Because I'm not asking you to *talk* to anyone, Hanan. I'm telling you to come down and show your face to the people who have come to show kindness to this family."

I flip over on my bed so my face is buried in the mattress. "But I didn't ask them to come and see this family," I groan.

Hooyo flips me back the other way so she's seeing my face again. "Ha i ceebeen, Hanan. That's the first and last time I'll say that."

Hooyo walks to the door and stands in the doorway. She turns to look back at me. "A beautiful character is made by adaab," she says quietly. "You know that, and your father and I raised you with that. Good manners are everything, even in the face of sadness. That's what makes a person. So, don't disappoint me." She shuts the door behind her.

I decide not to push my luck. I try make myself presentable, putting on my best baati and garbasaar, even though I'd rather stay in my unwashed clothes. I even go as far as to use some of Abooto's favourite attar and use face cream for the first time in a while. If I were to listen very carefully, I wouldn't be surprised to hear the sound of my skin rejoicing at the moisture.

I go downstairs and say hi to the people who are sitting in the living room. I don't really look at faces or mention names. I say thank you when they express their sympathies and say Alhamdulilah or Ameen, the words ready at the tip of my tongue. I go the kitchen and prepare a simple afternoon tea. I take a tray of steaming shaah in a Thermos, xalwo, doolsho and buskud. They compliment me on my shaah, tell me how great it is that I got the balance of cardamom and cinnamon right, how difficult that is sometimes, and I say thank you.

I look to Hooyo and she nods.

So, I leave. Not just the room, I leave the whole house, walking right out the door in my colourful Somali attire, not caring whether anyone looks twice at me. And, for the third time in as many days, I go to my willow tree.

When all the well-wishers are gone, and my house chores are done, I sit down in my room and cradle my phone in my hand. I've been looking at it for the last ten minutes, but I've still not managed to do the thing I want to do. The thing that I'd managed to do after Gertrude's encouragement but seems impossible now.

I hear Hooyo coming up the stairs, but her steps don't sound angry this time. The door opens and Hooyo comes in to sit on my bed. She runs her hand over my duvet repeatedly, not saying anything. I start to worry she'll notice I haven't bothered to change my bed sheets.

"You went outside without a coat again."

"I know, Hooyo, sorry." Her face is impassive. "I wasn't thinking."

"You've stopped thinking a lot lately." Her hands stop running over the duvet. "But have you ever considered whether any of this is easy for me, Hanan? Or for your Abooto? Or for your sisters? They're struggling to even understand what's happening."

I feel the air escape me. Tears jump to my eyes. I quickly wipe them away before they have a chance to fall.

"Have you thought, Hanan, for just a moment, that maybe the least you can do is survive for your family? To eat the food I make for you and drink the water I bring you so you don't collapse from dehydration?"

The tears spill over.

"Or to at least cover yourself against the cold when you go outside? How do you think I'll manage if I've already got one son in the hospital, barely alive, and I get a daughter in there for hypothermia?"

"Then I'll think that's good, Hooyo!" I scream. The tears are hot on my face but there is a heat coming from inside me.

A heat I've felt slowly build over the last few days – a long fuse that's finally reached its end. "I'll think I deserve it because Hussein is in there and he's nearly dead and it's my fault! I'll deserve it because I'm the one who put him there and then walked away! So why should I bother to eat or sleep or put a coat on when I go outside? Why, Hooyo?" My voice cracks. The rest comes out in a whisper. "There's isn't a reason to try any more…there isn't a reason to do anything. There's…nothing. There's nothing left."

Hooyo doesn't look taken aback by my anger. Her face is expressionless, and she is still, like she expected this. As if she's seen it building and building and has waited patiently for it to burst to the surface.

"If that's what you believe, Hanan, then you must think nothing of me and you must think nothing of qadr," she says. "You must think that your father's death left me overjoyed because I didn't let myself break and splinter in the way you're falling apart now." Hooyo pauses. "Do you think grief is simple? Do you think it exists alone, with nothing else?"

These questions do not disappear in the silence. They linger in the air between us.

"If you truly believe that then…" Hooyo sighs and turns away from me. "Life is a complicated thing, Hanan. You know this truth the same way your body knows how to breathe, so I don't need to convince you. You'll be challenged by so many different things in so many different ways and maybe your challenges will be harder because of who you are, because of what you look like and what you believe in…but I need to know that you will try to survive, whatever comes your way. I need to know that you will keep living, keep pushing forward." Hooyo's voice trembles. I want to reach out and hold her, but I don't. "I need to know that you won't break."

She runs her hands over the duvet one more time and sighs, bringing a hand up to wipe her eyes. "Listen to your father's words, Hanan. If you don't understand my words, maybe you'll understand his," she says, standing up.

"And change these sheets. Tonight. It's been weeks."

She leaves my room.

I get up to grab some fresh sheets from the wardrobe, the phone forgotten on the desk and Hooyo's words on repeat in my mind. And, although I try to avoid looking at the top drawer of my desk, my eyes land there too many times.

So, I go to Hussein's room across the hall and change his sheets too. Imagine him lying on this bed of solid pine with the scent of freshly laundered sheets in the air. Imagine him looking out of his window, looking for something different across the same landscape, like he did every night.

I open the window and let the wind into this room, stuffed with stale air, and try to imagine being him. To think what he might have thought and to see what he might have seen. *Maybe he was looking for a way out*, I think. Trying to see past the lines that divide Northwell, the lines that define allegiances and the lines that can get you killed if you cross them. The lines he had somehow, against all odds, found himself on.

Hussein was never meant to be on road. Of course, I'm sure most people who are on road never planned to be. But this life of dealing drugs and exchanging tainted money wasn't a life either of my parents saw in our futures. And it was a future Hooyo thought she'd succeeded in protecting us against.

I go back to my room and pick up my phone again, wanting to distract myself. It works for all of two minutes before my hand gravitates towards the top drawer of my desk. I pull it open and pick up the cassette inside, carefully, as if it's a dangerous thing. The label on it is yellow and faded but I can still make out my name in black ink across the front.

Hanan cadeey. Aabo's nickname for me.

I locate my old cassette player under a few piles of papers under my bed and dust it off. I lean against the bed frame that's held me up on so many of my bad nights and put the cassette in before I have a chance to second-guess myself. I take a sharp breath in and listen to my father's voice fill the room. If I close my eyes, I can almost pretend that he's here.

"Hanan cadeey, my daughter, if you are listening to this, then it is because I am no longer in this world. Your mother and I knew that this journey to Kenya would be a difficult one, but we decided to make the journey regardless, to give you all a better life. There is nothing that I would not do for my children and so, if you are listening, then I know that you have survived and that is all I have ever wanted.

"Your mother and I each recorded something to give to you children should either of you reach a point in this tumultuous life where you see the world for what it truly is. In all of its glory and beauty, but in all of its ugliness and evil as well. I want you to know, wherever destiny takes you in this life, that you are loved. Not only

by those lucky enough to stand in the shadow of your brightness, but also by Allah, the Almighty.

"But you must remember that destiny is a difficult thing, Hanan cadeey. We try to fight against what is written for us, what is meant to be, though know that we are only humans with very little power. Life won't ever stop turning and, from the little wisdom I have gained in my life, I know that we must turn with it, not against it, if we are to survive this world.

"And, though I have not been able to see you grow into the woman you are today, I know that because you came from your mother, you are every bit as beautiful, strong, determined and courageous as I imagine you to be.

"So, my daughter, I want you to shake the world with your brilliance and kindness. The very same brilliance and kindness that I have seen you run around with all your life. I want you to show this world what you are capable of. That you are the daughter of Leyla Abdullahi and Ibrahim Ali. That greatness lies in your bloodline. That greatness is your inheritance, even if those blind to it deny you.

"I am the proudest father to have ever walked this earth. Although we are all blessed in ways we cannot imagine, when I ponder my own blessings, I almost crumble under the weight of it.

"Remember your own blessings, Hanan, even when it seems as though there is nothing to be grateful for. There is always something to be grateful for. All that is required is a little perspective and patience. Sometimes when I need a reminder of that, I remember what Allah taught us in the Qur'an: that verily with hardship comes ease. Hold those words dear to your heart, Hanan, as I hold them to mine.

"I love you, daughter of mine."

I hold the cassette player for a long time after the tape finishes, hands shaking. I find myself thinking back to the last time I held it. It seems like a lifetime ago, but it's only been about a week since the anniversary of Aabo's death. When I laid down here on the floor of my room, in a cocoon of my own making, and gripped the cassette to my chest.

Somehow, it feels both light and heavy in my hands. Heavier still, when I think about how someone could be so calm about the possibility of death or welcome it, in fact, so long as the other pieces of their heart remained. And, though I try to fight it, the cassette reminds me of other things. Things I'd long forgotten. Like the smell of uunsi in our Mogadishu home; the earthy, intense smell of it that would cling to my dad. The goodbyes Aabo would pepper us with in kisses when he would leave, going where he was needed to save lives or deliver babies. Or the stories he would tell us when he came back, lettings whole worlds slip off his tongue into the dusty, humid air.

I take the player with me as I crawl into bed, being careful with it. I stare at the buttons and at Aabo's writing on the label, through the tiny window at the front. I find the answer to a question I thought I'd forgotten.

Grief doesn't exist alone. It can't.

Because if grief existed alone, what joy would there have been in Sumaya's birth after Aabo died? How would we have looked on with such wonder as she breathed her first breath with the memory of seeing our dad ripped from this earth?

How could we have welcomed her into a broken family and not crumpled under the weight of that new life?

How?

We did because we could. We did it without splintering because the fundamental truth is that being broken doesn't mean you're broken for ever. Maybe you've come apart, like scattered Lego pieces, but you can come together again too.

It means that while the world continues to turn, you don't resist the motion, however jarring it seems. However much it shakes you or makes you feel like the very ground underneath your feet might disintegrate. You turn with the world, in any direction it wishes to turn, and *you hold on*. Tightly, with both hands and with a string of prayers.

Verily, with hardship comes ease, I remind myself, picking up my new black leather notebook. I write the words I want to say and the words I don't want to say. I write what I have been holding back for most of my life.

CHAPTER THIRTY

My friends come over the next day after school and I tell them all about my grand plans. By the time I'm done, Nasra's jaw hangs, Andrea looks at me impressed and both Lily and Isha just stare at me aghast.

"So, what do you think?"

"Um…um," Nasra stutters. "It's just that, well, wow… It's a bloody—"

"It's a bloody big move is what it is," Andrea cuts in. "Why are you so lost for words, Nasra? You're not normally like this."

"Because this is Hanan we're talking about!" she exclaims. "Like, no offence or anything," she adds hurriedly, looking at me. "I just never in a million years would've expected you to do this."

"None taken," I laugh. "I just don't think I have anything to lose at this point, right?"

"You're not worried they might kick you out of school after this?" Lily asks, visibly worried on my behalf.

"They might do," I reply, shrugging my shoulders. "But my brother's in hospital and Mr Davies seems to care more about keeping up appearances than doing what's right so I thought maybe it's time I finally do what's right."

"I really think Mr Davies might just collapse after this," Isha laughs.

"He looks like he's been ready to collapse from day one to be honest," Nasra jokes. "Bright red all the time and with a tie that looks *way* too tight around a human neck."

I choke back a laugh but, for some reason, Isha's howling on the floor. It takes her a minute to compose herself. Nasra beams.

Andrea, Lily and I share a look. There's something about Isha and Nasra's relationship that I don't think the three of us will ever truly understand.

"Okay, enough chit-chat." Andrea claps her hands. She zeroes in on me. "Can we hear it then? I'm dying to hear it."

I pull out the leather notebook from under my pillow and wave it. "You think you lot are here for fun? I need ears on this. And you guys are some of the best ears in the business."

When my friends are gone, I find myself staring at the words I'd read out to them not once, twice, but three times. Each time I'd read it out loud, the words had changed. Sentences stripped and built back up again until the whole thing was perfect.

"Hanan," Sumaya calls out from their rebuilt duvet fort. "Do you wanna paint with us? We're doing a surprise. It's for Hooyo and Abooto."

Hafsa emerges from the fort a moment later, pulling on her arm. "It was meant to be a secret, Sumaya!"

"Oops, sorry." She smiles sheepishly. "But do you, Hanan?"

"Can't now, sis. Maybe later?"

They both snake back into the space they've crawled out of. I hear Hafsa berate Sumaya for her loose lips and I have to swallow back a laugh.

I turn my attention back to the words. They look…normal, on the page, as if they don't have any power written the way they are on these lines. But I wonder what will happen when I say them aloud one more time. When Mr Davies and the governors and the teachers and the parents hear what I have to say.

I'm glad none of my friends asked me why. That none of them said, *what made you decide to do this now, after everything, after so long?* Because, the truth is, there's so much that led me to it.

Yes, Aabo's words had something to do with it, but the match had been truly lit long ago. For so long, I believed that perfection would change how the world sees me. That being a good little girl and staying under the radar and Not Speaking Back was the answer to everything. But now I know the world may never see me the way I want to be seen and I know that the scarf on my head has everything to do with that.

I'm pressing send on an email to Mr Davies confirming I'll be at the meeting when the doorbell rings. Sumaya bolts out from the fort and makes a run for the door. I'll never understand what it is about people at the door that gets her so excited.

"Who is it?" I call out after her.

Hooyo and Abooto are at the hospital visiting Hussein which means I am the most senior person in the house. That means no one gets through the front door without my say-so.

Sumaya walks back in. Her face is half twisted in confusion. "Someone called Jusica? She told me to get you," Sumaya says. "Do you know them?"

"Jusica?"

"Yeah. Jusica. I don't know what that is."

"I think I do." I sigh, standing up. "Don't worry, you can go back to play—" I start to say, but she's gone before I can even finish my sentence.

The frosted glass of the front door means I can only make out a head and a body. I don't need clear glass to know who it is though. The doorbell rings again. I resist the urge to rip the box from the wall.

I squat in front of the door and pull up the lid of the letter box. "I think I made it very clear I don't want to speak to you."

The head disappears from the glass as the body outside descends. Her reply comes a moment later.

"I know." A pause. I hear her shuffling before she speaks again. "But I really need to speak to you. Can I come in?" Then, "Please?"

"Why is it only what you want that matters? I don't want to speak to you, Jessica. I don't know how much more obvious I can make it."

"I know that you don't owe me anything, but please. I have a few things I want to get off my chest, things I wanted to say to you at school actually, when I saw you the other day but that wasn't...that wasn't the best time to do it."

I don't say anything. Hafsa and Sumaya poke their heads into the hallway. They mime at me, wanting me to explain why I'm refusing to let this person in, but I only shake my head.

"I'm going to wait out here until you hear me out."

"Good. I hope you lose a toe to frostbite."

Hafsa purses her lips, disappointed. Thankfully, they stop their miming and slink back into the living room.

I drop the lid of the letter box, hoping that the sound hurts her ears, and sit down to lean against the wall. I hear Jessica drop her side of the lid too, but not any sounds that suggest she's leaving.

"Hanan!" Sumaya calls out from the living room. She sounds tearful. "I hurt my finger. Can you come look at it?"

I'd look at anything if it would get me away from the entitlement seeping through this door right now. I stand up loudly, hoping Jessica will get the message and leave.

"What's up?" I walk straight over to the fort.

"Nothing." It's Sumaya's voice. But it's behind me.

I turn around. "If it's nothing then why—" I pause. "Where's Hafsa?"

"Nowhere," she says coyly.

A second later, I see a flash of something darting from behind the sofa and running into the hallway. I sidestep Sumaya to follow but it's too late. Hafsa's already pulling down the handle on the front door. Jessica catches herself before she falls completely onto the floor, caught out by the door opening so quickly.

"This is great," she says, standing up and pulling down her skirt. "Thought I'd have to wait around much longer than this."

"So, you're Jusica?" Hafsa asks. She looks her up and down, as if trying to convince herself that that's a real name.

"No, it's Jessica," she corrects. "And you must be Hanan's sister?"

"Yeah, Hafsa. I'm the next oldest. Not the youngest. That's Sumaya."

"Cool. That's cool. It's nice to meet you."

"Nice to meet you too." Hafsa's head starts to turn towards me before she decides against it. "Do you wanna come in?"

The relief that sets in Jessica's face is undeniable. Her eyes flick over to me. "That would be great, Hafsa, thanks."

And then she steps into my home.

At the direction of my sisters, Jessica takes off her coat, places it on the hook, then takes her shoes off. They invite her to sit down in the living room and, despite her protests, they head off into the kitchen to get some snacks. They return with water in Sumaya's favourite pink glass and a bowl of Hula Hoops.

"This is amazing. Thank you."

Sumaya beams with pride. Hafsa pulls on her arm. "We're going upstairs to play, Hanan, okay?"

They leave without another word, ignoring my glares. Jessica puts the pink glass down on the coffee table. We don't look at each other.

"How's your brother?" she asks, looking straight ahead at the black TV screen. "Is he doing any better?"

I scoff. "You seriously want to ask me that when it was Daniel who created this mess in the first place?" Jessica's head turns. I'm not sure if she's building up to her brother's defence again but I don't want to hear it right now. "I don't care if he wasn't the one with the knife. He was friends with Jacob. *He* egged Jacob on."

I shake my head, wondering why the hell I'm having this conversation right now with Jessica, of all people. This is exactly what I didn't want to happen and why I'd avoided her at school to begin with.

"Anyway, since you're so concerned, my brother's nearly dead in the ICU. Just an FYI for you to spread around school, if you'd like."

Jessica winces and turns her head back to the TV. She looks at me from the reflection on the screen and, for a moment, I wonder what she sees.

A girl unbothered by her brother's condition or a girl scrambling to collect the shreds of her unravelled life?

"I'm sorry about your brother," she says. "I'm really sorry. I hope he gets better."

"Cool. Is that all you came here for?"

"Not exactly..." Jessica shifts a little in her seat, probably to get away from all the springs that have bitten their way through the leather. "You asked me a question last time I was here," she says, after a while. "You asked me why I hated you. Why I treated you the way I did. And it was a question I didn't answer."

From the periphery of my vision, I see her sat very still. Back straight and with both hands on knees. Unlike last time, she doesn't bother opening and closing her mouth repeatedly as if trying to get lies through.

"The thing is…you and I are very different people," Jessica begins. "I come from places where…where everybody looks like me, and people like you, they…they don't fit that description." Her hand moves up to pinch her thigh. Hard. But she doesn't flinch.

"I've always heard one thing about people like you, about Muslims. Not great stuff and, um yeah, pretty bad stuff for the most part. My parents will see someone who looks like you and then spend the next ten minutes ranting about how you're all the scum of the earth and how this country deserves better than you. All sorts of rubbish about how you're terrorizing this great nation and want to take over." She laughs. "It sounds ridiculous when I say it out loud now but, yeah, that's my family's take on Muslims, or anyone different, I guess. But, when I met you, on the first day of school…you didn't seem like any of those things. Like, I'd see your mum pick you up after school and give you the biggest smile and hug in the world and I used to think, how on earth are they going to terrorize us? And, in class, I'd always see you laughing with Andrea, or I'd overhear you guys talking about movies or weekend plans or whatever and it was never really like the image I built up in my head." She picks up Sumaya's pink cup to drink a sip of water. I'm sure I notice a tiny tremble in her hand as she sets it back down. But, when I look again, it's not there.

"Mr Fleming and my dad would get into it at home sometimes," she continues, "if he was around when my dad was going off on one of his rants. And I remember he'd say the same thing every time: you can't judge who you don't know." She starts picking at her thigh again. "But I always believed my parents. What they said stuck with me so, for a long time, I was pretty confused about you."

Her hand stills.

"Until I saw you at the memorial service."

I see her glance at me, probably to see if I'm looking at her. She looks away quickly.

"You know…Mr Fleming was really close to my family. More with my grandad and Daniel than me but, after he died I'd go home every day and there'd just be so. Much. Hate. All these people practically screaming about how this was the last straw, like, how could a foreigner do this 'on our land'?" she says with air quotes and sighs.

"Then I saw you and the rest of your family at the memorial, and none of it really made sense any more. Your whole family came there even with everything going on, even with all the hate and the resentment Muslims were getting, and it made me think… It made me think that maybe something wasn't right about what my parents always said. That maybe Mr Fleming had it right all along and that you really can't judge who you don't know. And I know this sounds like the greatest excuse in the world and there's no excusing me being a complete arse to you when I could've been better than the things I heard, but honestly, I think…I think

I was confused for a really long time."

I've never heard Jessica sound apologetic for anything, ever. Jessica is the kind of girl who runs in the opposite direction to remorse or guilt, yet there's something in her words now that seems to ring true. But I'm tired of being hurt by people.

"That's a beautiful speech," I say.

"It's not a speech. It's the truth."

I turn to look at her. She doesn't squirm under my gaze.

The funny thing is, I've imagined this scenario a thousand different ways in my head: the day when Jessica and I are no longer enemies. But, for the first time, I'm realizing that the years of her hating me has made me strangely comfortable with the unfriendliness, with the aggression, the whispering… What would the world look like if nothing ugly existed between us?

"Well, it's your truth," I say. "It's your truth that you've come in here with and that you're waving about now and trying to force me to accept. You were bad to me. That's my truth."

"I know that," she whispers. "Hanan, I know that, and I'll feel terrible about that for the rest of my life. But I thought it'd be better to be honest and answer your question than not tell you at all."

She looks at the untouched Hula Hoops on the coffee table. "I don't expect us to be best friends or skip into the sunset together, but it would be nice for our last year at Grafton to be different." Jessica stands up. She fixes her skirt again. "To be the way it should've been when we started together six years ago."

I don't tell her that there may not be a future left for me at Grafton. Or a future I want, anyway. In fact, I don't say anything else at all.

She leaves, closing the front door behind her.

Tonight, there are no nightmares. But no dreams either. Only sleep and, right now, someone is waking me out of it.

Hooyo's tear-stained face floats above me as I adjust to the sudden light in my room.

"Hanan?" Hooyo's voice wavers. "Did you hear what I said?"

I'm still crawling out of the sleep-space in my head. My mother's face looks blurry in front of me.

"No," I say, sitting up. "What's wrong? Is it Hussein?"

Hooyo nods and I feel that yawning hole open up in my chest again. She grabs my shoulders and hugs me, as if she senses it too.

"He's awake, Hanan," Hooyo says. Her warm breath tickles the back of my neck. "Hussein's awake. He's alive."

CHAPTER THIRTY-ONE

According to the information Hooyo got, Hussein is no longer in a coma.

Hooyo seems to believe that just fine. She buzzes around the whole house in the hour before we leave to see him, packing a bag of things he might've missed and food he probably hungered for. I don't tell her that the ten days he spent in the coma are not the same as the time we spent waiting for him to come out of it. And I definitely don't tell her that the things she wants to bring are things that will probably comfort her more than her son. I don't say these things because I'm grateful for the smile that lights up her face and I'll do anything to keep it that way.

But I'm a different story. Since that phone call from the hospital, I've been on edge. Teetering on the lip of a precipice, wanting to be pulled back to solid ground. Hussein being awake is a miracle, but it's a miracle that I need to see with my own eyes. I refuse to let anyone else allow me to be hopeful. Hope is something that can grow wild if left unchecked and I'd rather let it suffocate than grow to uncontrollable heights.

We're driving to the hospital when Hooyo gasps. "Did I bring his mango yoghurt?"

I check the bag on my lap. "Yeah, it's in here. But they might not let him eat it anyway."

Abooto clicks her teeth. "The doctors in this country know nothing. How dare they refuse the mango? There's nothing but good in God's fruit."

"Abooto, you know it's not like that." I feel like I've had this conversation with her a million times before, in some shape or form. "They just might not let him eat certain things. Or even eat or drink at all. I don't know. Let's just see what they say."

She clicks her teeth again and rolls down the window to let in some of the winter air.

We drive the rest of the way in silence. Hafsa and Sumaya have been dropped off at their school breakfast club so it's just me, Hooyo and Abooto on our way to the hospital.

Somehow, I'm strangely calm. My breathing remains steady, my hands stay dry, and I don't feel a sudden urge to run to the toilet. I quickly feel the pulse of my wrist to check there isn't anything seriously wrong.

The journey feels like it's taking hours, but I know that's just my perception. When you want something, when you're desperate for it, time seems to play games. The seconds and minutes like to hide away and, when you look at the clock again, you wonder how they slipped past you.

"Is that clock broken?" Abooto asks, pointing at the digital display above the AC.

"No," I sigh. "It's not." Guess I'm not the only one questioning how long this is taking.

Finally, we pull up to the hospital. I get out from the back, holding the bag Hooyo's packed to the brim, and pivot to help Abooto out from the passenger seat. She groans as she stands up. I duck back in to grab her walking stick and hand it to her.

Now that we're here, it suddenly feels like it's all happening too fast. Too fast, too soon, too much. I can feel the rope around my middle again, that sensation of something, or someone, tugging at me, like the first night I made my way to Hussein.

Hope flickers.

I squash it down.

I follow Hooyo and Abooto inside the hospital because I have no idea where we're going. I haven't visited Hussein since he was moved from his original hospital to this new one. It felt too painful to go and see my brother when I was convinced that he wasn't going to make it. I wish now that I had been to see him because if, *if*, the news about Hussein being awake is true, now it means I've been a terrible sister for no reason at all.

I trail behind them, slowly, slowly, and then even slower, as if I want to lose them in these corridors.

"Hanan?" Hooyo asks, confused. I think she's saying more but I can't hear her because I'm quite far behind them now. She marches back to me and holds my wrist. "You're precious cargo, macaanto. Please, keep up."

"Really?"

That twinkle that used to inhabit Hooyo's eyes, the one that's been gone for so long, is back. "Not *you*," she says with a smirk, pulling me along. "I mean that bag you're holding. Hussein's going to need all this if he's going to get better."

I purse my lips and let Hooyo pull me along.

They buzz us in when we reach the ward. One of the nurses asks who we're after.

"Hussein," Abooto says. She lifts the niqab slightly off her face, so her words aren't muffled. "Somali boy. Hussein."

"That's fine," the nurse smiles. "Go right ahead. I assume you know which room he's in?"

Hooyo nods and then it's just the three of us walking along the corridor. I feel my stomach constrict when I look at the next room coming up on the left.

"It's this one," Hooyo says, slowing down and pointing at it.

I feel her confidence melt away as she stands there, uncertainly gripping the handle but not pushing it down. Hooyo closes her eyes briefly. She opens them when Abooto's hand covers her own.

"Leyla, my daughter, your strength is a beautiful thing, but it's not the only thing," Abooto whispers. Though most of her face is covered, in her eyes, I see the vulnerability and the pain and fear that I've only seen once before in my life. "Family open the doors that are too difficult for one person to manage alone. We lighten the load, so it becomes easier to carry."

Hooyo sniffs and nods. She looks at me but I'm already there, standing right next to her, bringing my hand down over theirs.

We push down on the handle together. We lighten the load. We say Bismillah.

And we open the door.

* * *

The room isn't as dark as I expected it to be. I'd been prepared to see a Hussein barely alive, breathing noisily, with a flicker of life in his eyes. I'd thought I'd feel a sense of dread walking in. I thought…well, the worst.

Hussein is sat up in the bed. The expressionless face that I saw the last time is replaced by the face I once knew. He's leaning over something on the table in front of him. When we come in, he looks up. The card in his hand falls and a huge smile erupts. The jagged scar lining his cheek folds as the skin of it stretches and, in that moment, I think of how beautiful scars can be.

"What took you guys so long?" he says. His voice sounds the same. Why did I expect it to be different? "I hope you brought something to eat because the doctor said I could eat soft foods now and I refused to eat that dirty porridge they put in front of me." His hand moves to his stomach, over the knife's rip and stitches. "I'm legit starving."

I look to Hooyo, watching the unshed tears retreat back to wherever they came from. I see the switch in her eyes flick from *despairing mother* to *commander of healing* and I resist the instinct to step back from the determination that seeps off her in waves. It's a little scary to watch.

Hooyo gives her son a hug and a kiss. There are a lot of things unsaid in their embrace, things that I can see Hussein is scared to admit and things Hooyo is afraid to burden him with. But there are a lot of things said loud and clear too, like in the way they linger holding each other, in the way Hussein's shoulders loosen and in the way that Hooyo leans in to smell her son.

Hooyo moves onto the next phase of her motherly mission. She busies herself putting on a recitation of the Qur'an on low volume, opening a window and taking the bag from me to begin decking out the room with Hussein's things.

Like a family procession, Abooto is next in line. Her walking stick smacks against the floor as she makes her way to the bed. She lifts it up to hit the side rail of the bed, once, indicating the remote. Hussein dutifully grabs it and lifts the bed higher from the ground.

"Is that high enough, Abooto?"

Abooto bends to hug him. She lets the walking stick clatter to the floor and wraps both arms around him. It's when I notice her shoulders shaking that I realize she's crying.

I never knew Abooto could cry like that.

It's enough to set Hussein off too because I hear his sobs carry over their embrace. Neither of them says anything, they just hold each other and, when it's done, they dry their eyes and steady their breaths. Abooto sits down in the chair by the bed and, just like that, it's over.

Hussein looks to me now. Our eyes lock for the first time since I walked into this room and I can't help but wonder if, somehow, he remembers all the things I said to him when he was unconscious. If he heard me sitting across from him, praying, staring, thinking, breaking apart. I notice the card that I'd left on the table in his old room is here, on his lap, open.

"You not happy to see me, sis?" His smile widens. Ever the

serious boy. "Thought it was Hanan and Hussein, best friends for ever. That's what this says, anyway." He indicates the card with Sumaya's terrible handwriting.

I try to read his eyes from where I stand but I'm too far away. I have to see him see me, because what I find in his eyes might change everything.

"Thanks to you, it might not have been for ever," I say, moving to stand by the bed.

I don't know why I say this or why I say it like this. I think I'm trying to bait him, to unleash the anger that I'm so sure is there, beneath this skin of joy he's presenting to the world.

The smile falls from his face, like a sheet pulled by a magician's hand.

Good, I think. *Blame me. Hate me. It's my fault you're here.*

"I'm sorry," Hussein whispers. His breath catches on the roll of the *r* and I think he's about to leave it there, but he doesn't. "I am so, so sorry, Hanan. I'd say it a billion times if I could, but it would…it would never be enough. I know that, I'm not stupid. But I'll never stop saying sorry, I'll never stop asking you to forgive me." He wipes the corner of his eyes, looking away from me.

"You don't know how sick it makes me when I think about that night… When I think about what I put you through and how that piece of shit hurt you and tried to come after you…" He clenches his fist. "I was too caught up in my bullshit. That's on me. That will always be on me. And I'm okay with that."

Hooyo clears her throat. The corner of Hussein's mouth goes up. "Sorry, Hooyo. Sorry. Didn't mean to swear."

Hooyo gives a single nod and goes back to her mission.

There is anger there, it dawns on me suddenly. I could see it in his eyes before he looked down and I can see it now in the way he clenches his fists. An anger that is deep and wild. An anger that is unforgiving. But it's not anger at me. It's anger at himself.

"Oh my God. Is that what you think?" I whisper. For some reason, saying words loudly feels wrong. Like the air is delicate and loud words might break it and then it would be hard to breathe. I sit down on the edge of the bed. "Is that what you think, Hussein? That it's your fault?"

He sighs and runs a hand over his unruly hair. "What kind of a question is that, Hanan? Of course it's my fucking fault. I'm the big man who wanted to be on road and who thought that after everything Hooyo did to keep us off it, it would be a great idea. And then you followed me because I was acting booky, because you're a good sister, a good person, looking out for me and then…you know what happened then. I don't need to say it."

Hooyo clears her throat. Again. Hussein gives her a sheepish smile.

"I can't believe you think that," I say in disbelief. "How can you say that when I was the one who was meant to be at home? If I hadn't followed you, none of this would have happened in the first place." My voice creeps louder and louder. "I'm meant to be your sister, the one who looks out for you, who protects you, and all I did was get a knife stuck in you!" I breathe, feel myself deflate a little. "You're the one who should hate me,

Hussein…you nearly died. I nearly killed you."

Hussein laughs then, a huge, unexpected laugh that makes his head fall back. He wipes tears again from the corner of his eyes but, this time, they're not tears of anger.

"I'm sorry, did I say something funny?"

"No, no," he says, laughing. I notice him touch his stomach again as if in pain. "It's not right that we're each blaming ourselves. It's so fucked up." He beats Hooyo to it. "Sorry, Hooyo. I promise that was the last time."

"And?" I say.

"It's funny because it's not our fault, sis. Not really. But we're fully pointing the finger at ourselves like it's one of us." He shifts in the bed so he's directly facing me. "It was that little terrorist from your school! It was that prick who decided to come there with a knife. Not you. Not me."

"Jacob."

"What?"

"You're saying it's Jacob's fault."

"Listen, I said it was his fault, not that I wanted to hear his name. There's only so much progress a guy can make in a day."

I think about Hussein's words, measuring them up. It sounds right in my head. Simple. Yes, it was Jacob's fault. Anyone could say that, objectively, without any trouble. So why am I still blaming myself?

I know I did things that day I'm not proud of. I disobeyed Hooyo on a deep level, but I'd rationalized that being a temporary caasi would be better than letting my brother get dragged into some bad business. Still, me following Hussein wouldn't have ended the way it had if Jacob hadn't followed me. He'd set a different course of events in motion when he'd sent the email, when he'd followed me from school, and when he'd pulled out the knife. A course of events outside my control and outside Hussein's.

My mind keeps circling back to that newspaper clipping. The words of Douglas White in black-and-white that cancelled me and my brother. They were words that framed Jacob, and only Jacob, front and centre – an angel boy who'd snapped and hurt two random people in the process. We were afterthoughts to his victimhood, barely worth a mention.

I look at Hussein now and see he's right. It wasn't either of our faults, not really. I sigh. I'd spent so long hating Douglas White for blaming me, blaming my brother, when I hadn't even noticed that that's what I've been doing all along.

I tell Hussein about everything that happened after the attack, catching him up, and Hooyo sits down when she's done fussing over him. I make sure not to mention anything about the news report in the updates I give him. We've spoken enough about Jacob already and I don't think Hussein would react well right now to news of "angel boy's mental breakdown".

Abooto yawns after a while, probably bored of the conversation. I get an idea.

"Should we play ciyaar bilaw?"

Abooto perks up as expected. "That's the best idea you've had in a long time, Hanan."

"Ouch," I say, feigning hurt.

"Everyone pick a number?" Hooyo asks.

"Yeah, I'll go for 13," Hussein says. "But I have to request you guys take it easy on me. I'm very sick right now."

Abooto cackles, rubbing her hands together. "I won't make promises I can't keep."

Hussein visibly gulps.

We start the game, playing over and over again until all our hands are deadly sore. My number gets called a few times and when Hussein and I face off, I don't see any of the vulnerability he was claiming. He grins at me as he slaps my hands, hard, three times in quick succession.

"Feel like there's a lot of pent-up rage in those slaps."

He shrugs and smiles. "That's just the way I play, sis. Get with it or get out."

Later, when we're getting ready to leave, I ask him a question. "Hussein?"

"Yeah," he says, picking up the TV remote.

"That night, when, you know, when you came back for me…I remember you helped me up. You got me off the floor and then you turned and went to Jacob." He nods slowly, fingers roaming over the buttons on the remote. "Why didn't you run away?" I ask. "Why didn't we leg it to the main road to try and get help?"

I'd thought about that moment when I first saw him, unconscious and expressionless, in the hospital. When he'd turned away from me and turned towards the boy who nearly killed him. If he'd run away with me like he was meant to, he wouldn't be here right now, clawing his way back from the edge.

His hand rests on the ON button.

"Honestly, in that moment, I wasn't even thinking about that prick…I didn't even see the knife in his hand. My guy pulled that out after." A short, humourless laugh. "It sounds stupid but I wasn't even seeing his face. I…I was seeing Aabo. I was seeing Aabo and the guy that killed him and I was just frozen. I couldn't run away." He puts the remote down and sighs. "I just thought to myself: no, I'm not going to be a coward. Not this time, not ever again."

"You were just a kid back then, Hussein. We both were. You know that, right? There's nothing you could've done to save Aabo."

He shrugs. "Maybe not. But I wasn't going to let that happen again in front of me."

I nod, leaning over to squeeze his hand. If there's one thing I understand, it's how deeply the pain of the past can lodge itself in us and not let go.

We say goodbye, and Hooyo brings her goody-bag closer to Hussein so it's easier for him to reach. He rummages through it. We're nearly out the door when he squeals.

Hooyo jumps to attention. "Hussein? What is it?"

He holds the offending object in his hands. "How come no one told me my mango yoghurt was in here? It's warm now!"

I slide down the door laughing, gasping, my body suddenly floppy. It feels desperate and raw, like I've never laughed before and like I'll never laugh this way again. Hooyo clicks her teeth at me, glancing up and down the hallway nervously to see if anyone else is watching.

CHAPTER THIRTY-TWO

The police come knocking on Hussein's hospital room door the next day, breaking up the second part of our family reunion. Sumaya and Hafsa walk out of the room sulking, promising Hussein that they'll return the minute the officers leave. Abooto leaves with them.

It's the same officers from last time – PCs Patel and Lundy. They both greet me with smiles when they spot me standing near the window. I don't smile back.

They get their statement from Hussein. I can tell this process is uncomfortable for him because he spends the whole time biting the inside of his cheek. He faces the officers, not looking to me or Hooyo once. I don't need twin telepathy to tell me why. As much as I know Hussein wants to tell the truth about everything, it isn't easy when you think that truth might disappoint your family. A part of me wishes that I could pause this moment, walk up to him and remind him that, with family, disappointment comes with the territory. He wouldn't be off the hook, not for a long time. But there are other things that come with the territory too. Love, forgiveness, patience, acceptance…and aren't all of those things, together, worthwhile?

The line of questioning doesn't surprise me. I'd been expecting it and I'd warned Hussein about it too. It's not that I have the power of foresight (Astagfirullah) or anything, it's just obvious that these officers are only interested in hearing certain things. And I can't help but think they're resisting the bigger picture in front of them.

How can anyone paint a picture of a forest without the colour green? Simple answer: you can't. It's impossible. Without the green, without the leaves and leafy canopy, the picture will always be incomplete…and using any other colour in its place would just be wrong.

They ask Hussein about everything that happened that day and everything that led up to that moment. Where was he going? Why? And, for the first time, we hear everything in full.

Hussein's voice is flat as he answers.

Some guy told me there'd be good money. He said we wouldn't be doing much, just moving a few things about.

Just weed. None of that…none of that other stuff.

No, I didn't do any of that yet. I was…[*pause*] I was going that day, before everything happened, to get my first drop. Or whatever you want to call it.

Thank God, he wasn't already in deep.

Why? [*scratches head*] Honestly, the money was good.

I heard it was good anyway. And it was more for...more for my family, than anything else. We were struggling a bit at home. I got a job at the cinema. That helped. But the pay was still shit.

Hooyo looks away.

The new clothes and stuff, yeah [*laughs*]... No, that was my own money from work.

I'm not lying. The pay was shit but I was basically working there full-time.

[*takes deep breath*] I stopped going to college a few weeks ago, that's how.

Hooyo searches for something in her bag. She pulls out a pocket tissue.

No, I didn't get any of their names. [*Hussein's left eye twitches.*]

I think he's lying. I think he might be hiding the one name he knows. His friend, Ahmed.

Really. I didn't get names.

Okay. Listen. I've answered your questions now, but I feel

like I'm the one on trial. Can you ask me about that little prick, the one that stabbed me?

When are we going to chat about him?

The conversation loses steam after this. If I were to describe it as a thing, it would be like a fresh balloon morphing into a three-day-old half-deflated bag of air.

Okay. Cool. It was great to meet you too [*sarcasm*].

The balloon is popped. End of conversation.

We find out that Jacob is being charged with two things:
- possession of a knife
- grievous bodily harm with intent

We listen to all of this, nodding our heads, but all I can think about is the one thing that's missing. The thing that renders everything else meaningless without it:
- hate crime

When the police officers leave, it's like the life has been sucked out of the room. Hafsa and Sumaya skip back in, excited to get back to where they left off with Hussein, but they quickly notice that the vibe in the room is very different. That the Hussein they left isn't the same as the Hussein in front of them.

They entertain themselves instead, flicking through the TV channels at a dizzying speed, trying to find something to pique their interest.

Hussein stares out the window for a long time afterwards. His mango yoghurt lies in front of him untouched. When he notices Sumaya eyeing it for the fifth time since entering the room, he gives it to her without putting up a fight.

Hooyo and Abooto share a long look. They're right to. Hussein sharing his yoghurt with anyone isn't a miracle, it's frightening.

I move out of my chair and go to sit next to him on the bed. He shifts to make space for me, and I lie down next to him, staring out the same window. The view is a snapshot of sky and clouds that looks almost identical to the one I used to stare at from my own hospital room too.

"Why you so vexed, bro?" I ask, bumping him lightly before dropping my voice down to a whisper. "You know your face has more creases than Abooto's does right now."

Hussein smiles begrudgingly, remembering those same words he once said to me. "You got real jokes, don't you?"

"Always," I grin.

He shakes his head. "I just can't get my head around it, Hanan. I've been trying to figure it out, but I can't. Some guy tries to kill me because I'm Muslim and they're saying it's not hate… I mean, what the hell is it supposed to be then?"

I take his arm and loop it through mine, leaning my head on his shoulder.

"I know."

"I hate it," he says.

"I know."

"I really, really hate it." He wipes his eyes with the back of his free hand.

"I know," I whisper. "I really, really hate it too."

CHAPTER THIRTY-THREE

I'm in the middle of changing my sheets at home the next day when my phone rings.

It's Andrea.

She launches in, not bothering with niceties. "Hanan, I've given you space, right? Haven't I been a good friend and given you a decent amount of space? Roomy and nice and *spacey* space?"

I sit down on the naked mattress, trying to figure out and get ahead of whatever she's about to say.

"Um, sure. I mean physically, yeah, there's a lot of space between us. Probably like two-point-four miles if I had to be specific—"

"No! Don't be smart with me, I'm being serious."

"Okay, but honestly, I have no idea what you're being serious about. You're being so cryptic right now."

"Am I?" she says, genuinely surprised. She sighs. "Look, that's my bad. Guess we're not on the same page then. But honestly? That's kind of what I'm worried about."

Andrea takes my silence as an invitation to carry on, which is good, because I'm still very confused.

"Have you even been thinking about school and everything you're missing? This is our *final* year, Hanan. It's not a joke. Do you just not care about uni any more?"

Andrea doesn't sound judgemental, but I feel defensive for some reason. It's not like I could have thought about something as trivial as school with Hussein at death's door or spent time thinking about *my* own future when I didn't even know whether my brother would make it through the night. I couldn't have done any of those things, because the fear of losing Hussein was a paralysing, all-encompassing thing that felt like it almost swallowed me whole at times.

The future was paused when Hussein was hurt. There was no past either, only the present. I'd even thrown away the calendar on my wall without hesitation. Seeing it up there, with my test day circled in black ink, felt like a reminder of a different life. One that didn't feel like my own any more.

What's the point in trying to do anything, trying to *be* anything, if at the end of the day, I'll still be pushed down for who I am and what I believe in? If people like Jacob are still going to be able to do what they want and not get called out for it the way they should be? What's the point in trying at life if life just doesn't make sense?

I look up to my father's degree framed on the wall, and the empty space next to it. The space meant for me.

"King's was meant to be our together-dream," Andrea continues. "I'd be the one who'd brag about having such a brainy best friend and you'd parade me around as the creative drama soul that keeps you fun."

"I'm going to take that to mean you don't think I'm fun."

"Queen of deflection, huh? Nice try, but no," she replies. "Time's running out, Hanan. You can't be stuck in this out-of-school limbo for ever."

"I know…" I sigh. And I really do. Hooyo had broached the topic a few times already, but I'd shut it down as quickly as I could. Mr Davies had given up with calling the house phone as well. All he sent now were emails. I don't mention any of this to Andrea and I don't mention the emails from the exam centre either. The exam that's meant to be tomorrow and meant to have my name and ID number written all over it.

"I'm working on it, Andrea. I really am. It's just…it's hard. I don't have the energy, I don't care the way I used to, and I don't know how to get it back."

"You don't have to know," she says softly. "The hard part is knowing. The easy part is doing. So…just do. Come back to school."

"I'll promise to think about it. How's that?"

It's a weak answer, and probably a lie, but it's the best I can do right now. Thankfully, Andrea doesn't push it more.

"Fine," she says. I can hear her pout over the phone. "Guess I'll speak to you later—"

"No, wait. Hold up."

"Oh my God, please tell me you changed your mind!" Andrea screams so loudly that I have to move the phone away from my ear.

"No," I laugh. "I just wanted to see if you were down for a movie night?"

"Yeah, sure," Andrea says, layering the disappointment in her voice. I pretend not to hear it. "But I'm not watching any of those trash comedies you love so much. Sorry. I'm flexible, but I'm not that flexible."

I cross my legs on the bed, bracing myself for impact. "Actually, I was thinking maybe something a little more…vampire-y?"

Unfortunately, no amount of bracing is enough to prepare myself for the scream that follows.

The conversation with Andrea finds its way into the hospital the next day. Although, *find* probably isn't the best word. More like…is knowingly implanted by someone with a very specific endgame.

"How's old Graffy treating you?" Hussein asks, considering his next move in our game of Uno.

We've played this game too many times for it to be fun any more, but Hussein's doctor told us this morning that he'll probably be discharged by next week which means that, thankfully, Uno will be no more.

"Fine," I reply.

He puts a card down.

"You're bad at lying."

"I'm not lying," I say. "It's fine because I'm not there."

He looks up from his cards. "No one likes a smart-arse."

I shrug my shoulders and wait for him to take his turn. He doesn't. I look up to find that Hussein's put all of his cards on the table, facing up.

"Hey! What's wrong with you? I thought we were playing a serious game."

"We are playing a serious game, sis. It's called Being Honest And Not Being A Smart-Arse. Have you heard of that one before?"

"Yes, but I'm not really in the mood to play." I put my cards down too and stand up from the bed.

Although no one else knows, today's exam day. I'd hoped I could ride out the day here with Hussein and chill, take my mind off the fact that I'm not sitting it; that the test I've been preparing months for, that the dreams I've been holding for years, are disappearing today, right in front of my eyes, because I'm too scared to do anything about it but, clearly, Hussein doesn't want to give me peace today.

I turn to Hooyo.

"Hooyo, I'm going home. I'll take the bus back, don't worry."

Hooyo looks up from her phone and, for some reason, both she and Hussein share a nervous glance. Why are they looking at each other?

"No," she protests, standing up. She looks around for her bag. "I'll drop you home and come back to the hospital later."

"Hooyo, honestly, it's really fine, I don't mind—"

She puts a hand up to stop me and I know there's no point saying more. Maybe she's still nervous to let me go out by myself. To be fair, I haven't wanted to go anywhere by myself since that night anyway.

Hussein gives me a serious look as I put my coat on.

317

"You know running isn't the answer, right? Things will catch up to you eventually."

"Ha," I laugh. "When did you start trying to be all philosophical?"

I'm expecting a sarcastic answer because that's what we do. Sarcasm, back and forth, the kind of verbal tennis match that only siblings understand, twins even more. But that's not what I get this time.

"Since Hooyo and Andrea told me my sister's trying to throw her life away." He moves a playing card around in circles as he stares me down. "Since I heard you stopped giving a shit about school, about uni."

I look to Hooyo, expecting her to tell him off for swearing but she doesn't say anything. Seems like it's two against one then. Well, three against one, if I'm including Andrea.

I walk to the door, wanting to leave as quickly as possible, wanting to avoid being questioned over something I don't want to talk about, that I'm not *ready* to talk about, but when I push down on the handle, I turn around to say one last thing. The reasonable part of my brain screams at me to stop, to understand that my family, my friends, are coming from a place of love – true, unconditional, wholesome love – but the other part of my brain wins. The part that screams *betrayal* at me.

"I'm not going to take advice from someone who *actually* threw their life away and almost became a drug dealer. Wouldn't be very smart of me, now would it?"

* * *

318

The car ride home is quiet. Worse than quiet even, because quiet suggests neutrality. The words I threw at Hussein hang between us in the silence. Hooyo doesn't say anything. Maybe she thinks that the silence is punishment enough, but it isn't. I deserve to be berated and scolded and rebuked. Everything and anything that can pierce this silence and put me back in my place.

I'm struggling to process that I actually said those things to Hussein. That I'd flung dirt at him without batting an eyelid. I hadn't even apologized, just walked out of the room, gone downstairs to the car park and waited for Hooyo to join me.

There's a sick feeling now in my stomach. I look for some chewing gum in the glovebox but there's none there. I open my bag and rummage for my water bottle but when I pull it out, I find it's empty. I crank the window down a fraction, wanting to let the sound of circulating air accompany this silence.

After ten minutes or so, we're still driving.

That's weird, I think. We should've been home by now. We're on a dual carriageway but it's not one I recognize.

I want to ask Hooyo what's going on, but at the same time I don't. The last words that left my mouth have left a bitter taste. But, after another ten minutes, curiosity wins over.

"Where are we going?"

Nothing.

I ask again in case Hooyo didn't catch me over the sound of the engine.

"Hooyo, where we going?"

Nothing.

I turn my head to look at her. Her mouth is set in determination. I know she's heard me.

We continue driving for maybe another ten minutes before Hooyo takes a left. She drives through an area we've never been to before. Or one that I've never been to anyway. She slows down and parks outside a big, grey building. She turns the engine off, removes her seat belt and twists around in the seat to face me. I brace myself. She's probably driven me all the way out here to tell me off so badly that she doesn't want any witnesses.

"You have your exam in one hour," she says to me. "You can either wait here in the car with me or wait inside until it starts."

My eyes nearly pop out of their sockets. She grabs her bag from under the seat and hands me a paper wallet from inside. The label on there – *Hanan Ali* – tells me everything I need to know.

"Everything you need is there. Andrea put it together. Your ID card and pens and exam letter."

I look through it, pulling everything out one by one so they're lying across my lap.

"How did you know?" I ask, touching the items cautiously, as if they might catch fire. "That it was today."

"The school sent a letter a week ago. It was addressed to you, and I opened it." Hooyo looks out at the industrial landscape on her side of the road. "We don't keep secrets in this family, Hanan. Secrets are like poison. Except they take longer to kill you."

Hooyo unlocks the car doors. For a second, I imagine

getting out and running away. Not going into the exam centre but bolting past it and running back the way we came, towards the dual carriageway. Trying to flag down a car and attempt to hitch-hike. Maybe finding myself somewhere random, away from everything.

Because I'm not ready for any of this. I don't think I'm ready to walk back and press play on life again. Maybe I could be, if I could just see what was coming. If there was a skip-forward button that would let me jump ahead a little and get a glimpse of what's to come.

"We don't run away from things in this family. We face them head-on and we put our trust in Allah."

I pick up a pen, turning it over in my hands. The familiar anxiety that has befriended me for so long settles in my throat, almost closing it up completely.

"But what if I fail?" I whisper. "What if all of this trying and putting up with everything at school for all these years…was all for nothing?" My voice starts to shake. "What if I fail at the one thing we came here for? What if…what if Aabo died for nothing?"

I hear Hooyo's sharp intake of breath. Her hand reaches across to hold mine and the pen falls from my grip.

"Your father and I left for a better life, Hanan. A life away from the danger in Mogadishu. A life where we could all live in peace, so don't you ever," she says, with a vibrating anger, "ever, for even a second, think that you'll disappoint anyone. You are alive and that is enough. And that's all Aabo ever wanted for you, for all of you."

I nod, holding onto the conviction in her voice and letting that settle the worries fluttering inside of me.

She pulls at my hand. "You want to wait in the car then?"

"Yeah. I'll wait here."

"Good," she says.

The silence that follows then is quiet, and no longer tense. I watch the clock count down the minutes to the start of the exam and try to ignore the roiling of my stomach. I don't remember the last time I studied for this test but now, I'm supposed to go in there and give the best performance of my life.

"I think I should go," I say, looking at the clock, "and get registered."

"Okay. Good luck, macaanto," Hooyo says, pulling me in for a hug. "Say Bismillah before you start and remember that you can do this. You've worked so hard, and I know you'll succeed, whatever happens."

As I get out, the instinct to bolt floats up again but, when I look back to the car and see Hooyo waving at me, it disappears. I walk into the big, grey building.

I turn with the world and not against it.

CHAPTER THIRTY-FOUR

Sitting the exam felt like a huge weight had been lifted off my shoulders – good, but not in the way I expected. There was no instant relief or brief hysterical joy. There was just emptiness and a sense of not knowing what comes next, because the road map I once followed, the compass that was leading me to where I thought I wanted to go…disappeared. For a few short minutes after the exam ended, before we were ushered outside, I felt like Alice falling down the rabbit hole. There was a flurry of chaos all around, but me? I felt lost. Unsure of where I was going. Unsure of everything I'd been so certain of for most of my life.

I've tried my best to avoid thinking about the exam since then. To avoid that rabbit hole, to stop plotting and thinking and losing myself in a future that no one can see or predict anyway, and I think I've done a decent job of it so far. Because, if the last few weeks have taught me anything, it's that life is unpredictable and my new mantra, after a bit of tweaking, is this: The future is the future. Whatever it looks like. And I'm now at peace with that. Plus, it hasn't hurt that I've had plenty of other things to be preoccupied with anyway – like getting ready to bring Hussein home.

"You're clutching that book like a lifeline," Hooyo remarks as she packs away Hussein's things in his hospital room, making use of the time he's spending getting ready in the toilet. "Are you sure you want to do this?"

I look down at my fingers curling around the spine of the black notebook. The notebook that Andrea gave me and whose pages I thought would for ever remain empty. I put it aside and stand to help clear up. The holdall bag fills quickly, and I wonder whether it might've been smart to bring a second. Hussein's comfortably amassed a lot of things while in hospital, but these things will all need to leave with us today.

"I have to. I made a promise to Mr Davies."

Hooyo busies herself with untangling the impressive collection of charging cables near the wall. She disappears as she bends down to tackle it and her voice sounds a little further away when she speaks. "I hope you know you don't owe that man anything. If you're doing this, do it for yourself. Not for him."

I put down the empty plastic yoghurt cup I'm about to throw away. "Can I ask you a question, Hooyo?"

She grunts as she stands back up, holding four separate cables triumphantly in her hands. "Of course, macaanto."

"You know how you always said af daboolan dahab waaye? Like, if something happened when we were younger and me and Hussein were fighting, you'd say that. To try and get us to stop?"

Hooyo nods. "I'm sure I remember an entire week when you two were twelve years old and that maah-maah were the only words that left my mouth."

I smile awkwardly, remembering that week vividly. It had not been a good time for Hooyo. Hussein and I had been at each other's throats on a bad level.

"Do you think that's always true? Because I'm starting to think…" I shake my head and look up at the ceiling, searching for answers to a question I don't know how to ask. "I'm starting to think that it's not true. At least, that it's not true all the time. I think sometimes there's gold in opening your mouth."

"Ahhh." Hooyo sits down on Hussein's empty bed, pulling the holdall bag over and putting the cables away carefully, tangle-free. "I think I understand what this is about." Her eyes flick over to the notebook on the chair. "Are you worried about what to say in front of all those people?"

"I'm not worried about what to say," I sigh. "I know what to say. I'm just not sure I should say it."

Hooyo nods, still staring at the notebook, as if she can see through its leather to the words that I've marked on the page.

"There are a million maah-maahyo out there, Hanan, and they're not all the same." Hooyo looks at me and smiles. "When I said those things to you growing up, it was because a closed mouth *is* gold when it comes to petty things. Especially when it comes to two stubborn children. But I don't want you to believe that's a rule of life – that it's better to stay silent than to speak at all." Hooyo looks at the notebook again. "I don't want you to be scared to be honest with these people or with yourself."

I go over to the chair and pick it up. "I'm not scared," I say, turning it over and appreciating for the first time that *yes,*

I'm not actually scared. "I just…don't know how these people will take it."

"People will take it how they want to take it, macaanto. That's out of your hands. They may accept you, they may reject you, but that's up to them." Hooyo zips up the bursting holdall bag. "Shall I teach you another maah-maah? This one is probably better for you to understand."

"Sure."

"Dhagax dhunkoo, ama dharbaax, waa isugu mid."

It takes me a few moments to translate the saying in my head before I can confirm that I actually understand it.

"Kiss a stone or slap a stone…it's still the same? Okay, I think that's the weirdest one I've ever heard, Hooyo."

Hooyo laughs. A big, warm, carefree laugh that I haven't heard in a long time.

"It's the English that does a bad job of capturing the meaning. It means that a stone will always be a stone: a kiss or a slap changes nothing."

"You're going to have to connect the dots for me here."

The smile on Hooyo's face stretches as she keeps herself from laughing again. "I'm saying that you can kiss these people, as you have done for all these years, or you can slap them, and it may not change anything. I'm saying that a stone will always be a stone. These people may never understand you and may never change, but it doesn't mean you should stop yourself from being honest."

I nod, finally understanding and, in my mind's eye, I see the stones of my life: Mr Foster, Mr Davies, Daniel, Jacob, Jessica.

Okay, maybe not Jessica, not any more.

Hussein comes out of the toilet. He leans against the door frame, looking thinner and frailer than he's ever looked before. He's dressed in his regular clothes, not the flashy ones I last saw him in.

"You guys ready to bounce?"

"Yep. Are you sure you're up to coming to the school though?"

He scoffs, walking slowly over to the bed. "I was born ready, sis, so that's kind of a stupid question."

I smile at him, grateful that we're now back in the normal swing of things. Hussein isn't one to hold grudges. He'd let me off the hook quite quickly when I'd come to apologize.

"Alright then," I say, gripping the spine of my notebook. "Let's get this show on the road."

The Great Hall at Grafton Grammar looms ahead of us, tall and foreboding. Near the entrance is a blackboard with a sign for the parent–governor meeting and an arrow pointing towards the double doors. A few parents are milling about the entrance. They laugh in their clusters, happy, unbothered. Not a care in the world. For them, this meeting will be just another insignificant thing on their schedules.

"I know you asked me if I was okay before…but are you sure *you're* okay to do this?" Hussein asks me, eyeing the school warily. This is the first time he's seen beyond the gates of Grafton Grammar and it's nothing like his own college.

"This place is…intense. I feel bait here, I can't lie."

"Story of my life," I sigh, looking up at the roof of the Great Hall. The school flag whips wildly in the wind. "But yeah, I'm sure. Let's go in."

Hooyo smiles at me in encouragement. She grips Hussein's arm tighter to support him. The three of us make our way through the double doors, and through the foyer of the Great Hall.

I spot Mr Davies in the centre of it all. He sees me at the same time and smiles widely, excusing himself from his company and walking over to greet us. I catch myself staring at the man who's standing next to Mr Davies. Something about him feels very familiar.

"Hanan, it's so wonderful to see you're doing better!" Mr Davies says. He turns his attention to my family. "It's great to meet you again, mum, and…" He squints. "You must be Hanan's brother?"

Hussein's mouth twitches. He extends a hand in greeting.

"Yes, that's me. Hanan's brother and survivor of knife crime." As the red begins to creep into Mr Davies's face, Hussein adds, "Oh, don't worry, I'm not fussed about that label."

It takes a few moments for Mr Davies to recover but, even then, he still stumbles over his next words. "I'm…yes, I'm of course aware of the recent events and I…I am shocked and appalled and disgusted at what you've had to go through, particularly at the hands of someone from this school. We're all incredibly shocked here at Grafton."

"Naturally," Hussein says, with an air of manufactured grace

328

that makes Mr Davies squirm. "But thank you for the kindness you've shown me, and my family, in such trying times. Hanan really is quite lucky to have someone like you leading such a brilliant school. Marvellous, really. It's all very marvellous."

Mr Davies smiles hesitatingly. "Well, that's very kind of you. Thank you." He turns around, looking for a quick escape. "I'll just finish doing the rounds and start getting everyone inside soon. Hanan, I'll introduce you first and then get you to come onto the stage. Then you can say a few things about yourself and your experience at the school. Hopefully after that…well, we'll see how the vote goes on the Integration proposal."

His smile is a little strained as he says goodbye, and then he's gone.

I swat Hussein on the arm. "What's your problem? Stop sounding so uppity."

"What?" he says defensively, leaning forward on his crutch. "This is what you sound like when you're around these people. I'm just trying to blend in."

"Hanan!" It's Andrea's voice but it takes a second to locate her in the foyer that's quickly filling up. "Over here!"

I turn around and see her snaking her way through the crowd on my left. Her mum and dad follow behind.

"Phew," she breathes, when she reaches us. Our parents naturally gravitate towards each other, leaving the three of us standing in an arc.

"There are loads of people here," she says. "Way more than I expected."

"Guess people are very passionate about an Integration

Policy for twenty students who all happen to be Muslim," I reply drily.

Andrea laughs. "Good joke. Keep that one for when you start your comedy set in a few minutes." She turns to Hussein. "Hey, Hussein. How you doing? Feeling better?"

He shrugs. "I'm doing alright. To be honest though, I'm more nervous about seeing one of your other friends." He looks to me, trying to remember. "Hanan, you know that one. The one you say is always—"

"Guys!"

It's Lily. Hussein looks to me, eyes wide. *It's her*, he mouths. *The obsessed one.*

She sidles up to us, Nasra and Isha following quickly behind.

"We've dumped our parents on the other side of the Hall," Isha says, by way of greeting. "Just thought we'd come to say hi and good luck."

"You guys are cute but I'm not nervous, honestly. I'm actually feeling…calm, I think."

"That's good…" Lily trails off. Her eyes shift away from me. Seems like my time in the spotlight is over. "So, Hussein."

"Hmmm."

"Long time no see," she says. She swaps places with Isha, who stands the closest to him.

"Hmmm." Hussein grips the handle of his crutch more tightly.

"How've you been?" she asks sweetly.

Nasra cuts in. "The boy's been stabbed, how do you think he's been?" She moves across the circle to grab Lily by the arm.

"Come on, let's go before you make the rest of us cringe to death."

Isha smiles at my brother apologetically.

"But, Hussein, if you ever want to grab a coffee, let me—" The rest of Lily's words are cut off as the three of them exit the circle.

Nasra shoots me a look over her shoulder as they make their way back to the other side of the Hall. I nod.

See you up there, I mouth to her.

See you, she mouths back. Then, she disappears into the crowd.

I look at Hussein. Beads of sweat have somehow already formed over his brow. He dabs at it with the corner of his jumper.

"Yeah, that's what I was nervous about."

Just then, Mr Davies begins shepherding everyone into the main hall. His voice carries over the noise and people break off to start heading in.

"Come on," Hooyo says. "Let's go and get the good seats before they all disappear."

We choose our seats near the front – my family next to Andrea's. Nasra, Lily, Isha and their families sit behind us in the row we've saved for them.

When most people are seated, Mr Davies makes his way to the stage. He lets the other man stand at the podium first and speak – the one who he'd been standing next to when we first walked in.

That's when it clicks.

He'd looked familiar, although I couldn't figure out why. But now I know who it is, because the answers are there in his features; in the grey of his eyes, which I can see so clearly from where I sit, and the sharpness of his face.

It's Jessica and Daniel's father. He must be a school governor.

"Thank you all for attending Grafton Grammar's parent–governor meeting. As you know from recent communications, we're here to discuss the issue of implementing a policy for integrating students who may be finding that process difficult here at Grafton for whatever reason."

Though he's sugar-coating his words, it's clear what Mr Roberts means and who he's really talking about. I can feel the heaviness of people's looks on my back. Not just on me, but on my family too.

"Recent events have concerned most of us, I'm sure, so this evening is really just to air those concerns and discuss best steps moving forward. Our aim is, and always has been, to protect the welfare of our students here at Grafton Grammar. With that, I'll hand over to Mr Davies now, our head teacher."

Mr Davies thanks him and steps forward to the podium. He clears his throat and pulls on his tie nervously. He introduces me and, somehow, doesn't collapse under the weight of Mr Roberts's glare.

"…one of our star pupils, who has been a tremendous student since her admission six years ago. Hanan is a prospective medical student…"

He goes on like this, listing my achievements and accolades, parading me to these people as though I'm proof of their success and, when Mr Davies is done, he invites me to the stage.

Hooyo squeezes my hand. I stand up, gripping the notebook, and walk towards the stairs that will lead me to the stage. My friends and family whisper words of encouragement and, as those words reach me, I feel steadier with each step.

I walk right past Mr Roberts without acknowledging him and stand at the vacated podium. I put the notebook down, open on the sixth page. The first few pages of writing had been an experiment almost, but it was really the sixth page and beyond that carried the words I wanted to say. That captured everything perfectly. It's those words that I stare at now, in front of the people who love me and the people who hate me, all in the same audience.

"I have thought about what I wanted to say for a long time," I begin, keeping my voice steady. "I was hesitant to speak, at first, when Mr Davies asked me to do this. That might sound cowardly to you, but I don't think it's easy for anyone to speak for a whole group of people. In fact, I don't think it's right to speak for a whole group of people, to speak for all the Muslims at Grafton Grammar, so I'm not going to do that. I'm just going to speak for me."

I can feel the tension in the air, taut and unyielding. Mr Davies coughs and I hear him shuffle uncomfortably on his feet behind me. Perhaps he senses that this won't be going the way he expected.

I'd found it strange, but not surprising, when he didn't mention anything about my life in his introduction. About what I've had to go through in the last two weeks or who was behind it. But the very fact that I'm standing here is a testament to the truth that I tried to pretend wasn't my problem or would one day change. That it's fine when Muslims are the villains but, when they're the victims, no one pays attention. No one cares. Nasra's voice, her words, from what feels like a lifetime ago, ring in my ears again.

The world doesn't give any fucks for you, does it? So why do you keep bending over backwards for it?

"I know what I'm expected to say," I begin, staring at the words I've long since memorized. "I know I'm expected to tell you about how great I am, how many A*s I have, how lucky I am since this school took a chance on little-refugee-me. I know I'm expected to say all these things at a meeting deciding the future of people like me – people who believe in the same things I do – with the hope that my words change your agendas. I know that I'm meant to be a voice of reason, wrapped up in a headscarf. I know I'm meant to be an exception."

The disgruntled murmurs coalesce, echoing around the room. I look up briefly, even though everything in me is saying not to, and see Ms Williams and Ms Al-Khansaa standing behind the last row of seats. Ms Al-Khansaa stands with both hands clasped under her chin. Ms Williams smiles and gives me a single nod. I breathe in, keeping my hands on the notebook, and continue.

"But the truth is, I'm not an exception. I *can't* be an exception because there is no rule that says people like me can't do well. Or that people like me are inherently evil. There is no rule that can paint a whole group in a single colour, because that would be impossible. That would be prejudiced and bigoted and cruel." My voice cracks on this last word. I quickly clear my throat. There's too much left to be said, and too many eyes watching, for me to fall apart now.

"Still, that's exactly what happened over the weeks since Mr Fleming's death. A death that was painful and unexpected and one that will hang over Grafton Grammar for a long time. A death that was caused by another man, another human, because he was a criminal, not because he was Muslim."

I look back down at the words in front of me and close my eyes for a brief moment. When I open them again, the ink is smudged in the corner.

"Yet it was this tragic death that has led me to be standing here today to discuss a policy on achieving integration. But what does integration even mean? To me, it sounds like something fancy people say when it really means trying to make everyone the same. But isn't that a disservice to our diversity? If we try to make everyone the same, are we saying there's no room for any difference in the world? And if we continue to fear the things we don't understand, can there ever be space for growth and humanity?"

I look down and see Hooyo and Hussein. Hooyo grips Hussein tightly. I can read her nerves from here but, strangely, her nerves don't add to mine. They help to steady me. I look to their right and see a bright light where Andrea's face should be. The light that means she's recording the words I'm letting loose, on my own terms.

"The reality is some people are only willing to accept a certain amount of difference. Because too different seems threatening. I *seem* threatening. My faith seems threatening when, to me, it's the complete opposite. To me, it's freeing. To me it's light. It's beauty and joy. To me, it's my truth. And it's the truth of my being that my school is hoping to strip away from me with this policy. A policy that's born out of a misinformed fear and a fear that can have terrible consequences for anyone who chooses to be different."

There's a scuffle on the stage where Mr Davies and Mr Roberts are standing, near the wings. Mr Roberts leans back from whispering in Mr Davies's ear, a furious expression on his face. I can't tell what they're saying from the podium, but I can tell Mr Davies is reluctant to do whatever Mr Roberts wants him to.

My hands start to shake, and I grip the notebook harder. I can feel the sweat beginning to drench my hijab.

They're going to kick me off, is all I can think before I see Ms Williams and Ms Al-Khansaa emerge from the wings to join Mr Davies and Mr Roberts. After a few seconds, Mr Roberts storms off, thundering down the steps. Mr Davies takes out a pocket square and dabs it across his forehead.

I breathe a sigh of relief and turn back to the audience.

"And I've already had to face a lot of the consequences of that fear. Consequences that have for ever changed mine and my family's lives. Ones that people would rather not hear about, because who'd want to hear that the hate from this school put me in hospital? Or nearly killed my brother? Who'd want to hear that the prejudice and bigotry that would be reinforced by this policy has very real and ugly consequences and can leave deep scars?"

Someone shifts in the periphery of my vision. It's Hussein. The crutch he's been holding has fallen from his grip, clattering to the floor. He stares down at it.

"I've carried a lot of pain with me these few weeks, my family too, and especially my brother, since we survived what happened. But, even then, I somehow still had a job to do... to prove something to you all. I couldn't understand why, for a long time, but I understand it better now. I understand that I don't owe anything to any of you."

I close the notebook, fingers curling around the leather spine, and look at the faces of the people I love floating beneath me. The people who will love and accept me without me having to prove myself.

"I may be many things, but I can promise you that one thing I will never be is your good Muslim. The fact is my being doesn't belong to any of you." I take a deep breath before I say the next part, careful to glance at Jessica. "And you don't have to like me, but you do have to live alongside me, because we're in this world together, whether you like it or not."

I catch Nasra's eye when I say this and nod. She makes her way up to the stage, with the kind of flair that only she has, and stands next to me. She covers the microphone and leans in to whisper.

"Are you sure about this?" she asks, eyebrows arched and uncertainty in her eyes. "I don't want you to get in trouble or anything."

Someone from the audience shouts. I'm not sure who it is at first until I squint. It's Sophie's dad. I recognize him from the memorial.

"Can someone get these two off the stage?" he roars. "This is absolutely ridiculous! I don't know what this is but I refuse to sit here and listen to it." Sophie tugs on her dad's arm, but he pulls away from her. "No! I'm not having this. You two get off now and—"

Nasra taps the microphone. The shrill feedback is enough to stop Sophie's dad for a moment.

"Excuse me, sir," Nasra says calmly. "You're making quite a scene. If you could please sit down and let the rest of this meeting continue in a more dignified fashion, that would be great."

Nasra covers the microphone again as Sophie's dad splutters. No one else comes to his rescue, miraculously, and when he realizes that, he reluctantly sits back down.

"That's about all the refined I can manage for now," she whispers to me.

I shake my head. "Refined is just a bunch of crap," I say, squeezing her hand. "And, yes, I'm sure about this."

Nasra smiles.

She turns back and clears her throat. "Good afternoon, everyone. My name's Nasra and I'm also a Year Thirteen student here at Grafton. I'm here today because Hanan's invited me to say a few words about this policy you'll all be voting on. She's pretty much said it all, but I have a couple more thoughts I'd like to share."

Unlike me, Nasra doesn't have anything written down. She stares ahead at the audience – at the people who stare daggers at her and at the people who smile at her – certain and unafraid.

"I once told a friend a pretty basic piece of advice. It wasn't true, but it was the only thing I could think to say at the time because I felt hopeless and angry and confused. I told my friend that the world doesn't give any fucks for you. That it was better to stop being flexible for everyone else and do your own thing."

Nasra pauses here as the murmurs from the audience reach us. She glances at me and smiles knowingly.

"And while I think there's some truth to that, I also think it's a little more complicated than I first made it out to be. Yes, maybe it seems that the world doesn't care, but I've come to realize there's much more to the world than what we see at first glance. So much kindness and compassion and… goodness. I think Grafton Grammar could be one of those places, with a bit of work, and so my advice to my friend would be to never give up hope in the goodness of people. To never lose hope in what they could be and not to feel lost because of what they are." She glances at me again, briefly, but my eyes aren't on her. They are on my blurred feet.

"I would tell my friend that she doesn't need to prove anything to anyone, except herself, but to hold out hope that one day people will stop expecting her to be perfect. That they'll stop expecting her to be what they want her to be, instead of what she is."

Nasra's words sit heavy in the silence. They weigh the air

down and weigh the murmurs, so they no longer reach us. But there's a lightness around us too. There is optimism and dreams and faith. There is wishing and conviction and promise.

There is possibility. I can feel it.

Nasra leans into the microphone and waves her hand. "Also, on a final note, in case this isn't already obvious, this policy you're all voting on is *hella* racist. It's not the greatest look for Grafton, unless racist-oppressive-bigotry is the look you're going for, in which case, you governors have hit the nail on the head. That's just me saying it in black and white in case anyone has been tone-deaf the last ten minutes." She crosses her arms. "Now, I'm not sure who came up with the idea for this or who backed it, but I'd recommend firing said person. Or people," she adds.

She says this with such authority that I almost forget she's a student at this school.

"Thank you," she says, with a note of finality, moving to step off the podium. "That is all."

We swap over.

When I stand at the podium again, my eyes find Hooyo's. Her nerves seem to be gone now, replaced by a fierce pride that sets her back straight and a love that makes her eyes glassy. She smiles at me and, in that smile, I see the joy of both my parents. A smile that is so wide and feels so endless that I almost feel like she's smiling for Aabo too.

Hearing Nasra say all those things, I can't help but remember my dad's words too, his wisdom imprinted on loops of tape. His steady voice in my ear, as if he's right next to me.

I take a steadying breath before I speak about the man I never imagined I'd invoke in this school, in the presence of people who have tried to push me down for too long.

"A great man once told me I would reach a point in life where I'd see the world for what it truly is: in all of its glory and beauty, but in all of its ugliness and evil as well. And he was right. But, like Nasra, I hope we can make Grafton Grammar a place of more beauty than ugliness. A place where we can all be ourselves, without making each other smaller."

I smile back at Hooyo's joyous face. "That great man, my late father, also told me to shake the world with my brilliance. To show everyone what I'm capable of and to never hold back. I intend to do just that and make him proud."

I've been so exhausted for so long, trying to bend and fit myself into a mould that hurt me more than it helped me but, as I stand on this stage and under this skylight, I find myself determined to exist in this world freely, the way I want to, the way I'm *meant* to. To be me and own my truth with open arms and focus on the glory and beauty and goodness that exists in this world.

Because it *does* exist, even if it's evaded me for so long.

"Right," I say, into the microphone. Steady voice. I look down quickly. Steady hands. "Any questions?"

Unsurprisingly, there is dead silence when I ask this. I look over to Mr Davies to see if he wants to take charge of the stage again, but he looks a little lost standing there. He's turned a funny shade of purple, his tie almost completely undone.

My eyes scan the back of the audience, who sit frozen in

their seats, faces painted with either looks of horror or pity...
except for one.

Jessica sits between her brother and a woman I assume is
her mum. She smiles at me. It's a lonely smile. A single smile
between the grimaces of her family. I smile back. Not quite a
friendship, but a truce.

My eyes land on Hooyo, Hussein, Andrea, and the rest of
our friends and family, who stand side by side now, clapping
and cheering for us, the loudest people in the room.

CHAPTER THIRTY-FIVE

Hooyo cooks up a welcome-back feast when we get home. Aromatic, delicious bariis iyo hilib with a side of banana. My mouth waters just at the smell of it but I resist making any comments about how excited I am to eat. Hooyo will probably rope me into chopping or frying something if she hears anything from me.

The evening rolls around quickly and we all sit together in the living room, quietly enjoying the feeling of everyone together again.

Abooto breaks the comfortable silence after a while, halting her rhythmic bead counting. "I have a story to tell," she says, injecting a little mystery into her words. "If anyone wants to hear it."

Our grandmother has always been a master storyteller, believing in the gift of the Somali people to bring stories to life. She says ours is a culture moulded by spoken histories and tales, and that the richness of our oral tradition needs to be kept alive. She always makes it sound so poetic, as if tradition has a beating heart that needs to be nurtured across time and place, across centuries and across the globe, where our people are scattered.

"It's a story I haven't thought about for a long time. One about your father."

We all perk up when we hear that, including Hooyo. When Abooto tells a story about Aabo, it's a story unmatched and often one none of us know. So, it feels like magic every time we hear one, like we're discovering another fragment of him, one we didn't even know existed.

Abooto closes her eyes. When she opens them again, I sense some of her is lost to the past.

"When your father was born, we already knew he was something special. We just knew, your grandfather and me, deep in our bones and…we were right. Your father grew to be kind and generous and compassionate," Abooto says, her eyes becoming unfocused as she pulls on the tendrils of her memories.

"Now I'm not sure, even to this day, where he got it from, because it certainly didn't come from his own father and neither did it come from me. But it was something he had, and it was something special. People would always come up to me and say, 'Hawa, how did you birth this child?' or 'Hawa, how did you raise this child?' 'This child did not come from you,' they would say. 'This child came from something greater.' But I was never insulted when I heard them say that because how could I be? Your father did come from something greater; he came from the will of Allah."

Abooto pauses, perhaps to recall the story or maybe just

to help the mystery further along. Either way, it works. I lean forward, instinctively.

"It was a kindness that I always worried would be his undoing. I was worried he'd be abused or walked over or that people would think he couldn't hold his own. Every day, I breathed a sigh of relief when he came home, safe and untouched by the cruelty of this world. I only stopped holding my breath when he married your mother," Abooto says. She smiles at Hooyo. "Because I knew she would protect him from the world if she had to."

Hooyo discreetly wipes a tear away from her face as she continues to listen intently, re-imagining the man who she loved and continues to love.

"But there had been a day when he came back home, and I could see that the cruelty of the world had touched him. I was beside myself, wondering what had happened but he refused to tell me until I calmed down, saying that the hysteria was making me unbalanced. Imagine that! Calling his own mother unbalanced," Abooto says with a chuckle. "So, instead, I just tended to his wounds, washing away the blood and bandaging the deep cuts, and when I calmed down, he told me what had happened."

I can tell that Abooto's already lost Hafsa and Sumaya. They can only do Somali in small doses and this story is clearly too much for them. They lose themselves in a thumb-war instead.

"He had said that some of the boys in his class at school had been ridiculing him for his kind nature. Calling him names when he helped another student or teacher with this or that.

Or laughing at him in the market when he helped another habaryar with her heavy shopping. Until one day, that same day, they stopped doing all of that and instead they decided to see what Ibrahim Ali was made of. They wanted to see if he was made of flesh and bone, if he was man, or if he was something else entirely. So, they beat him up by a quiet road outside of school. There were two of them, Ibrahim told me, and they each took turns. Each time they landed a blow they'd look at him curiously because although he blocked off their advances, he didn't strike at them. And they became more enraged the more he refused to fight them and at this point, I myself was enraged, worried that I'd raised a boy who would allow himself to be pummelled to death." Abooto shakes her head and sighs.

"But Ibrahim...he told me something extraordinary then. He said one of them heard a popping in their shoulder as they prepared to land another blow, and that he fell, hard, brought to his knees because of the pain. His other friend rushed to him, forgetting about your father and only remembering why they were there when Ibrahim approached them. They jumped, of course, out of fear that their vulnerability now gave him an edge. Yet, instead of hurting them like they expected, your father just told the boy to lie down and then popped his shoulder back into place for him. They couldn't believe that someone they hurt was now helping them and, in that dusty street, both boys cried, begging for your father's forgiveness and he gave it to them," Abooto says, her face dominated by a mother's pride.

"It was after hearing that story that I truly understood what a man your father really was. It was then...it was then that I truly understood that cruelness will never triumph over kindness, although kindness may take a pummelling first."

Abooto looks pointedly at Hussein and me when she finishes the story, but I can't hold her scrutinizing gaze for long. I look away.

Although I'd known Aabo was a lot of things, I'd never known the extent of his kindness to be so vast, to extend to everyone and everything. It makes me think about the hate I feel unfurling in my own belly when I think of Jacob. I want nothing more than to extinguish it, but I know I can't do it the way my dad did. I don't know how to be that kind in the face of viciousness. But maybe there's something else I can take from this story.

Aabo had chosen to be that way with so much facing against him. He'd *chosen*. And, hearing this story now, it reminds me again of how powerful choice is and can be. When it's in your own hands, not in the hands of someone refusing to give it to you. And it reminds me again of that feeling on the stage in the Great Hall when everyone was looking at me and I *chose* to speak the truth that I'd spent six years letting people deny. When I chose to stop running from what would make other people uncomfortable because I thought it would make for an easy life.

We all sit quietly for a long time, each of us holding onto this new part of Aabo. When Sumaya begins to doze off next to me, Hooyo stands up, ushering the girls to bed. I offer to help Hussein get upstairs, an offer he graciously accepts. It takes us a couple of minutes and, by the time we reach the landing, Hussein's forehead is plastered in sweat. I help him get into bed and it takes all of a minute for him to sleep. His light snoring follows me as I cross the hallway to my own room.

It feels weird walking back into my room. Physically, it's still the same. The same recently changed bed sheets, the same stacked folders on my desk and clothes strewn haphazardly over the floor – a consequence of my morning rush to find a suitable "hospital discharge" and "school speech" outfit, all in one. But…it's the world that's different. I'm no longer in the same world, the one that existed the last time I lay in my bed. My old life doesn't exist any more and probably will never exist again, because everything has completely shifted. I felt it the moment I closed my notebook and looked out at the faces in the audience, the moment Mr Davies called me Miss Ali, instead of Hanan, the moment people stood up to cast their votes for the policy and the moment Andrea's video of me hit a thousand views online after only a few minutes.

This new world, whatever it'll be, is one that I'll need to navigate differently and, when that dawns on me, I realize what I have to do. I fish for the business card that I tucked in my bag earlier today. Though it only has a few lines, I've already read it countless times: *Samira Ahmed, freelance journalist.* Below that is a list of contact info.

I'd only seen Samira's face for the best part of a minute before she'd disappeared in the Great Hall. She'd walked right up to us, ignoring our confused looks and held the card in her outstretched palm.

"Hanan, Nasra, great speech," she'd said matter-of-factly. "It was fantastic. Gave me goosebumps and everything. I was certain the vote was going to go the other way but you two really knocked it out of the park."

Nasra had stepped forward. "Are you trying to be sarcastic? Because if you are, read the room, lady. There's no place for sarcasm today."

Samira had shaken her head. "No. No sarcasm. It was genuinely fantastic." She indicated the card in her hand again. "I used to be a governor at the school, until all of this," she rolled her eyes, "which is why I'm here today. But I'm also a freelance journalist. I'd love to do a piece on school leadership, student identity, grammar schools…the whole shebang. I think you two would be perfect for it."

I'd looked down at the card. "You want to write about us?"

Samira had smiled. "I'd love to write about the culture of things in places like these and after seeing you today and how you've both managed to kill this proposal? Yes, I think you'd have brilliant perspectives. But there's no pressure. Take the card and think about it. You can drop me a line if you have any questions."

Andrea had swiped the card from Samira's hand. "Thank you. My clients and I will take it under consideration."

I look at the card again now. The idea of doing anything like this would've terrified me before everything happened. To speak to someone about the kind of things I've been hiding away from, pretending didn't exist, would've had me running in the opposite direction. But then I think about Douglas

White. The man who painted with words before he had all the colours of the story. And I think about Mr Roberts, who's so desperate for everyone to fit into a box that he doesn't care about what collapses in the process. And I think about Mr Fleming. My friend, who was my friend despite the oceans of difference between us.

Optimism and dreams and faith, I remind myself.

I write Samira an email. I don't hesitate. I make a prayer and press send.

THE END

GLOSSARY

SOMALI WORDS/PHRASES

Aabo – Father

Abooto – Grandmother

Aboowe – Brother

Adeer – Paternal uncle

Afkaaga xir – Close your mouth

Baati – Cotton house dress with a loose fit
and short sleeves

Bajiyo – Fried snack made from black-eyed peas

Bariis iyo hilib – Rice and lamb

Bur – Fried dough snack

Buskud – Biscuit

Caasi – Disobedient

Cadeey – Light/clear

Ciyaar bilaw – Game played socially

Doolsho – Cake

Garbasaar – Colourful shawl

Ha i ceebeen – Don't embarrass me

Habaryar – Maternal aunt

Haye – Yes

Hikmo – Wisdom

Hooyo – Mother

Ilko boqol – One hundred teeth

Kaalay – Come here

Khaat – Leafy green plant consumed as a stimulant drug

Maah-maah(yo) – Saying(s)

Macaanto – Sweet

Maqaayad – Restaurant

Miskeen – Someone to pity/deserving of empathy

Qalbi furan – Open heart

Sambuus – Samosas

Shaah – Tea

Shaash – Headwrap (f)

Shukaansi – Dating

Suugo – Pasta sauce

Tusbax – Prayer beads

Uunsi – Incense

Xalwo – Popular sweet treat

ARABIC WORDS/PHRASES

Adaab – Islamic etiquette of having good manners and character

Akhirah – Afterlife

Alhamdulilah – Praise be to God

Allah – God

Ameen – Amen

Attar – Fragrances in oil form

Bismillah – In the name of God

Dua – An invocation; an act of supplication

Hijab – A headscarf (f)

In shaa Allah – If God Wills

Jilbab/Abaya – A full length outer garment (f)

Ka'bah – A building at the centre of Islam's most important mosque, in Mecca

Niqab – A veil covering all of the face apart from the eyes (f)

Qadr – Concept of divine destiny in Islam

Qamiis – Ankle length garment (m)

Qur'an – Central religious text of Islam

Surah Ad-Dhuha – Chapter 93 of the Qur'an (The Morning Hours)

Taqiyah – A short, rounded skullcap (m)

Wallahi – I swear by God

Wudhu – A type of ritual purification

Ya Rabbi – My Lord

A NOTE FROM THE AUTHOR

Dear Reader,

When I first started writing the story that eventually, and painstakingly, became *You Think You Know Me,* I really had only one thing in mind and that was getting to *"the end"*. But, as I slowly waded through, other thoughts began to crop up, ones that also vied for attention, aside from the desire and driving force to finally write the two most beloved words to a writer.

There are too many thoughts to name here but there were certainly a few that kept me up at night – ones that I worry about still and likely will for a long time to come.

Would people, knowing what this story is about, give this book a chance?

Would Hanan's story be met warmly, with understanding, with compassion?

And, undoubtedly, the biggest of all, was I doing justice by all those I had hoped to represent with Hanan's identity? Would those people, wherever they were in the world, feel seen?

I hope the answer to at least some of these questions, when you reached *the end*, is the same as I'd hoped.

Writing *You Think You Know Me* has been the biggest

challenge of my life. It has been a labour of love as the first book I have ever written and an experience I will never forget. But the idea for this story did not just come from a single experience or memory or Eureka! moment. It came quietly, over days and weeks and months – almost a whole year, in fact – before I felt compelled to do something with it. And while there are countless unnamed things that led me here, it would be remiss of me not to mention two pivotal moments that tipped the scales: specifically, the tragic deaths of Shukri Abdi, a 12-year-old Somali refugee, and Lee Rigby, a British Army soldier. If you are yet to read their stories, I encourage you to do so.

Like most Muslims in the West, I have never forgotten the first time I experienced Islamophobia. I have been lucky enough to live in diverse cities all my life so I've, thankfully, been protected from more frequent vitriol, but the fear of being abused because of my faith has always been a constant shadow (and more so after "terrorist" incidents in the UK and abroad). I wanted to explore this in *You Think You Know Me*, and also consider how different this experience might be from the point of view of a refugee who has already faced so much in a difficult world.

The representation of Muslim characters in Young Adult books is dire. It's made even more dire when you consider the lack of characters who are visibly Muslim or who actively practise their faith. But I believe it is so *vitally* important that representation of all groups is shown across the spectrum of lived experiences. In *You Think You Know Me*, Hanan wears the hijab, prays, reads the Qur'an – she is actively choosing her faith. It's a beautiful part of her character that I was excited to write and for readers to see and I hope, too, that it proves educational for people who may not know much about Islam.

Another facet of Hanan's identity that I hold close to my heart is the Somali culture. The language, food, clothing, community – it is beautiful and vibrant and loud and wholesome. It is everything that I never read in books growing up but that I hope puts a smile on the face of a young Somali if they happen upon this book.

Much of this story is centred around "issues" – from Islamophobia and institutional racism to gang culture and bullying – but a large portion is also dedicated to Hanan's pursuit of medicine as a career; for herself, her family and to honour her late father's legacy. As a medic myself, I can confidently say that medicine is not for the faint-hearted. While it's a hugely rewarding career, it is also mentally, emotionally, and financially demanding – in ways most people do not expect, or realize, before embarking on this path. It is a career that is often misunderstood and excessively glorified in entertainment.

In *You Think You Know Me*, Hanan is very much set on this career path but she, like all of us, does not know what the future will hold. Maybe Hanan will find herself at university, disillusioned with medicine, and find herself on the path to becoming a scientist or psychologist or teacher instead. Or maybe she will stick with it, and become a doctor, because that is what she is meant to be. Regardless of her choices, always be conscious of yours. Do what you want to do because it's your dream (for the right reasons) and not because it is anyone else's.

If you are beginning to wonder when all of this will begin to wind down, it has. We have reached the anticipated end. Thank you for indulging me and thank you for reading this book. You have my eternal gratitude and I hope, whether or not you enjoyed Hanan's story, that it left you a little differently than when you first picked it up.

With love,
Ayaan

If you want to find out more about the experiences of refugees coming to the UK, or if you or someone you know needs help in this area, you may be interested in the Refugee Council.

The Refugee Council is a leading charity working with refugees and people seeking asylum in the UK. Founded in 1951, following the creation of the UN Refugee Convention, we exist to support and empower people who have been forced to make the heart-breaking decision to flee conflict, violence and persecution in order to rebuild their lives here in the UK.

We work with over 13,000 women, men and children each year who are desperately seeking safety. From the moment refugees arrive in the UK – we are here for them in several important ways:

Our children's services ensure unaccompanied children are able to access their rights as they claim asylum, as well as provide therapeutic counselling, support for victims of trafficking, an age disputes project and a safe space for children to simply be children again;

Our integration services support newly recognized adult refugees who have arrived in the UK outside of formal resettlement programmes. This group often faces disproportionate levels of destitution and homelessness, and so we provide vital crisis and early intervention advice services to ensure they can access their entitlements to welfare;

Our therapeutic services provide extensive specialist and culturally sensitive therapeutic support to adults and children;

And our resettlement services see us working in partnership with local councils to provide life changing support for some of the world's most vulnerable refugees. For at least 12 months we provide refugees with a full package of support, including taking them to their new home, providing personalized support for access to the job market, education and training, healthcare and other mainstream services.

On top of all of this, the Refugee Council campaigns, carries out research and lobbies government to fight for the changes needed to improve the lives of refugees and people seeking asylum in the UK.

For more information about our work, go to
www.refugeecouncil.org.uk
Or follow us on
Twitter @refugeecouncil
Facebook *www.facebook.com/refugeecouncil*
Instagram *www.instagram.com/refugeecouncil*

ACKNOWLEDGEMENTS

This book has been so many things to me over the last several years: incommunicable joy, headache, unsuspecting blessing, sleep-thief, somewhat of a semi-autobiography, my first, my therapist, my debut. But it wouldn't have been anything, first and foremost, without the guidance of Allah. Though it can be difficult, sometimes, to realize when your duas and prayers have manifested, that wasn't the case in writing and publishing this book. Alhamdulillah. I am forever grateful.

To Hooyo, my beautiful, strong, resilient mother, I love you. Thank you for always reassuring me. Thank you for raising me to believe I could achieve anything I could ever want, if that was what was written for me. Thank you for sharing your stories with me, for listening to me, for being not just my mother, but my bestest friend.

To Aabo, if I could bottle up your pride and keep it with me for ever, I would. Thank you for being excited, even when you didn't always understand. I'm sure I could never count the number of strangers you've told about this book. Thank you for being my number one cheerleader.

To my second mother, Habaryar Sahra, you have been with me for so long I did not even realize your transformation into fictional Abooto. I am beyond grateful for your steadfast presence in my life. Thank you.

Asli, my big sister, you are my Hussein. We aren't twins but we are as close as you can get. I am so grateful that we have grown up and shared so much of this world together. You are my rock.

Ibtisam, my darling, I think you know that, without you, this book would not exist. When I think back to those early drafts, I am overwhelmed just thinking about how much I leaned on you, my thirteen-year-old sister. You are my sounding board, the one who expertly manages my near-nervous breakdowns, you *are* this book. And I will always tell anyone who listens.

Ibtihaj, my sister from another mother. You are half-Hafsa, all-Sumaya. I am so grateful to have another bookworm in this family. Thank you for zooming through this book, while I was still debating whether you were old enough to read it, and for loving it.

Imaan cadeey, my baby, I love you so much. Of course, you don't know anything about this book, but I really hope you love it when you're older, in shaa Allah.

To Naima, I am so grateful to have a friend like you. I won't ever forget your love and support – it is priceless in a world like this. I remember I promised more than a decade ago I would give you a book shoutout if the day ever came. It feels surreal I get to keep that promise.

To Saima, I want you to know you got me through the hardest point of this book. That day you called me, and I told you I was stuck, you pushed me over the hurdle. Thank you so much for helping me write that chapter (even though it eventually got cut, so peak).

To Duha, Anisha and Serena, thank you for the friendship that let me write authentically about what it is to be a teenager. I am so grateful for the daily belly-shaking laughter, the inappropriate antics, and the serious moments we shared together. I wouldn't have been able to write without any of those experiences.

To my 360 Harbaes, I don't know how you survived the last couple of years with me. I am in awe of your resilience. Thank you for believing in me, Chevonne, when I struggled to believe in myself. I am so lucky your door was always open for me to knock on and that you never tired listening to my worries. Sharon, you don't know how much it means to me that you did the impossible and read a book, *my* book. I think that might be my biggest flex. Thank you for everything, Darkwa, including tolerating my weirdness.

Feyi, my unofficial publicist, I hit the jackpot with a friend like you. I am so grateful to have someone "scriming" from the rooftops about my book but, most of all, I'm just grateful to have met an amazing hugger (second, only, to me of course).

To Suzanne, thank you for gifting me the thing I kept coming back to during some of my lowest moments (even though you probably don't remember!). For a future writer, you said, and it is what kept me going, time and time again.

To Clare, the person who, quite literally, made my dreams come true! I will never forget where I was when I got that fateful email from you, the email that set everything in motion: eating dinner in front of my laptop. I don't know if there are any words to really express how grateful I am you took a chance on me. Thank you for seeing something in my book, for believing in Hanan and, also, in me. You are a brilliant agent and human.

Sarah, my fabulous editor, your love for this book has always blown me away. I cannot believe I get to work with such a dream editor and publisher. I am so thankful to have had someone who understood, at every level, what I wanted to say. Who pushed me and made me really think about the bigger picture. This book is stronger with you.

Thank you to the whole DACBA and Usborne team. To Will, my amazing designer. Teara, my copyeditor. Hannah and Fritha, marketing and publicity extraordinaries. Thank you to everyone who made this book be what it is today.

And, finally, I owe a huge debt of gratitude to Wasima Farah. The gifted, incredible artist whose work graces the front cover of this book. Whose work is Hanan. Allahumma baarik. Thank you for letting us use your creation.

A LOVE STORY
EIGHTEEN YEARS IN THE MAKING

THE
RUMOURS

IT'S TIME TO
EXPOSE IT ALL...

Love this book? Love Usborne YA

Follow us online and sign up to the Usborne YA
newsletter for the latest YA books,
news and competitions:

usborne.com/yanewsletter

 @UsborneYA

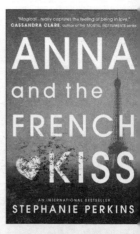